IF YOU DARE

What Reviewers Say
About Sandy Lowe's Work

Party of Three

"In the world of erotica, Party of Three is like a day at the fair—cotton candy sweet with plenty of fun rides. It'll leave you exhilarated and a bit out of breath. I sped through this book in one sitting because everything clicked. It's sexy, cool, and funny all at once. If you've never considered reading an erotic romance, this is the perfect novel to get your feet wet. …When you want to spend a quiet night in and need something a little more raucous than a Hallmark channel rom-con, check out *Party of Three*."
—*Lesbian Review*

"I really enjoyed this book. It was well written and gripping, and each section had good character development and a strong story arc. …I really enjoyed the author's tone and writing style, and I look forward to her next book."—Melina Bickard, Librarian, Waterloo Library (UK)

"If you're looking for a fun and light read with a few sharp bits, this is it. Of course it's steamy hot, but it's also pretty romantic in its own way. Come for the sex, stay for the romance or come for the romance, stay for the sex, either way you win."—*Jude in the Stars*

"If this is a taste of what's to come, I am excited to see what's next from Sandy Lowe."—*Les Rêveur*

"The book is broken down by each lady's journey and each part gave all the emotions, sweetness, and smoking hot sexiness!"
—*Steph's Romance Book Talk*

"One hell of a party!!! ...A great read if you want fun, flirty, and a little erotica in an easy story that allows you to really experience the fun being had and the feelings of the characters."—*LESBIreviewed*

Girls on Campus—*Edited by Sandy Lowe and Stacia Seaman*

"[U]nbelievably hot and the perfect book to keep on your bedside table. ...This was an awesome book of short erotic stories. I loved that I got to read so many stories from so many of my favorite authors, but also got introduced to a few new ones to follow as well. ...They were hot, and sweet, and romantic, and hot! Definitely worth it."—*Inked Rainbow Reads*

Escape to Pleasure: Lesbian Travel Erotica—*Edited by Sandy Lowe and Victoria Villasenor*

"[A] very pleasurable read—especially whilst on holiday!" —Melina Bickard, Librarian, Waterloo Library (UK)

"Irresistible"

"A best friends to romance story line that is not only incredibly loving but also sexy and passionate. Almost like an awakening, this book is going to capture your heart."—*Les Rêveur*

Visit us at www.boldstrokesbooks.com

By the Author

Party of Three

If You Dare

IF YOU DARE

by

Sandy Lowe

2020

ISBN 13: 978-1-63555-654-4

THIS TRADE PAPERBACK ORIGINAL IS PUBLISHED BY
BOLD STROKES BOOKS, INC.
P.O. BOX 249
VALLEY FALLS, NY 12185

FIRST EDITION: DECEMBER 2020

CREDITS
EDITOR: CINDY CRESAP
PRODUCTION DESIGN: SUSAN RAMUNDO
COVER DESIGN BY TAMMY SEIDICK

Acknowledgments

They say that doctors make terrible patients. Well, editors make, if not terrible writers, then certainly neurotic ones. Mega thanks to the superlative team at Bold Strokes Books. You manage to make publishing look easy, and that's never true, especially when the book is mine.

Thank you to my editor, Cindy, for reading another billion really long sex scenes written by your coworker and not being weird about it. This book is better for all your wisdom.

Thank you to my superstar romance writer beta readers Nell and Jaime for your excellent advice to ensure I had all the right parts in all the right places. Sending my draft felt a bit like sending Picasso a finger painting. Your kindness and enthusiasm made me feel less like a rookie.

Thanks to Eden, who writes horrible kissing. Uh, I mean horror with kissing, and CGH, who writes the occasional to-do list. You guys are awesomely supportive friends. You still have to buy a copy, though.

Thank you to erotica writing goddess, Meghan. You're the writer I want to be when I grow up. I'm so lucky to have begged my way into a critique. There are some things that only the Queen of Sex can teach you.

Lastly, thanks to Radclyffe. You deserve hazard pay for listening to my long and copious complaining about how this manuscript just wasn't working, and then my longer, and even more copious, whining about why all your suggested revisions sucked. I mean, you're only the most prolific author/editor/publisher of lesbian fiction ever. I have no idea why you thought you could help. Did I mention I'm neurotic? Sorry. At least it's over now.

Dedication

For the one with whom I dared.

CHAPTER ONE

Christmas sucked, the small town of Sunrise Falls sucked, and the blame fell squarely on Santa's jolly shoulders. As far as Lauren West was concerned, Santa could take his holiday cheer and shove it up his red polyester-covered ass.

She swung the SUV rental car into the rutted lot of the Grumpy Goat and snagged the last spot, pulling between a Ford pickup so rusty the bed looked ready to collapse and a Subaru Crosstrek in eye-searing orange. Grumpy's was the only bar in town, and mercifully, open on Christmas Day night. Nothing sold shots quite like a culturally mandated holiday with family you got whiplash avoiding the rest of the year. Bars and hospitals were sanctuaries on this holiest of holy days. Lauren didn't have any family she wanted to stab with a decorative reindeer antler, but she needed a vodka tonic. Like *needed* needed. She wasn't going to think about that. The baby Jesus's birthday was today, which meant Lent was way off. If she swore off her vices this early, she'd never make it through April. She winced as her boots landed in two inches of muddy slush next to the car. *Hello, December in upstate New York. Oh, how I haven't missed you.*

Lauren spotted Roxie Courtland the instant she pushed through the door. Rox was hard to miss. Miles of bottle-blond hair piled as high as gravity and hair product would allow, and the shortest skirt of anyone in the place, rivaling even the gaggle of barely-legal girls crowding the bar. She smiled. Old friends were the best friends.

She kissed Rox on the cheek and dropped her ancient messenger bag on a chair at Roxie's table. "You never change."

"Why would I change when it's so much fun being who I already am?" Not satisfied with the cheek kiss, Roxie threw her arms around Lauren and pulled her in for a bear hug worthy of an actual bear.

"That's a point." Lauren sank into the jasmine and hairspray scent that was Roxie. The scent of safety. Of friends that were as good as family. Of people you didn't have to explain yourself to.

"Want a drink?" Lauren let her go and fished in her bag for her wallet. She'd missed Roxie like an amputated limb since moving to the West Coast, but they weren't the kind of people who actually *admitted* to missing each other.

Roxie held up a highball glass with the requisite sprig of holly poking out the top. "I'm covered. You might want to wait for table service, though. Those chicks at the bar are a hundred pounds soaking wet, but what they lack in body fat, they make up for in elbows."

Lauren eyed them and weighed her odds. High heel wearing, hair tossing, fake-nice girls. The kind of girls who grew into the kind of women she used to work with. "I can take them. I'm going in."

Roxie saluted her and Lauren made her way into battle. By Christmas miracle, a spot opened up almost immediately, and she squeezed between Selena Gomez, pre-drug addiction, and her bestie, Winter Vacation Barbie. Lauren almost smirked. She didn't, because what if these girls were actually nice? You never knew, and she tried not to judge. But her lips twitched.

She waited the eternity it took the potbellied, prematurely balding bartender to make his way over to her. That bartenders were only ever hot in movies was a first world injustice, but still a damn shame.

She ordered her drink, and Selena Gomez ordered a vodka gimlet. Lauren was impressed for the minute it took the girl to down a gulp and squeal, "Oh my God, Kara. You were so right. That's gross." They doubled over laughing and stumbled their way to the throw-rug-sized dance floor tucked into the corner of the room. Ah, the good ol' days, when lime juice was your biggest problem and your best joke.

She took her drink back to the table and plopped her butt down across from Roxie. "Thanks for meeting me."

"Hey, friends don't ignore nine-one-one texts. You okay?" Roxie sipped from her glass and did an admirable job of keeping her eyes on Lauren and not the gangly, brown-eyed guy across the room Lauren had caught her eye-sexing.

"Santa's my problem. White-bearded, bell-ringing, carol-singing Santa Claus."

Roxie blinked. "You've lost me."

"Mom and I went to the YMCA Christmas dinner." Lauren took a gulp of her drink and the burn of vodka down her throat made her eyes water. The bartender might not have been a Hemsworth brother, but he seemed to understand that if you were at a bar on Christmas Day, your drink ought to be stiff.

"How was it? I tried to get Dad and Carleen to go, but you know how Carleen is about cooking on Christmas." Roxie rolled her eyes, a gesture Lauren knew Roxie'd never dare make in front of her well-meaning but overbearing stepmother.

"Awful. Everyone stared at me. I'm pretty sure Jessica Norman called me a home wrecking slutface. So, you know, holiday spirit, good cheer, peace, and all that."

Roxie winced. "Slutface? Who calls someone a slutface? What does that even mean? Is your face sluttier than the rest of you?"

"Well, I'm pretty good with my mouth, but I prefer the use of my hands too. I'm ambidextrous you know." Lauren wiggled her fingers.

Roxie rolled her eyes again. "You should take that show on the road. Wit is such a comforting defense mechanism when your life's in the toilet. Now, why am I here?"

"Do you remember Douglas French?" Lauren asked, ignoring the rest of Roxie's comment. She and Doug had been best friends in kindergarten. In the pre-boy-germs era, they'd bonded over a shared love of who could bounce the highest on the death trap of a trampoline in his parents' backyard. It was a miracle they'd both lived. Roxie hadn't transferred to Sunrise High until the tenth grade, and by then Doug had been the sophomore's most eligible bachelor and far too popular to be hanging out with the likes of Lauren. No one was wealthy in Sunrise Falls, but some were poorer than others. Lauren and her mom had been the kind of poor people described as dirt. Trailer park, Salvation Army, food stamp trash. Being dirt trash tended to make you wildly unpopular at the age when a North Face jacket was the difference between cool and ostracized.

"Doug? Sure. He's the general contractor. He replaced the porch last year. Took over the business from his dad, I think," Roxie said.

"Well, apparently, he and Gayle have been dating. *My* Gayle." Lauren charged on, well aware of what Roxie would say about her biggest crush and not giving her the chance. "He rigged the whole thing so that Gayle's Secret Santa present was actually a gift from him. He got her diamond earrings. What kind of person buys a woman they're dating diamond earrings, anyway?"

"The really generous kind?" Roxie suggested.

"Douchebags who want to buy love, that's who. Then there was Santa hell-bent on making a bad situation worse. He basically forced them to kiss. Right there in public. In front of me. Everyone in the place goes *aww*, like Dougie's just given her a basket of kittens instead of sucking on her face."

She finally ran out of steam and Roxie pounced. "Lauren, no. Just, no. Your Gayle obsession isn't healthy."

"I'm not obsessed. I just like her."

"In an *I'll be the one in the tree outside your window watching you undress* kind of way."

"If I'm going to be there when she's naked, I definitely want to be closer than that. I'm not a creeper, I'm just…"

"Obsessed with a straight girl who doesn't know you exist?" Roxie said.

"Gayle isn't straight." Lauren refused, as always, to budge on this point.

Roxie's head dropped into her hands like a hammer. "How many times have we had this conversation?"

"At least twenty million." Lauren took another sip of her drink. She'd marry the bartender later, if she was still standing.

"You need to move on. All you do when you come home is follow Gayle-fucking-Wentworth around like a duckling. It has to stop. You need an actual life, with someone who actually wants to sleep with you, Ms. Slutface. If only Jess Norman knew the truth."

Lauren stabbed the sip stirrer into the bottom of her glass. First, Sunrise Falls was the farthest place from home. Maybe she'd had the misfortune to grow up here. Maybe, for some reason she would never understand, her mom still wanted to live in the shithole of America. But it would never be home. Second, Jessica Norman had narcissistic personality disorder and wouldn't know the truth if it hit her on the head. Third, Lauren could have all the sex she wanted. It just so happened she wanted it with Gayle. Was that a crime? Some people might even say it was romantic.

She stabbed her glass so hard the plastic stirrer bent in the middle. "How long have they been dating?"

"Eight months," Roxie said, gentler now.

She didn't get it. She'd known Gayle was bi, but Lauren had been the recipient of Gayle's very passionate, very sexy kiss. No woman kissed like that if they weren't into you.

"Why?" Lauren wasn't stupid. She knew if romance was in the cards for her and Gayle it would've happened a long time ago. But their kiss was right around the time Lauren left for California. She'd always kept the flame alive, hoped more than a little that when she came back to visit her mom, Gayle would kiss her again. That she'd get the *I have to feel your body over mine* quivers. But Gayle had been nothing but polite and friendly the couple of times Lauren had dragged herself back. Polite was the worst. Give her anger, give her pissed off Gayle who was mad she'd moved across the country instead of kissing her every day for the rest of her life. Politeness, though, had all the hallmarks of being a stranger.

"Because she likes him," Roxie said. "You need to find someone who likes you like that. You'd look good in diamond earrings."

Lauren shrugged. "Dating's too complicated and casual sex just leaves you disappointed."

Roxie shot a look at the brown-eyed guy again. "Casual sex doesn't have to leave you disappointed."

Lauren turned in her seat to study him. "That guy's the splitting image of Ashton Kutcher's character on *That '70s Show*. He needs a decent haircut."

Roxie just smiled.

"You going to ask him out?"

"I'm thinking about it," Roxie said. "Can you ask someone out on Christmas Day? Is that right, do you think?"

"Every made-for-TV movie ever says yes," Lauren said.

Roxie's phone pinged on the table by her glass and she glanced at it. "Dad's drunk again. I'm so not going home now."

Roxie's dad, Simon, wasn't exactly an alcoholic. Not in a fuck-up-your-life kind of way. But he got pretty shit-faced on a regular basis. Luckily, he was an adorably happy drunk who just wanted cuddles and intense conversations about the meaning of life. He was completely harmless, really. But after twenty-five years of long conversations, Lauren figured Rox was due a break.

"Want another?" Lauren picked up her empty glass.

"I'll get this one. I have to pee anyway," Roxie said.

As she walked away, Lauren zeroed back in on Gayle and the total abyss that was her love life. On the way she'd managed to screw up everything back home in San Francisco and earn herself the slutface moniker. She'd hurt a man she'd respected, gotten herself fired from her dream job, and wound up back in the last place she wanted to be. Her only goal since the age of ten had been to escape this town and the poverty no one ever let her forget. And yet somehow, here she was, sitting in Grumpy's, tipsy on one drink, single, broke, and wanting eyeball replacement surgery after watching her biggest crush make out with her ex-best-friend from kindergarten.

God might be blowing out two thousand years' worth of candles on his kid's birthday cake tonight, but he sure as hell made some time to laugh at the mess she was in.

Merry freakin' Christmas.

Chapter Two

I'm serious about finding you a Gayle replacement, only attracted to you." Roxie slid another vodka tonic across the table to Lauren.

"The last thing I need is to fall for someone in Sunrise. You think my obsessiveness is bad now, just wait until it's *love.* You'll never hear the end of it."

Roxie huffed. "Not fall in love, you idiot, that's for people over thirty. I'm talking about dating and sex. You know, that stuff other people do?"

"My life's a hot mess and you want me to start taking strangers out on dates?"

"What've you got to lose? May as well put your shiny new rep to good use. And, more importantly, what else do you have to do? You're staying through the New Year, right?" Lauren squirmed and Roxie nailed her with a wounded look. "Right?"

"Yeah. Mom needs me." That was putting it mildly, or she would've been on the next plane to anywhere.

"So, what's stopping you? Have some fun. Get I-Like-Penis-Too Gayle out of your system for good."

"Really, you had to go there?" Lauren scrunched up her face.

"Penis, penis, penis, penis," Roxie singsonged, laughing when two burly guys with beers glanced over at them.

"Would you please shut up?"

"Not until you agree to a Christmas fling."

"Now you *sound* like a made-for-TV movie. I don't want to date. My shady past doesn't exactly make me the most eligible bachelorette," Lauren said.

That stumped Roxie for a second. "Okay, not dating. We'll give you some time to lick your wounds. What about sex?"

"What about it?"

"How long's it been?"

"Roxie!" Lauren laughed.

"What? I tell you when I have sex."

"Yeah, but that's because you want to. In far more detail than I ever want to know."

Roxie shrugged. "It's your duty as my best friend to listen to the details. It's not my fault you're gay."

"A duty I perform with sacrificial heroism."

"Spill," Roxie said without sympathy.

Lauren thought about it and mentally eye-rolled at having to search her memory. "Six months ago. The blonde who worked at Macy's and got me an awesome discount on the dress I wore on Memorial Day. Sophie-something."

"Oh, I remember her. The I'm-known-for-it girl," Roxie said.

"I'm known for my phenomenal kissing." Lauren mimicked Sophie-something's puckered lips.

"I'm known for being so adventurous," Roxie chimed in, giggling.

"I'm known for going down on women in the shower." Lauren shook her head. "Nothing like being told what you should want in bed wrapped in a reminder of all the women she's ever been with. Aside from that fatal flaw, though, the sex wasn't that bad. She *was* pretty good at going down on me."

Roxie frowned. "You do know *wasn't that bad* isn't a benchmark you should aspire to."

Lauren just shrugged. She missed sex, but it was a vague, undefined feeling that lacked urgency. More akin to lazy, apathetic melancholy than a genuine desire for mind-melting orgasms. Missing sex was like living on the East Coast and missing sunshine in the middle of January. You knew it was amazing, could recall the way your skin warmed and your spirits lifted, could all but see the blaze in the sky. But, well, it was freaking January, and pining for something that was months away did no one any good. Sex was sunshine, and Lauren's horizon was dark as night.

Roxie ran her finger around the rim of her glass. "I'm worried about you."

"I'm *fine*," Lauren said, for the billionth time. She'd lost her job, but she was fine. She was down to her last hundred bucks, but she was fine. She was home for the holidays, but she was fine. She hadn't realized when her life fell apart that she'd spend as much time making *other* people feel better about it as she did coping with it herself.

"You are so not fine," Roxie said. "You're miserable and you need to shake things up."

Lauren eyed Roxie suspiciously. Roxie was her best friend, her bury-bodies-together, I'd-jump-in-front-of-a-bus-for-you, best-of-the-best, ride-or-die friend. But she was two parts enthusiasm and one part daredevil. In comparison, Lauren was a little old lady afraid to cross the street. "Shake what up, exactly?"

"Your sex life," Roxie said like it should've been obvious. "You need fun, and sexy times, and toe-curling can't-stop-the-rush pleasure. I'm not taking no for an answer."

Lauren raised her eyebrows. "Gosh, Rox. Why didn't you tell me you felt this way? I'd do you in a heartbeat."

Roxie delivered another of her signature eye rolls. "Not me, and you know it. Plus, if it *was* me we both know I'd be the one doing *you.*"

Lauren thought about that for a second, but the image made her brain want to implode so she stopped. All things considered, Roxie probably would want to be the one doing her.

"You want me to take some random girl home?" Lauren asked.

"I want you to take some random girl home and have so many orgasms you see God."

"God's a bit busy, today of all days."

"Sex so good God shows up for it," Roxie said with enough conviction to make Lauren laugh.

"You're a weirdo."

"That's why you love me."

Completely true.

"Truth or dare?" Roxie asked.

"Huh?" Lauren said.

"Truth or dare? Or are you too chicken to play?"

Lauren groaned. "Come on, that's for twelve-year-olds at slumber parties."

"Okay then, chicken." Roxie tipped back in her chair and started making exaggerated clucking noises, louder and louder until Lauren worried people would think she was hallucinating.

"Okay, okay, geez. But you go first. Truth or dare?"

"Dare," Roxie said, just like Lauren knew she would.

Lauren scanned the room for inspiration and landed on Ashton Kutcher. "I dare you to kiss that guy without saying a word."

Roxie didn't hesitate. She snagged a cocktail napkin and scrawled on it. Then she was out of her chair and halfway across the room before Lauren had taken her next breath. God, how she wished she had half of Roxie's confidence. Ashton was standing with his back to a pool table older than time, chatting with half a dozen guys. Lauren knew zilch about what it took to impress guys. She noticed every woman between sixteen and sixty-five within a fifty-foot radius, but guys were just guys. Interchangeable and largely pointless in her world.

In Roxie's world though, they were cotton candy covered in crack.

Roxie brushed aside the men in her path like they were the pages of a book she was flipping through and zeroed in on her target. She didn't just kiss him, she went full-on movie star and grabbed his face, pulling him for a lip lock worthy of not just Instagram, but the front page of *Us Weekly*. If they'd actually been movie stars and not total strangers in the smallest of small towns, that is.

Roxie broke the kiss before Ashton knew what'd hit him, tucked the cocktail napkin into his back pocket, and gave his ass a squeeze for good measure before sauntering back to their table like the twenty feet of beer drenched floorboards was a runway in Milan. "I should definitely do that more often." Roxie ran the tip of her tongue over her bottom lip. "Guys don't kiss enough."

Thinking about kissing guys gave Lauren a really unfortunate mental image of Doug and Gayle doing just that, so she changed the subject. "Bonus points for the paparazzi worthy technique and added flourish of the hair toss."

Roxie grinned. "Go big or go home. Hopefully, he's plenty big, and he'll be taking me home."

Lauren shook her head. "Your one-night stand prospects are much more promising than mine, that's for sure."

"Time to fix that. Truth or dare?" Roxie asked.

Tension curled like an angry fist at the base of Lauren's neck. This was supposed to be fun, she knew that. But fun wasn't a word she'd associate with her life right now, and the last thing she wanted was another awkward situation in a bar. "Rox."

"It's going to be fine." Roxie wasn't giving her a chance to back out. "Can't-stop-the-rush pleasure, remember?"

Lauren sighed. The whole sex thing was overrated. Orgasms were the genital equivalent of a sneeze. Maybe it *was* impossible to stop the rush once it got going, but in the morning all you had was a foggy head. She had enough to regret already. "I'm not doing this. I appreciate your concern, but this is a terrible, immature idea."

Roxie folded her arms. "I did it."

Lauren waved a hand at her. "You *wanted* to do it."

"Doesn't matter. Fair is fair. If you don't follow through…" Roxie paused as if to consider what heinous fate would await Lauren. "You'll have to help me serve hot chocolate at the Christmas parade Saturday."

"Wasn't that last week?" Lauren had timed her visit so she'd miss the damn thing.

The Christmas parade was a Sunrise Falls tradition, as sacred as the virgin birth itself. In a town where emergency services spent more time rescuing cats from trees and glad-handing for charity than tending to actual emergencies, any excuse for lights and sirens was an occasion you didn't mess with.

"Too much snow, they had to postpone it," Roxie said.

"Until *after* Christmas?" Lauren asked.

"Not the point." Roxie pointed a finger at her. "You're stalling. Truth or dare, or hot chocolate?"

"I'm not freezing my ass off for two hours handing out cups of poop-colored water."

Roxie just stared.

Lauren knew when she was beaten. "Truth."

"What *really* happened with James and Caroline? Not what was reported in the media," Roxie asked.

Lauren closed her eyes as her heart sank into her shoes. She tried her best to ignore the stab of hurt and failed miserably. She'd hoped Roxie wouldn't go there. All anyone had wanted to do for the last three months was go there. Her whole life had imploded exactly at the intersection of those two names. She'd hoped that of all people, her best friend would understand she didn't want to talk about it. But, no, nothing was quite as salacious as a full-blown scandal that wasn't your own.

Lauren would rather freeze her ass off listening to "Jingle Bell Rock" on repeat than replay the moment her life fell apart. Option number two was her only choice.

"Okay, dare," Lauren said.

Roxie pumped the air with her fist and grinned.

Lauren narrowed her eyes. "You set me up. You knew I'd pick truth, so you asked the one question you knew I wouldn't want to answer."

"I'm *worried*," Roxie said, as if that made up for it.

"That was low."

"I'm sorry." Roxie sounded like she meant it. She squeezed Lauren's hand. "Now, on to your dare."

Roxie had the heart of a golden retriever and the attention span of a goldfish. She scanned the room and frowned. Clearly, no one caught her interest. Lauren was relieved right up until Roxie said, "I dare you to sleep with the next woman under the age of forty-five who walks through the door."

"*What*? No way." No wasn't strong enough. No to the eleventh power.

"Come on, it's not that crazy. If she's really awful you don't have to do it," Roxie said generously.

"But I only dared you to *kiss* someone. You're really daring me to have sex with a woman I haven't even seen yet?" Lauren asked.

"You need it more than I do. You need to feel good. Get out of your head for a bit."

Lauren stared at her. "You're insane."

"I'm right," Roxie said with all the conviction of an insane person. "I'm not going to force you to go through with it, if you *really* don't want to. But at least see who walks in. Try, okay?"

Lauren could only shake her head. Sex wasn't going to make her feel better. Rewinding the clock three months, waking up as anyone else, anywhere but here, might help.

But sex? What was the point?

The overly cheery tinkle of bells sounded when the door swung open right on cue, as if Roxie had planned it that way. Despite herself, Lauren's heart picked up and her palms went damp. This was stupid. She wasn't actually going to go through with it. Likely, Mrs. Leery from next door would come bustling in for her nightly glass of sherry and Lauren and Roxie would fall all over themselves laughing. *Can you imagine?*

But it wasn't Mrs. Leery. It was Emma Prescott.

She frowned. She frowned so hard she could feel her forehead wrinkle. What was little Emma Prescott doing here? Lauren had to search for a solid memory of her. Emma had been in the year behind her at Sunrise High, a wisp of a thing, dark hair and big eyes. She'd been bookish, and shy to the point of mute, all but running away whenever Lauren came within ten feet of her. In fact,

Lauren had seen more of the back of Emma's head than she'd ever seen of her face. Emma'd been...pretty unremarkable. But pretty unremarkable Emma had turned into a very remarkable woman. The hair she'd used to hide behind now framed her face in a long bob, just touching her shoulders, and so shiny black it gleamed in the overhead light. She was still tiny, but it suited her, her smallness sexy in that way of bodice ripper romance novels, all I-big-and-beefy-You-small-and-trifling. The kids at school used to call Emma Casper for her light skin. Those same girls would be jealous now. She had a complexion Disney princesses dreamed of, as smooth as cream and just as pale. Lauren pushed aside a twinge of insecurity. Emma might be compact, but she was all curves. Soft and supple, and woman in a way Lauren's taller, lankier frame just wasn't. *Lush.* That was it. Lush, and lusciously so. There was no denying it, Emma was hot. Like how had Lauren never noticed before now, hot hot hot.

Roxie waved a paper napkin in front of Lauren's face. "For the drool that's trailing down your chin."

"I'm not drooling." But Lauren wiped at her chin just in case. Emma Prescott's sexiness deserved drool. What was she doing at Grumpy's on Christmas Day?

"No way," Lauren said. "I'm never going to win the dare with her. It's a waste of time."

Roxie tapped a finger to her chin. "I don't know, you might be in with a chance. She's a librarian, you know. How's your Shakespeare?"

Lauren shot her a look.

"Brontë? Dickens? At least tell me you've read Jane Austen. Everyone and their mother has a crush on Mr. Darcy," Roxie said.

"I'm a lesbian. Mr. Darcy has all the allure of burnt toast. Does watching the *Jane Austen Book Club* movie count?" Lauren asked.

"Did you learn *anything* in high school?"

Lauren held up three fingers and ticked them off. "French kissing, beer pong, and how to scrape a B minus in chemistry without singeing my eyebrows."

"Seriously?"

Lauren shrugged. High school had sucked, Roxie knew that. Hell, everyone in Sunrise Falls knew that. Lauren scraped an acceptance to college and was gone before the ink had dried on her diploma. Acing her classes hadn't exactly been top priority.

Emma greeted the bartender like a long lost relative she actually liked, even hoisting herself up on the counter to kiss his stubbly cheek. *She knows the bartender?* They chatted for half a minute until a busboy came out of the back with a Styrofoam container and slid it across to her. Emma smiled and Lauren's breath did a woozy backflip in her throat. Emma was nineteen-fifties pinup girl hotness. When she smiled she was Marilyn Monroe in a Colgate commercial.

"If you don't hurry up she's going to leave." Roxie kicked her in the shin.

"Ow. No, she's not." Except, Emma was in fact leaving. She'd turned around with her mystery container and was heading for the door.

"For Christ's sake, Lauren, don't let a girl you're actually, dare I say *obviously*, attracted to walk away because you're too dopey to make up your mind." Roxie kicked her again for good measure.

Lauren glared at no one in particular. It wasn't that she couldn't make up her mind, it was just, it was *Emma Prescott*. No one was more a hometown hero. More beloved by all she met. Emma was so Sunrise Falls they should've made her the mascot. Lauren grinned. A librarian mascot, in a pencil skirt, wielding a ruler. Now there was spirit she could get behind.

She got up to catch Emma before she left. She'd had no intention of delivering on the dare. Sex wasn't a game. But that was before Emma walked in. Shy, sweet, run-away-from-you Emma had gotten all gorgeous since graduating high school, and suddenly the prospect of sex tonight didn't seem like such an insane idea after all.

Not when Emma Prescott was the one she'd been dared to seduce.

CHAPTER THREE

Playing nice was getting her nowhere. Emma needed a plan B. Well, actually, at this point more like a plan J, but who was counting. She loved this town the way you love your spouse by your twentieth wedding anniversary. Some days were sunshine and rainbows, and other days you wanted to hightail it to Nebraska. Was opening an e-book lending program so damn space-age no one could comprehend the value? That she had to get the town council's approval, and that the council comprised a motley crew of octogenarians who didn't even know what an e-book was, was a pain in her ass. It was Christmas Day and instead of enjoying Christmas crackers and gingerbread, she was rewriting her damn proposal. Why bother calling it a proposal? They should've just cut to the chase and called it what it was: a permission slip.

She bumped her shoulder against the door of Grumpy's trying to push it open without sending her purse and her grilled cheese sandwich dinner to the floor. As the door started to swing, a hand shot out to push it for her, sending Emma stumbling. The arm connected to the hand caught her at the waist to steady her, and a warm body pressed along her side. Emma nearly jumped out of her skin. The scent of ripe tangerines twined around her senses, so exotic, and so out of place she lost her bearings completely.

"Whoa, you okay there?"

Breath coasted against Emma's cheek when the woman spoke into her ear. Emma shivered and every ounce of sense she'd ever possessed evaporated. Her purse landed sideways on the floor, spilling paraphernalia. The grilled cheese flew from her grasp as she struggled to compose herself, landing a foot away on the floor that hadn't had more than a cursory mopping in ten years.

Diagnosis: not okay. Possible mental instability characterized by loss of motor control, inappropriate shivering, and head swirlies.

Could this day get any worse? She righted herself and turned to glare at the unhelpfully helpful perpetrator. Her swirling head had only just caught up with itself when she fell into the soft gray eyes of Lauren West. Well, there was her answer. The day could definitely get worse, and she'd just boarded the express train. Destination: mortification.

"Sorry." Lauren let her go quickly, as if prolonging their contact might cause Emma to spontaneously combust this time. She bent down to scoop Emma's stuff back into her purse. To her credit, she didn't even blink at the prescription bottle for Valium or the tampon still in its flowery paper. She just shoved it all back in and handed the purse to Emma. "I was actually trying to help and ended up making everything worse. Story of my life."

Lauren's smile was all I'm-so-charming-please-forgive-me.

Emma had no idea what to say. She couldn't ever seem to say anything to Lauren, even when she wanted to. She just stood there like an idiot with her mouth open and the imprint of Lauren's body along her side embedded with enough heat for a branding iron. Her cheeks grew steadily warmer and sweat broke out across her forehead. *Say something. Don't just stand there.* But the voice inside her head was all bark and no bite, a drill sergeant with no authority. Emma managed a halfhearted smile but couldn't make words around the lump ballooning in her throat. Story of *her* life. She turned back to the door that had caused all the trouble in the first place, preparing to flee.

"Wait." Lauren's hand was back, preventing the door from opening this time. "Emma, right? How are you?"

Surprise had Emma spinning around, words popping out of her mouth before she had time to think about it. "You know who I am?"

Lauren shrugged. "Yeah. How are you?"

"I'm *fine*." Emma drew out the word so one syllable became three. How was she? What kind of a question was that? No one went around asking people how they were.

"Good," Lauren said. "I'm not. But then you probably already knew that. That's why you can barely look at me. You and everyone else in this town."

That was so not why Emma couldn't look at Lauren. But she wasn't about to tell her the real reason, not when she was still all tingly. Now that she'd managed actual words, others came a bit easier, even if she did deliver them to the floor. "It sounds like you've had it rough. I'm sorry. I'm not going to judge you. I mean, we all make mistakes." Lauren's mistake had been quite a bit heftier than your average screwup, but Emma only knew what she'd heard, and hearsay wasn't always reliable. She wasn't going to judge Lauren until she knew if there was something worth judging.

Lauren opened her mouth like she wanted to say more, then closed it again.

"What?" Emma asked. For some reason, Lauren censoring herself bothered Emma. *Yeah, right, because someone as beautiful as Lauren is going to confide all her deep, dark secrets standing by the exit of a bar with greasy cheese at her feet.*

"Do you want to dance?" Lauren asked.

"What?" She really had to expand her vocabulary beyond that word. Finally getting up the courage to talk to Lauren was a level of awesome she never thought she'd achieve. Gaping at her like a carp, though? Totally ruining it.

Lauren gestured to the dance floor like Emma needed the visual to make sense of her invitation. "Do you want to dance? I promise not to step on your toes." She smiled her charming smile again.

Emma frowned. Lauren grabbing her so she didn't faceplant, she could buy, but dancing? They'd known each other for years. Well, she had known who Lauren was anyway, but Lauren had barely spoken to her before tonight. Now she wanted to *dance* with her? It made no sense.

The silence hung expectantly between them and Lauren's smile wobbled. "Never mind. Let's get this mess cleaned up at least." Lauren grabbed a stack of napkins from a nearby table and managed to scoop the sandwich back into the Styrofoam container, then three-pointed it into a trashcan. "Sorry I ruined your dinner. Can I buy you another?"

"Doesn't that line have something to do with a drink?" Emma asked.

Lauren stepped closer, and the door behind Emma became less of an exit and something more enveloping. The air grew heavy, pressing in on her, implausible humidity in the middle of winter. Lauren wasn't touching her, but she was so close Emma barely had to use her imagination to feel the weight of Lauren's body against hers again. Her blood heated and she bit her bottom lip. This was bad. This was really, really bad. She focused on her breathing.

"Okay, can I buy you a drink?" Lauren asked.

Emma didn't need one. Not with the way her head was spinning and her stomach was dipping. "Why? I mean, you barely even know who I am."

Lauren paused as if giving the question an honest evaluation. "Maybe I want to know who you are. You're beautiful and I'm having a pretty lousy week. I'd like some company from someone who won't judge me."

Emma scoffed at that. "I'd say lousy is an understatement, and I'm not beautiful, anyway."

"Have pity on me then."

Lauren thought the only way Emma would have a drink with her was out of pity? Was she insane? "Don't do that," Emma said.

"Do what?" Lauren asked.

"Put yourself down. You don't need a pity drink. Half the girls here would love to drink with you. Or dance with you."

Lauren touched her lightly on the shoulder. The gesture wasn't the least bit sexual, but it spoke volumes. "But I want to dance with you."

Emma swallowed. Apparently, this had nothing to do with other girls. She didn't get what was going on here and that wasn't good, not with the way her imagination was always running away with itself. But, on the other hand, did that really matter right now? Unrequited crushes were the most painful kind. Hope and hopelessness in constant tug-of-war, and the outcome never quite certain. For whatever reason, drunk, or lonely, or just having a bad night, her unrequited crush wanted to dance with her. Was Emma really going to turn her down because... There was no *because* except her own inner monologue. Damn if she was going to get in her own way this time. That settled the argument that had never required settling in the first place.

"Let's dance," Emma said.

Lauren led her to a token dance floor some enterprising soul had wrestled into an unused corner of the room. The lighting was low and the music was old school country. Emma was relieved that when Lauren had said dance, she hadn't meant anything with actual steps. They fell into the swaying shuffle typical of people who'd never learned anything more. Dancing was one of those skills that had gone the way of letter writing, so old-fashioned as to be quaint.

"You're so beautiful," Lauren murmured against her ear as she pulled Emma in closer than was friendly.

Emma fought a bubble of panic when Lauren's arms came around her. Her heart pounded against her ribcage like a violent inmate. She was holding herself too stiffly and telegraphing her awkwardness. Why didn't she just hold up a sign that read *this is a really big deal to me.* They were barely touching, but she was so aware of Lauren they may as well have been stuck together like Post-it's. Why in God's name did she think she could dance? She could barely *breathe.*

Emma shook her head. "Please don't do that. I know I'm not beautiful. You don't have to pretend. I'll still dance with you."

Lauren pulled back and stared directly into her eyes. Emma felt herself blush, yet again. It had been a very long time since anyone had really *looked* at her, and never quite the way Lauren was.

"You're beautiful," Lauren said. "So what if you're not some cardboard cutout, California Barbie doll princess bikini model."

With that little declaration out of the way, Lauren settled Emma back into the bend of her body and moved them in a lazy circle. She willed herself to relax. Every time she got even halfway there Lauren's thigh would brush hers, and distracting sparks of heat would make it impossible to focus on anything else. How was she supposed to have a good time while simultaneously ignoring the rush of *Iwantyoubad* taking over her body? Somehow, she had to manage not to make a total idiot of herself.

"I'm not sure *anyone* is all that."

"You know what I mean. Some fucked up version of femininity gracing the cover of *Insecurity* magazine. You're unique and quirky, and you have curves for days."

Wow. Lauren West thought she had curves. She seemed to think this was a good thing. If this was a dream, Emma never wanted to wake up. "Thanks."

"Thanks for dancing with me." Lauren trailed her fingers down Emma's spine one vertebrae at a time like the rungs of a ladder she was descending. The lower Lauren's fingers went, the weaker Emma's knees grew. If she made it all the way to her tailbone, Emma was going to fall to the floor in her version of a swoon, kind of like dropping a sack of potatoes from a great height. Lauren stopped respectably mid-waist and Emma was simultaneously disappointed and relieved. Her fantasy brain wanted Lauren to keep going, to cup her ass, bringing their bodies together, and kiss her senseless. But that was the thing about fantasies, they weren't reality for a reason. If Lauren *had* cupped her ass and kissed her, Emma's reality brain would've thought it was mightily presumptuous, because what kind of person gropes a woman on the dance floor? The gross lecherous kind, and that would've ruined everything.

Emma shook her head slightly, as if she could dislodge the thoughts. This was exactly the kind of thing that made her different from other people. She finally had the opportunity to spend quality time with the girl of her dreams, and instead of enjoying it, she was pondering the inexplicable meanderings of her own brain, forever getting in her own way.

The music wound around them, a crooning melody of love everlasting and they swayed to it with no particular rhythm or skill. Lauren caressed her back every now and then, and Emma's lips were only an inch from the tantalizing column of Lauren's throat. Her skin lit up, sensitive and tingling wherever Lauren touched her, until she had to close her eyes and focus on her breathing. Her palms were sweating so much she didn't dare touch Lauren. She wanted to stop dancing. She wanted to dance the night away. She wanted time to compose herself. She wanted to lose herself in the moment. She wanted to be cool and sophisticated and witty. She wanted Lauren to see the real her and like her anyway.

Undecided, she hung limp in Lauren's arms, breathing like she needed a paper bag. Her anxiety had to be sexy as all fuck.

The music eased to a finish and Lauren stepped back, looking into her eyes again. "Are you okay?"

She wanted to sink to the floor, then curl up in a ball and never move. "I'm sorry. I'm…" *Certifiably ridiculous, and also kind of in love with you.*

But she couldn't finish her apology because the look in Lauren's eyes wasn't mocking, not even close to that irritating brand of concern most people adopted in the face of her unease— all pity, wrapped in sympathy, and sprinkled with condescension. Lauren was looking at her like…like it'd been the best dance of her life. Lauren ran a hand through her chestnut hair calling attention to the way her chest rose and fell, not exactly steadily. Huh, that was interesting.

Lauren touched her fingers to Emma's cheek. "You're so pretty when you blush."

Emma groaned. "Stop. You'll make it worse. I look like a clown."

"It's pretty."

Emma shifted uncomfortably. "I've been sitting on my ass all day, my clothes are wrinkled, and I can't remember if I brushed my hair this morning. I must look like a street urchin."

Lauren's fingers curved around her jaw, caressing her face. "You look sexy, like I've just fucked you."

Emma blinked. Every drop of blood, every cell in her body, every *everything* she had, rushed between her legs and began to pound madly.

But, also, *what*?

Lauren jerked back, her expression going from sensual to horrified in a nanosecond. "Oh my God. I'm sorry. Fuck. I'm so sorry. I didn't mean that. I would never...I...oh my God."

Lauren closed her eyes briefly. "I'm sorry. I can't believe I said that."

"Neither can I," Emma said, then burst out laughing.

She wasn't sure why she was laughing, it wasn't funny, but the tension that had been building since the moment Lauren had cornered her by the door escaped out her mouth in uncontrollable giggles until she was gasping.

Lauren smiled slowly. She started laughing too, and they stood there, in the middle of the dance floor, laughing like loons and holding each other up.

"I'm so sorry," Lauren said again.

Emma grinned. For some reason Lauren saying something so undeniably inappropriate made her feel better about her own inexhaustible list of embarrassing qualities. "It's okay. I mean, my blushing makes women lose their minds. It's a thing. I'm used to it."

"It does," Lauren said right as she got control of herself and her giggles died.

It does. *It did.* Her laughter melted away as that mind-blowing little fact pulled out a chair and made itself at home in her brain. Lauren thought she was pretty. And not just pretty, but sexy. She thought Emma looked like a sexily rumpled after photo in a makeover. Or maybe, the after shot in a porno, depending on Lauren's preferred level of dirtiness. Emma really, really wanted to know what level of dirtiness Lauren preferred. Was she slow and romantic? All candlelight and rose petals. Or was she impatient and demanding? Shoving her lover up against the closest vertical surface and making her forget about comfort. Was she vanilla or kinky? Dominant or submissive? Vocal or quiet? Emma'd wondered these things for years, but knowing that Lauren found her attractive turned the wondering into obsession.

She should be annoyed, offended even, that Lauren looked at her and thought about sex. Emma was smart and nice and kind to animals. All those things should matter a hell of a lot more than being sexy. She knew this. She believed this. But she was still ridiculously flattered.

The pulsing between her legs that had started when Lauren said, "like I've just fucked you" wasn't going away either. She was wet. This wasn't a news flash under the circumstances. She'd been wet around Lauren countless times in her humiliating high school years. Lauren's endlessly tan legs in running shorts, her perfect breasts in tight T-shirts, her mouthwatering wicked grin—they could all make Emma wet. But she was shy. This was a fact she'd lived with since preschool and it didn't really bother her that much, except that unfortunately, her shyness escalated to king-size proportions around Lauren. Her shyness was linked to her hormones in some masochistically destructive fashion that ensured she never got laid, least of all by the person she desperately wanted to notice her.

And now, here they were, a handful of years later, with Lauren admitting her attraction in the most awkward way possible, and making Emma so damn wet she was going to faint from all the blood that wasn't in her head. The idea that maybe Lauren was just as self-conscious as she was made Emma like her even more.

Lauren took her hand, and Emma realized they were still standing in the middle of the dance floor. "We should—" she started, but Lauren cut her off.

"Come home with me."

Emma swallowed back the *fuckyesanywhere* that was her first instinct. Home. To a house with a bed, or a vertical surface, or any surface that wasn't public. "Lauren—"

"I know it might be the last thing you want, considering what a moron I just was. But I like you."

Emma raised her eyebrows. "You like the way I *look*. You don't know me."

Lauren opened her mouth to argue but closed it again. "Yeah, okay. I like the way you look. It's hard to deny that now. Is that so bad?"

Good was the opposite of bad, but good didn't come close to describing how much of a dream come true it was that Lauren wanted her. She bit her lip. She wanted Lauren more than she wanted oxygen right at this second. But...

She shook her head. "It's not bad. There's nothing wrong with having sex because you're attracted. But that's not me. I'm just not cut out for one-night stands. I'd feel weird having sex with someone I didn't really know." That last part was a little bit of a lie, but Lauren didn't need to know that. She didn't need to know that Emma was afraid that if she had sex with Lauren she'd never want to stop, that she'd want more, and that Lauren wouldn't. She'd get hurt, and doing something you know will hurt you was just stupid.

Call her crazy, but her fantasy brain wanted to hold on to this moment. She wanted to keep it safe in one of those snow globes protected by heavy glass. Something she could pull out every once in a while to shake up her boring life. No amount of mind-melting sex was worth the I'm-done-with-you-now that would surely follow and break her fantasy to pieces. Going home with Lauren would result in the world's most satisfying orgasm, but the morning after would destroy her heart. *Not* going home with her would leave her wondering just what might've been for the rest of her damn life. She wasn't sure which was worse.

CHAPTER FOUR

At nine in the morning, Lauren and Roxie were ensconced at a table at Down Home Diner, smack-dab in the center of town. Roxie's eyes were so huge she looked as if she were imitating a stuffed animal. "You said *what?*"

Lauren covered her face with the palm of her hand. "I know. I have no idea what I was thinking."

"Um, sweetcakes, we all know exactly what you were thinking." Roxie couldn't stop laughing.

"You're the worst best friend ever. Aren't friends supposed to be supportive in a crisis?" Lauren poured half-and-half into her Americano.

"She was right not to sleep with you." Roxie sipped from her caramel coffee, mocha whip, skinny whatever concoction that was three percent caffeine and ninety-seven percent sugar. "*You look like I've just fucked you*, is categorically, the worst line I've ever heard delivered to a virtual stranger. Vince Vaughn in a chick flick has better lines than you do."

"It wasn't a line." Lauren defend herself, for all the good it wouldn't do her. "I didn't mean to say it. She's just so unsure of herself. She really has no idea how hot she is."

"And you thought it would be a fantastic idea to tell her by way of expressing your interest in fucking her." Roxie was holding a hand to her chest like that would keep the laughter inside so she could speak. "Actually, fucking her in past tense, which is even weirder."

"Shut up." Lauren swiped a finger in the whipped cream spilling from Roxie's drink. "I wasn't thinking. She's just..."

Roxie rolled her eyes. "Let me guess. She's just that hot."

"Well, she *is* that hot." Lauren licked the cream off her finger. "But she also doesn't know she's hot, and that makes her hotter. She's really sweet."

"Hot and sweet. She sounds edible."

"She probably is," Lauren said. "Not that I'll ever know, now."

"Well, she laughed at you instead of punching you in the nose, so you never know."

Lauren just shook her head. "I told Emma she looked like I'd just fucked her. I actually said those words to her face. There's no coming back from that."

Roxie collapsed into laughter again. "I wish I could argue, but I'd say you're well and truly fucked."

"Worst. Friend. Ever." Lauren downed her coffee like it was Grey Goose.

"So, you passed on truth, and the worst pickup line in the history of the world means that you failed your dare with Emma, so you're going to have to accept your punishment. I'll see you Saturday around five. Meet me at my place. We have to lug the giant thermos ourselves." Roxie stood up.

Before Lauren could plead for mercy, someone dropped their mug, and broken china and coffee splattered all over the floor, some of it landing on Roxie's sneakers. She whirled around, ready to reprimand the clumsy person, and found Emma's deep brown eyes staring accusingly back at her. *Oh, holy mother of fuck.*

Everything stopped. She didn't move. She didn't speak. She didn't even breathe for one heart pounding instant. Then everything went from stopped to spinning as the weight of what Emma had just heard came crashing down on Lauren like an avalanche of all the stupid decisions she'd ever made in her entire life. She leapt out of her chair. "Emma, no, it wasn't like that..."

But Emma had spun around and bolted out the door before Lauren could finish explaining herself. What she'd been planning to say, she had no idea. It *had* been like that, from the outside. She'd asked Emma to dance as a precursor to charming her into bed. That'd been the dare. Can't-stop-the-rush pleasure with Emma. But from the second she'd wrapped her arm around Emma to stop her from falling, it hadn't felt like a dare. It felt real. She'd screwed it up and said something inane exactly *because* being with Emma felt so good. Dancing with her, holding her, stroking her back and imagining her naked skin had turned Lauren's brain to fuzz. She'd stopped thinking. Stopped obsessing about Gayle. Stopped caring that her life was a train wreck. Stopped feeling like a total loser. All she could think about was the sexy way Emma bit her lip. The gorgeous way Emma's cheeks reddened at the slightest provocation. The way Emma's fast breaths had felt against her neck. She'd wanted her and that had absolutely nothing to do with the stupid dare. Only now Emma thought it did.

She fell back into her chair, dread a physical pain in her chest. What was wrong with her that she screwed up everything good in her life?

"Guess she heard me," Roxie said quietly.

Inexplicably, ridiculously, Lauren felt the sting of tears behind her eyes. "I guess so."

Sunrise Falls might suck, but she was starting to think she was the reason why.

Emma pushed a copy of *The Iliad* unceremoniously between a dieting book and a romance novel. Women who only cared about being skinny and falling in love could use some literature in their lives, even if she had to trick them into reading it. There were some things that were more important than being a size two, or having your heart go all pitter-patter. Maybe if women broadened their horizons they'd actually learn something important from a book once in a while. The female gender were idiots really, all of them. Just superficial idiots with not a care in the world for anyone but themselves.

She rubbed angrily at the tears that marched like watery traitors down her cheeks. She wasn't upset because it hadn't meant anything, it was just a dance. Lauren had said nice things and danced with her as some *dare*, like they were seven-year-olds on the playground. What adult person thought that was okay? It wasn't okay, but she didn't care, because the dance hadn't meant anything.

She whipped around when someone knocked softly on a bookcase three feet away. She wasn't all that surprised to find Lauren standing there, slightly out of breath, and looking like a puppy about to be kicked. "Hey."

"What are you doing here?" Emma asked, even though it was pretty obvious. "The library isn't open."

"The door was unlocked," Lauren said.

She mentally kicked herself. She'd been so upset, she must've forgotten to lock it behind her. "We aren't open. You can't just come waltzing in here. You can't just do whatever you want, whenever you feel like it."

"I know," Lauren said. "I'm sorry."

Emma blinked hard to stop the tears. "This is a town establishment." Her voice wavered but didn't crack. "I could call the police and report you for trespassing."

"Okay," Lauren said, her face blank.

The remoteness of her expression just pissed Emma off even more. She wasn't going to be made to feel like some overly emotional *girl* just because Lauren had all the sensitivity of a wet dishrag. If she was here to apologize, then she was damn well going to apologize, not stand there with all her shields up like she expected Emma to flatten her. "I should call the police and tell them you blocked the door and prevented me from leaving last night. That you said crude things to me. Maybe then you'd understand how it feels to have your trust violated."

Lauren looked as if she'd expected her to do exactly that. "Okay. I'd deserve it. I'm really sorry."

Emma stomped over and shoved her. The shove was about as effective as a shovel in a snowstorm, but she did it anyway. Lauren let her. Standing silently, not fighting back, with no expression on her face. "Don't just stand there. Don't tell me you're sorry like you don't even mean it. Do something," Emma said, when what she really meant was *feel something.*

"I'm sorry," Lauren said. She pulled Emma into her and wrapped her in her arms. They fit together as if they'd been made from the same mold. Her skin warmed against Lauren's, her thoughts blurred, and a desperate ache settled in her chest. All too much, too close, too raw.

Lauren whispered, over and over again into Emma's hair, "I'm sorry."

"Let me go." Emma cringed. The demand had no substance. She *should* want Lauren to back off, but everything inside her yearned to hold on.

Lauren stepped back in an obvious display of respecting her boundaries.

Emma sniffed, her clogged nose making her head hurt. "I don't know you well, but I know enough to believe you aren't a complete moron. What the hell were you thinking leading me on as part of some dare?"

Lauren winced. That single fissure in her composure mollified Emma the way a thousand sorrys never could. Lauren reached toward her but let her hand fall before she touched her. "It wasn't a dare, not really. I was feeling crappy, and Roxie was just having a laugh, daring me to sleep with a stranger to feel better about myself. I wouldn't have actually done it, I promise you. Sex might be her pick-me-up, but it doesn't work that way for me, even if I'd wanted it to."

Emma narrowed her eyes. "And yet you asked me to go home with you."

Lauren took her hand cautiously, not holding it but rather trailing her fingers over Emma's knuckles in a light caress. "Is this okay?"

Warmth radiated from where they touched. Her brain started to buzz, but from anxiety or anticipation? She couldn't tell the difference. Emma nodded.

Lauren squeezed her hand like her life depended on it. Emma let her. She didn't know why Lauren had to touch her, but it was obvious she did.

"I went over to talk to you because of the dare. But I swear, I didn't ask you home with me because of it. I asked because I wanted you."

"And I'm supposed to believe that." She watched as Lauren twined their fingers together and wished it didn't have to feel so good.

"You don't have to believe anything, but it's the truth."

"And all that bullshit about how beautiful I am? What was that? Just a bunch of smooth lines you practice in the mirror?"

Lauren stared at her. "It was the truth. I think you're beautiful, and hell, Emma, you think I practice a line like 'you look like I've just fucked you' in the mirror? If I did, I'd be a frustrated virgin."

That was a pretty decent point, as points went.

"If this was all some dare, why did you say that? You had to know it would blow your chances."

Lauren brushed her thumb across Emma's knuckles again. "Because it wasn't some dare. I wasn't thinking, and I just said what was true. Stupid and inappropriate, but true. The second I touched you, I forgot all about the dare. I forgot all about everything."

Pleasure swelled in Emma's chest, threatening to overflow the wall of bitterness she'd so carefully cultivated while re-shelving books. Her hormones were all set to let that wall topple, but her inner cynic knew better. The words coming out of Lauren's mouth might be pretty ones, but Lauren didn't much know or care about her feelings, and as good as sex would feel in the moment, casual had an expiration date. Maybe what Lauren was saying was true.

She didn't have any reason *not* to believe her. But hashing it out was pointless, it really didn't matter either way, it changed nothing. "Okay. Well, thank you for apologizing. Let's just chalk it up to too much alcohol and poor life choices."

Lauren didn't let her go. "And if I don't want to chalk it up? If I want another chance?"

"I can't do that." She looked down at their hands again, at Lauren's fingers wrapped around hers. At how *connected* they were even when they were so far apart in every other way. "Everyone has damage. Mine has to do with not trusting in…physical situations. I can't give you another chance, I'm sorry."

Lauren looked stricken. "Oh God, you weren't… Did someone…"

"No," Emma said firmly. She squeezed Lauren's hand for good measure. "Nothing like that." She didn't owe Lauren an explanation. No thank you, meant no thank you, and Lauren didn't deserve anything else after everything she'd pulled. But she wanted to tell her anyway. Why did she feel so comfortable with Lauren? Maybe because Lauren hadn't tried to fob her off like the dare was nothing. She hadn't said that Emma was overreacting, or minimized her feelings. Maybe that was why Emma trusted her, even when she shouldn't.

"I was played. Someone embarrassed me on purpose." Emma shut her eyes briefly as the memory resurfaced. She spoke to the floor, unable to look Lauren in the eye and reveal the extent of her humiliation. "They mocked me for my attraction to them. I was the butt of their joke. I believe you, that last night wasn't about the dare. But it's too close. It brings up too much for me. I can't go there again."

Lauren slid a finger under her chin and tilted her head up. "I'm so sorry. I can't even imagine how much that must've sucked. How you must've felt thinking you'd been nothing but a dare to me. I'm really sorry someone hurt you. I'm really sorry *I* hurt you. I mean it when I say I want you."

She'd expected Lauren to probe for more details, but instead she just accepted what Emma had shared.

She nodded. "I believe you, and yet, I don't believe you. That's not your fault. That's me and my fucked-up past. I hardly even know you. I just know what I feel, and I know that when I want someone, I usually end up regretting it."

"Do you want me?"

Of course Lauren zeroed in on the one thing that Emma hadn't meant to say.

Heat suffused her cheeks. That Lauren enjoyed seeing her blush only made her burn hotter. "You know I do."

"Do I? You turned me down."

"I wanted…" *More.*

"Tell me what you wanted."

Emma closed her eyes again like maybe that would make the question go away. She pressed her lips together to stop them from trembling. Lauren was up in her personal space now, expecting her to say something sexy about how she wanted to be teased or seduced. Nothing could be further from the truth. The truth was as sexy as taxes in April, and just as real. "I wanted you to ask me out."

She was the biggest loser in the history of losers. Wherever losers hung out, she should go there to make them all feel better about themselves, because no one was more of a freak than her.

"Oh," Lauren said, like asking Emma out on a date instead of asking her to bed hadn't even crossed her mind. And that was the point, wasn't it? Asking her out really hadn't occurred to Lauren. She'd seen a nice face, an available body, and she'd wanted a good time. An hour or two of forgetting about her own problems. Emma wanted sex, but she also wanted *Lauren.*

Lauren ran a hand through her hair. "God. I'm a complete ass, aren't I?

"You'd hardly be the first person to try to pick someone up in a bar." Emma shrugged.

Lauren shook her head. "You're not just some person."

"You don't even know me."

"You keep saying that. What is it that I don't know?" Lauren asked.

Nothing. Everything.

"It doesn't matter." Emma stepped back and let go of Lauren's hand.

Lauren didn't push, but she stared into Emma's eyes in that way that made her certain Lauren had x-ray vision and could see inside her head, into all the dark places and the dusty corners no one else knew existed, let alone had any interest in. "Why do you end up regretting the way you feel?" Lauren asked instead.

"Because the people I want never want me back. They—"

Lauren kissed her. It was so fast Emma would've thought she'd imagined it if Lauren's mouth hadn't been so close to hers. "I want you back." Lauren bushed her lips against Emma's. "I want you so much."

Emma couldn't help the tiny whimper that escaped when Lauren's mouth moved over hers. The moment was perfect. Every moment that wasn't this moment was administered an instant inferiority complex, a grade B report card, a token participation trophy. She tried and failed to ignore the tingle in her lips and the intensity in Lauren's eyes. Every inch of her body ached to be touching Lauren, or to be touched by her. When Lauren stroked her tongue against Emma's, her dignity rolled over and showed its belly, surrendering to Lauren's hot assault. The fight wasn't even remotely fair, and if things went any further, she'd get played again. She was trying hard to care about that, but her worries were fading, obliterated by how fucking turned on she was. "But the dare."

"No, it was an excuse to talk to you. When I did, nothing else mattered," Lauren said.

Emma made a sound, kind of like a groan, or kind of like a sob. So embarrassingly needy. Unable to stop herself, she melted against Lauren, her brain issuing frantic orders for damage control while her body smoothly staged a coup. Temptation was a heartless bitch, flaunting herself mercilessly, making Emma want when things were only going to end in suffering. But right now, there was just Lauren. Lauren's lips on hers. Lauren's hands in her hair pulling at the elastic of her ponytail. Lauren's body all taut and trim and so very close. No bar full of people to keep them in check. Pain shot up her shoulder as they fell against the bookcase behind her, but she didn't care. One second Lauren's mouth was soft on hers, and the next she was everywhere all at once, like she'd turned the dial from tender romance to erotic onslaught. She sank her hands into Emma's hair and held her still, kissing her with a ferocity that should've scared Emma, but excited her instead. It was too hard, too forceful, too overwhelming, for a first kiss, for *any* kiss. She went molten. There had to be something wrong with her that being trapped against a bookcase, having her body positioned, her mouth plundered, would make everything inside her clench into a fist of need. She was probably doing a terrible job of kissing Lauren back, she could barely keep her feet under her, let alone concentrate on her technique, but Lauren didn't seem to mind. She pressed her body along Emma's, using the tight space to her advantage, closing her in. "Don't you dare believe that I don't want you," Lauren whispered against her lips, her hands moving to Emma's hips, fitting their bodies together.

Emma's ragged breathing and swirling head made words almost impossible. "You just want sex. You can get that from anyone."

Lauren groaned. She bent her head and put her lips to the hollow of Emma's throat. "I can't have you with just anyone."

Emma sucked in a shallow breath as Lauren kissed her there. She had no escape, wedged against the new releases section of the library. Lauren was most definitely a vertical-surface type girl. Emma's hair had been pulled from its tie and was falling around her face. She was being handled like Lauren thought she had a right to touch her. Why the hell did that turn her on so much?

Lauren's bent head, her lips on Emma's throat, her admission that not just anyone would do, weakened Emma's resolve. "I'm good enough to fuck, I'm just not good enough to date," Emma said, and instantly wished she hadn't. Right now, being good enough to fuck was five hundred kinds of appealing.

Lauren's head whipped up. "Why would you say that?"

Emma shifted, painfully aware that Lauren hadn't let her go. "It's true, isn't it?"

Lauren shook her head. "I'm only in town for a couple of weeks. I'm coming off a really bad...situation back home. I'm not up for dating anyone."

"But you're happy to fuck," Emma said.

Lauren's smile was rueful. "I have a pulse, and we have enough chemistry for a nuclear weapon. But that's not the point. Any girl would be lucky to date you. You're beautiful and sexy and you know what you want. You're definitely good enough to date."

"You're just not that lucky girl." She knew when she was being placated.

Lauren sighed. "I like you. I like you more than I should like Sunrise Falls' hometown heroine. But I'm going back to San Francisco."

She let her head thunk back against the shelf. She could hardly blame Lauren for not wanting to uproot her life five minutes after meeting her. *She* might've nursed a crush for way too long, but Lauren hadn't. Emma didn't even know if she actually wanted to date Lauren anyway, she was impulsive and had a reputation for landing in bed with inappropriate women. She'd managed to screw her life harder than it was possible to ever screw a woman. Lauren hadn't exactly turned out to be dream girl material. Emma had standards.

"I don't want to be some notch on your bedpost," Emma said.

Lauren brushed the hair out of Emma's eyes. "What do you want to be then?"

She thought about it. Not easy to do with Lauren crowding her, Lauren's fingers in her hair, Lauren's gaze so direct she had to look away so her throat would work. "Nuclear chemistry sounds amazing, but I want dinner first."

Lauren frowned. "You're hungry?"

"No. Tomorrow, I want dinner before sex. Not a date exactly, but not a casual fuck either. I want filet mignon, and interesting conversation, and possibly candlelight."

"You want a date that's not a date." Lauren's forehead wrinkled.

Emma rolled her eyes. "Do you do anything but one-night stands? I want to *matter* enough to have dinner with. And besides, you owe me, you never did replace my grilled cheese."

Lauren smiled slowly. "Oh, I see. You want me to work for it."

"Well, if it's work, then forget it." She made to duck under Lauren's arm but wasn't fast enough. Lauren's mouth covered hers like the seal on a promise.

"Emma," Lauren murmured against her lips. "Would you by chance be free for dinner tomorrow night?"

"I'll check my calendar," she said before sinking into the kiss.

CHAPTER FIVE

Lauren pulled her SUV to the curb in front of Emma's bungalow. Of course Emma Prescott lived in a picture-perfect cottage, with a cozy little porch, subtly tasteful Christmas lights adorning her carved antique front door, and a warm glow filtering through partially open curtains. December was a bleak month. Everything green and living had died, or was on its way there, and the air was heavy with blah. That was the only way to describe it. Just a whole big bucket of blah. Once the holidays passed, there was nothing to look forward to but endless winter, and the ab workout you got trying not to break your neck on the damn ice. Smart people resigned themselves to it. They shut their doors, shuttered their windows, and abandoned their gardens until spring.

In contrast, Emma's house was positively welcoming. It belonged on a postcard or a puzzle, not stuck between Baker's house and a colonial that got more and more derelict by the year. You couldn't even see the house the front walk was such a graveyard of broken down, rusted out heaps of junk. Baker's place just looked fed up and mopey. The paint was peeling, the lawn was a mud pie, and the sag in each side of the porch took the shape of a frown if you squinted a little. Emma's house was all class. Not big, and not pretentious, but meticulously maintained, charmingly decorated, and suited Emma completely.

Lauren grabbed the bouquet of daisies she'd picked up at the 7-Eleven on the edge of town and got out of the car, suddenly crazy nervous. What the hell was she doing taking someone like Emma to dinner? Emma's house screamed *I have my shit together.* She washed her windows for God's sake, in *December.* She had a solid job, the respect of her community, and the most gorgeous mouth in all of history. Lauren grinned. God, that kiss had been hot. She'd been so desperate to convince Emma that the dare hadn't meant anything that she'd just lost her mind for a second. Just a tiny kiss. A trial kiss. Free and easy, no purchase necessary. But then Emma had kissed her back, had all but melded into her, making noises in the back of her throat that had blotted out the possibility of taking things slowly. She hadn't bargained on Emma being so drench-her-panties enthusiastic. She figured Emma for shy and reserved, a little too jumpy to really let herself go. But Emma vibrated with passion, and Lauren threw caution to the wind, pouncing on her like a seventeen-year-old nerd pounces on the prom queen in the back seat of a beater. She probably should've attempted some finesse instead of throwing her up against the bookcase, but, well, it was difficult to regret a kiss that spectacular.

Lauren gave the house one last long look before making her way up the path to the front door. She wasn't the kind of girl someone like Emma should date, but hell if she was going to pass up the opportunity to hear what other sexy sounds Emma could make. *Sex* she could more than deliver on with that kind of inspiration.

So, filet mignon it was.

Lauren rang the bell and took an involuntary step back when it was opened by Brenda Baker aka the Cupcake. Her heart plummeted. What was *she* doing here? Feeling ridiculous holding a sad little bouquet of service station daises, Lauren cleared her throat. "Hi there. Is Emma home?"

The Cupcake stuck a hand on her generous hip and looked down her nose at Lauren. "She is. That girl is under the impression you're taking her out to dinner, Miss West."

Lauren fought the urge to roll her eyes. "She's pretty smart like that. May I come in?"

The Cupcake didn't budge. "Now, do you really think that's a wise idea?"

"Okay. I'll wait here if you'll let her know I've arrived." Lauren smiled her fakest smile.

The Cupcake dispensed with her not very niceties and got to her point. "I have half a mind to slam this door in your face and let Emma think that you've stood her up."

Oh, hell no.

She didn't care if some snobby, only-Christian-on-Sundays, judgmental nitwit wanted to give her a hard time. She'd been getting the signature Sunrise Falls treatment all week. But this witch masquerading as a sweet old lady would *not* hurt Emma's feelings. She rested a hand on the doorframe, leaned into the Cupcake's space, and lowered her voice. "You could do that. But if you do, I'll call Emma from right here and explain to her exactly what happened. You wouldn't want her to think you're intentionally ruining her date, would you?" Fuck that it wasn't an actual date. As far as the Cupcake needed to know it was an intimate seduction that would end in a marriage proposal. After that, they'd be moving to Paris.

The Cupcake narrowed her raisin eyes to slits so small it looked as if she were squeezing them shut. "You listen here, little miss. That girl is a good sweet girl. She doesn't need someone of your reputation waltzing in to sully her."

"I'd say that's Emma's decision, not yours."

"Emma doesn't understand the situation."

"Everyone with a smartphone understands the *situation*." Or at least the version the media had slathered like grease all over the internet. "Emma doesn't agree with your assessment, does she?"

Lauren smiled, irrationally pleased.

The Cupcake shoved her face into Lauren's until their noses were almost touching. "That sweet girl thinks everyone in the world is as good as she is. But I know better. The apple doesn't fall far from the tree, and you're bad news. Literally."

Before Lauren could open her mouth to respond, Emma spoke up from the top of the stairs. "Hi, sorry I'm running a bit late."

Lauren looked over the Cupcake's shoulder and swallowed really, really hard. She'd said it before, but Emma Prescott was unbelievably hot. She descended the stairs like she was Kate Winslet in *Titanic*. Emma put her hand on the Cupcake's shoulder. "Thanks, I've got it from here. I appreciate you dropping off the minutes from the meeting. I'll make sure the library takes the town's insights into consideration." Emma spoke to the Cupcake, but she hadn't stopped looking at Lauren.

The Cupcake stiffened but stepped past Lauren out the door. "Of course, sweetie. I know you have the town's best interests at heart. We've made some excellent improvements on your suggestions. I'll see you at the parade tomorrow night." She glared at Lauren for an awkwardly long beat before descending the stairs and crossing the yard to her own.

Emma's smile tipped the corners of her mouth. "Hi."

Despite just being informed she was one step down from pond scum, Lauren's answering smile was genuine. "I hope you don't mind me saying, you look absolutely amazing."

"I don't look like you've just fucked me?" Emma's tongue peeked out to lick her bottom lip.

The air flew from Lauren's lungs and disappeared into the night, leaving her breathless. "Not yet."

Emma's eyes widened and she sank her teeth into her bottom lip, that outrageously erotic blush emerging on her cheeks. She twisted her hands in front of her, as if she didn't know what to do with them, but said nothing.

"You look beautiful." Lauren cursed herself for making Emma uncomfortable. The lines of communication between her brain and her mouth were unreliable at the best of times, but around Emma they were AT&T in a windstorm. Emma's sapphire blue dress clinched at her side, the folds draping across her body at sharp angles like an artfully arranged handkerchief. Her shoulders were bare, and her dark hair swung freely. She didn't look at all like Lauren had just fucked her. She was entirely fuckable, though.

"These are for you." Lauren proffered the bunch of daisies that she'd brought on impulse because they made her think of Emma. She liked daisies. Among a deluge of showy flora, daisies were sweet, pretty, and as honest as they came.

Emma's eyes lit up. "Thank you. I can't remember the last time someone gave me flowers. I love them. Come in, let me put these in water before we go."

Emma headed to the kitchen with Lauren trailing her. Under other circumstances she would've been interested in the kind of home Emma had created for herself, but the instant Emma turned around she only had eyes for her ass. The dress might've been draped in the front, but the back was *snug*. Her mouth watered. She had to think of something to say before Emma faced her again or she'd be caught staring with her tongue hanging out. "Your hair looks great down like that. Very glossy." Not exactly scintillating conversation, but it would do.

Emma opened a cabinet above the stove and reached to retrieve a glass vase. The heartfelt, "Oh," was out of Lauren's mouth before she could stop it. She would buy Emma flowers every damn day if she got to watch her reach up on her tiptoes like that, her dress inching up the back of her thighs.

Emma spun around. "Oh, what?"

"Nothing." *Fuck.*

Emma gave her a long look before running the tap to fill the vase. She unwrapped the bouquet and clipped the stems before arranging them. "My hair looks better up with this dress, but I got the impression you like it loose, so..." Emma let the sentence trail off, leaving Lauren to her own conclusions.

"You wore your hair down for me?" Lauren was still preoccupied with Emma's luscious thighs.

Emma shrugged. "It was you that pulled my hair out of its ponytail the second you touched me, wasn't it? That seemed like a statement."

Had she? She didn't remember freeing Emma's ponytail, but she did recall how gorgeously silky Emma's hair had felt wrapped around her fingers.

Emma wasn't looking at her, busy fussing with flowers that were already perfectly arranged.

Lauren waited, but Emma didn't respond. She was beginning to suspect that Emma's silences weren't always because she was uncomfortable. Lauren skirted the island to where Emma stood facing the sink. She put a hand on Emma's hip and ran her other through Emma's hair. Emma wasn't wrong. She did like loose hair, always had. Why women wanted to muck it all up with spray and gunk she'd never understand. Soft hair you could run your fingers through, that felt good sliding against your skin, that you could use to angle a woman's head in just the right way, was just about the sexiest thing she could think of right at the moment.

"Emma?" she whispered, her lips half an inch from Emma's ear.

"What?" Emma's voice was all squeak.

"Did you dress to make me hot?"

With a hand on her hip, she could feel Emma shudder. "Yes."

The admission was a simple one, just one little vowel squished between two consonants. But Emma said yes like she was admitting to the kinkiest and most daring of escapades. Lauren went hot all over. Very hot, and very wet. She kissed the shell of Emma's ear. "I like that you thought about what I would enjoy. It's very sexy."

She moved in closer behind Emma so she could wrap an arm around her waist. With deliberate care, she traced a line across Emma's abdomen from hip to hip. "Did you make any other decisions you thought I would approve of?"

Emma's breathing was fast, her chest rising and falling quicker than usual, quicker even than was appropriate for this moment. Lauren frowned. She eased back, then slid her hand back to Emma's hip again. She ran her fingers through Emma's hair until it draped to one side. "I make you nervous, don't I?"

Emma nodded. Lauren could see their reflection in the window in front of them. Emma had her eyes closed and she was gripping the edge of the sink like it was holding her up. "Good nervous or bad nervous?" She needed to know because Emma seemed a slippery slope away from a panic attack.

Emma opened her eyes, and they stared at each other's reflection. "Good, but…"

Lauren bent and kissed the nape of her neck. "But?"

Emma breathed in deeply and let it out slowly. "I get a bit anxious. It's mostly under control, but sexual situations tend to make me more nervous than most people."

Anxious. That explained a lot. Lauren ran a hand up and down Emma's arm. "And right now?"

"I feel a bit like you're knotting me up and unravelling me at the same time." Emma laughed shakily. "I'm sorry. I must seem like a crazy person. It's not a big deal, really. I can usually breathe through it."

Lauren turned Emma in her arms. She liked being behind her. Emma's ass snugged into her crotch was sending a waterfall of tingles between her legs, but their conversation had turned from sexy to serious and she needed to see Emma's eyes. "What can I do? You know we don't have to do anything you're not comfortable with. You be in charge."

Emma smiled. "Uh-huh. I'll be in charge until the cavewoman lurking in there," she poked Lauren in the chest, "comes out and corners me against a bookcase."

Lauren winced. "I'm sorry. I—"

Emma cut her off by reaching up and brushing her mouth against Lauren's. "Don't be sorry. I liked it."

Lauren's wet tingling pussy clenched like Emma had slid the words inside her. She bit back a moan. *Emma liked it.* "Did you?"

Say it again. And again, and again.

Emma nodded. "The nervousness makes it hard to let go sometimes. Even when I want to. You taking charge like that, it helped. I didn't have to think."

Lauren buried her face in Emma's hair. She needed a couple of seconds to pull herself together so she didn't just spin Emma around, hoist her up onto the island, shove her dress up, and show her exactly what it would be like when she took control. Or perhaps it was more accurate to say when she *lost* control. The difference was starting to blur. But Emma wanted them to get to know each other first, and this was prime *getting to know you* territory. "I'd never have guessed you were nervous when you were kissing me," Lauren said.

Emma shrugged again. "At some point the balance tips, and I forget myself and just focus on…"

Emma trailed off at exactly the wrong moment, leaving Lauren craving the rest of her sentence the way an addict craves their next hit. "You focus on what?"

The blush was back, spreading across Emma's cheeks like sunrise. "On the way I feel."

Lauren's skin was so hot and tight she expected to burst into flames at any second. Emma's natural shy-but-eager combo was killing her one sexy admission at a time. "How did you feel when we were kissing?"

Emma bit her lip again, her breathing unsteady. "Lauren—"

"Tell me. Take it slow. Breathe if it helps. But I want to know."

Emma made a sound that got caught somewhere between a squeak and a whimper. She breathed purposefully for a few seconds and said, "I felt good and sexy and clumsy and desperate."

"All good adjectives." Lauren shoved her hands into her pants pockets so she didn't use them to fuck Emma blind. If they kept this up, she wasn't sure even a herd of angry buffalo could prevent her from touching Emma. "But they don't tell me anything about sensation. About how it *felt*."

Lauren watched Emma's throat work as she swallowed. "I was wet. Is that what you want to know?"

On the word *wet* Lauren's panties instantly drenched with desire. Fuck. What was she doing? She was drowning, gasping for air, so so close to losing her thread of control that it was as insubstantial as wet spaghetti. She wanted to know if Emma was wet again right now. She wanted to feel it on her fingers. She wanted to not be going to dinner tonight. "Much better." She brushed the damp hair off Emma's forehead. "I'm sorry if that was hard."

Emma shook her head. "You're the best immersion therapy I've ever had."

Lauren shoved her hand back into her pants so Emma wouldn't see her fingers tremble. She needed to get them out of this damn kitchen and on their way to dinner. "We should—"

"Will you kiss me again, please?" Emma asked.

Lauren groaned. *Fuuuck.* "Emma, you wanted to go out to dinner."

Emma began twisting her hands again. "I know. I still do. I just want to feel what it's like again. The kiss."

Patience was the virtue Lauren hated the most, especially right now. "If I kiss you again, we won't make it to dinner."

Emma's eyes darkened. "No?"

Lauren couldn't help herself, she backed Emma up against the sink, pushed Emma's dress up to mid-thigh, and then slid a leg between hers.

"If you play with fire you'll get burned," she murmured, her mouth so fucking close to Emma's she could already feel the kiss.

Emma gasped and squeezed her eyes shut. Her breathing was ragged again, but this time it didn't appear to be nerves. "Please." Emma leaned into Lauren's thigh so her pussy pressed against Lauren's pants. *Ohfuckyes.* "I want you to kiss me."

Lauren did the only thing possible. The only thing anyone with half a brain and a functioning mouth would do in this situation. She gave the girl what she wanted.

Emma's mouth was searingly sweet, chili pepper wrapped in candy cane. Lauren planted her hands on the back of Emma's head and kissed her hard, harder than she should have. Emma gasped and she took advantage of the opportunity to slide her tongue inside Emma's mouth, discovering every inch of her with nips and thrusts. She tugged on Emma's bottom lip until Emma moaned and went liquid against her.

"Is this what you wanted?" Lauren asked between kisses. "You want me to kiss you like I'm going to fuck you?"

Emma whimpered and rubbed her pussy jerkily against Lauren's thigh. "Yes."

She pressed her forehead to Emma's and caught her breath. Caught her common sense. Caught her fucking sanity that had taken the keys and was currently on the joyride of its life. Emma wanted this, she wanted *her*, that was clear. Kissing her until Emma came riding her thigh was blow-her-brains-out sexy, and she couldn't believe she was stopping. If this were a movie, she'd be screaming at the actor right now. *Just fuck the girl, you moron.* But she couldn't do it. She couldn't actually *seduce* Emma. Not when Emma'd made her desires clear.

I want to matter enough to have dinner with.

Lauren stared at Emma flushed and sweaty. Emma's thighs wrapped around her leg. Emma's pussy tight against her. So beautiful and so gloriously *undone* from nothing more than a kiss. She wanted to see what happened when they more than kissed. When she stroked Emma's naked skin, sucked on her nipples, pushed her tongue inside Emma's pussy. The weight of her need was making her dizzy and tempting her to be careless.

Lauren kissed her again, but this time the kiss wasn't driven by force. It wasn't hard or demanding or consuming. She kissed her the way she'd planned to, *after* dinner. Not an I-want-to-fuck-you kiss. Rather, an I-like-you kiss. A you're-special kiss. An I'm-lucky-to-be-kissing-you kiss. She traced the curve of Emma's jaw, trailed her fingers slowly down Emma's throat until they rested on her shoulders. Emma sighed and wound her arms around Lauren's waist until they rested at the small of her back. The kiss was lazy and languid, the heat rising slowly like steam from a sauna, engulfing them.

Lauren stroked her shoulders and kissed her as tenderly as she knew how, savoring the warmth, sinking into a moment she wanted to capture and never let go. She studiously ignored the churning in her belly that told her, in no uncertain terms, this kind of kissing was a very bad idea. Sex was simple, yet somehow, even with Emma's pussy pressed to her leg, this didn't feel like fucking. Lauren might be about to take her to dinner, but caring wasn't on the menu.

CHAPTER SIX

The restaurant Lauren had chosen was small and homey. A converted factory with centuries old tin ceilings and wide plank floorboards patchy with four shades of stain. The half dozen tables were solid oak, covered in cheap red cloth, and the walls boasted black-and-white photos of the Sunrise Falls of yesteryear. The hostess led them to a table by the window, thankfully far enough from the bar that Garth Brooks was merely a rumble.

Lauren pulled out Emma's chair. "No candlelight. Sorry."

"I didn't mean for you to take me literally." Emma sat gratefully. If she was sitting down she wouldn't have to concentrate on keeping herself upright and walking in a straight line. Sexual arousal had a way of pulling her focus. It's not like she had eons of experience with sex, but she hadn't been living under a rock. Other people somehow managed to do two things at once. Christian Grey could tie up Anastasia Steele with a raging hard-on, so why couldn't Emma talk dirty, or touch Lauren back, or walk in a goddamn straight line when she was out of her mind turned on? The question mattered. She really wanted to enjoy dinner, and the throbbing in her panties had claimed squatters' rights and was there for the duration.

"I like to give you what you want." Lauren had a look in her eye that suggested they weren't really talking about candles.

"Lucky me." Emma pulled the menu toward her and studied it like she'd be taking a test. God. Had this been a bad idea? She'd spent the better part of two hours getting ready, choosing just the right sexy but not slutty heels, agonizing over the perfect shade of lipstick, fussing with her hair that wouldn't sit smoothly. She stifled a grin. The fussing had been both futile and completely worth it. Lauren had liked her hair, and Emma was surprised to discover that she'd liked Lauren running her fingers through it. Weird the things that made her hot sometimes.

She was looking forward to learning more about Lauren, about who she was, what mattered to her. All the things that led her to be the person she'd become. She'd been ridiculously excited for the not-a-date. But then Lauren had traced a line along the edge of her panties and all at once the very last thing she wanted was conversation. She'd wanted to stand there forever and let Lauren's fingers roam wherever the hell she intended for them to roam. Sunrise Falls wasn't exactly brimming with girl-meets-girl romantic possibilities, but she had a few lackluster relationships up her sleeve. Being turned on wasn't a new sensation. But she'd never felt such desire to be *taken* before. Not outside of her wildest fantasies, at least. And Lauren didn't make it easy. She hadn't been content to let her stand there a passive reveler in the pleasure. No. Lauren had wanted to talk. She'd wanted Emma to admit how it had all felt out loud.

She'd wanted to *know*.

Lauren's questions were caresses that sent sensation blazing a trail down her stomach and between her legs. The fire catching and spreading until her entire body was engulfed. Emma hadn't been able to say very much, getting halfway there and then trailing off in embarrassment. Her heartbeat pounding in her ears and her tongue Velcroed to the roof of her mouth.

What did Lauren see in her? She wasn't the least bit sexy. But Lauren seemed to enjoy touching her anyway. Kissing her, sliding her leg between Emma's. Hadn't that been the most perfect torture. She'd lost all sense of herself, rubbing against Lauren with shameless desperation. She could feel her face heating and willed it away. Her cheeks were the freaking town crier advertising her dirty mind.

Lauren smiled at her over the top of the wine list. "You're awfully quiet over there. Not having second thoughts, are you?"

She was, but not the way Lauren meant. Her second and third and fourth thoughts revolved around ditching dinner and rolling into bed. "I was thinking we want the same thing, you and I."

"I'd say that's an accurate observation."

"*Not* what I meant." Emma smiled. "I wanted to have dinner tonight because I wanted to get to know you. For you to get to know me, so that, if or when we did have sex, it would mean more than…"

"Friction?" Lauren supplied for her when Emma trailed off.

Emma nodded. "I'm not a random fuck kind of girl."

"Noted and appreciated and cured by filet mignon," Lauren said.

Emma nodded again. "True. But it's not just me, is it? You want to get to know me too. Just in a different way, with a different language."

Lauren put the wine list down and rested her chin in her palm. "Go on."

"Well, okay, so back at the library you had to hold my hand, right? I mean, you *had* to. You couldn't be open without touching me."

Lauren frowned. "Well—"

"Just hear me out. It's a good thing. Tonight, you couldn't help touching me again, and yeah, some of that was seduction, but you'd already agreed to dinner, so it wasn't really necessary. Asking me about being nervous in social situations wasn't about sex. Asking if there was anything you could do to help wasn't about sex. Asking me how I felt when we were kissing *was* about sex, but it was more than that too. You actually wanted to know. Like the answer mattered."

Like she had mattered.

Lauren's frown was so deep, it looked engraved. "Well, yeah. Obviously, it matters. Anyone you get naked with should matter, at least to the degree that you can appreciate what attracts them, what makes them hot, what they want from sex."

Emma wasn't sure she'd ever met anyone who actually lived by that principle, let alone been in bed with them. The whole point of casual sex was that it didn't really matter, right? Wham-bam and move on. She'd never understood the appeal. If you were just in it for the orgasm, wouldn't it be easier to load your vibrator with a couple of double A's and invest in some adult entertainment? Orgasms were nice and everything, but for her sex was about *connecting*, and she thought that maybe Lauren agreed. Talking about sex, asking questions, that was connecting, right? Only with kissing instead of dating.

"Okay, yes," Emma said. "I want the same thing too. But my version is superior because it involves steak and also, your entire backstory starting with where you went to preschool."

"You call that superior? Mine involves those delicious little sounds you make when I touch you. And screaming orgasms."

Emma half expected the room to tilt when all her blood rushed between her legs and began to pulse there as if her heartbeat had officially changed address. The suggestion that Lauren could make her come so hard she screamed had her fighting back a moan. Somehow, she managed to raise her eyebrows. "What makes you think I'll scream?"

"Eternal optimism."

Emma grinned at that. "So, can we compromise here? Pair some verbal knowledge with some physical?"

"I don't see why not," Lauren said. "I went to the Sunrise Falls pre-K on Main Street. What else do you want to know?"

The waiter came and took their order, then gathered up the menus, leaving Emma with nothing to busy her hands. She took a long steadying breath and put a mental barrier between herself and thoughts of sex. There was in fact one specific thing she wanted to know, but it wasn't the kind of how-ya-doin' question that dropped easily into conversation. It was a hand grenade dropped into a packed elevator.

"I need to know what happened with Caroline Bennett. I'm not saying it will change my opinion, but, well, getting naked with someone is a big deal in my world, and I want to know you."

Dead silence for thirty seconds and counting. Emma could hear herself breathing. Lauren didn't look as if she was breathing at all. All expression left her face, like Emma's words had wiped it clean. She was standing in front of a firing squad with Emma holding a riffle. "Knowing what happened with Caroline doesn't equate to knowing me." Lauren's voice was precisely measured. She didn't fold her arms, but she might as well have for the wall that flew up between them.

"That's true," Emma said carefully. "But knowing what you've been through does. Our histories shape us."

"That's not the same thing as defining us."

Emma twisted her hands in the cloth napkin in front of her. "I'm sorry. Forget about it. I shouldn't have intruded. It's none of my business."

"No," Lauren said. "It really isn't." Then she sighed. "But I can understand why you might be hesitant to have a sexual encounter with the woman who had her face plastered all over the media for seducing the wife of one of the richest men on the West Coast."

Emma tried to smile. "One could take that as an endorsement of your skills. You must be *very* good to have been able to seduce Caroline away from her billions."

Lauren didn't smile back. She sat stony faced and still as a statue. She looked *scared*, and that had Emma's heart contorting itself into complicated yoga poses. Whatever had happened back in San Francisco, she didn't fit the temptress-vixen-seductress mold the media had created for her. Emma wished she hadn't asked. Lauren wasn't some skanky girl in a too-tight dress purring dirty words into the ear of a wealthy and powerful woman. She was gorgeous and considerate and an excellent kisser. Not just melt her brain to sticky toffee kisses, either. Nice kisses. Sweet kisses. Kisses that took care and touched her deeper than skin. Emma needed to know what'd happened. Talking was her language. But she didn't need the answer to be sure she liked Lauren, that she wanted Lauren. Touching was Lauren's language, and when they'd touched tonight, she'd already told Emma all she'd needed to know.

Emma reached across the table and wiggled her fingers. "Give me your hand."

"Why?"

"Because I'm going to hold it while you tell me what *really* happened. I already know the stuff in the media is bullshit."

Lauren stared at her. "How do you know that?"

"Because you wouldn't have done what they say you did."

Emma wiggled her fingers again.

Lauren's stomach was executing flailing belly flops into a concrete pit, but she put her hand in Emma's and tried for a smile she wasn't sure she'd managed to pull off. She didn't know why she was surprised. She should've known that Emma would ask. Should've expected it. Been prepared for it. It's not like she hadn't spent the last three months anticipating it, and then getting it, from every single person she came into contact with. Well, not every person. People like the Cupcake judged first and didn't bother with silly inconveniences like questions. Emma hadn't judged her. Hadn't asked before tonight. But Lauren should've known that was too good to last.

"I guess you know I was his assistant." Lauren only realized she was squeezing Emma's hand once her fingers had started to ache. She let go and Emma promptly picked her hand back up again.

"Yes. That's a great job at a company like BennCorp. You must be talented."

Lauren shrugged. Talented, sure, but not all that special at the job outlined in her contract. She'd been *talented* at not letting James Bennett's authoritarian dictatorship get to her. If you worked for the boss at BennCorp you did things his way, whether or not it was the right way. Lauren got that. Hell, she'd respected that because more often than not James's way *had* been the right way. That some people got their panties in a twist when they were told what to do hadn't been her problem. James was more likely to ask if you'd woken up stupid that day than he was to overlook even the smallest human error. Lauren hadn't minded. She hadn't wanted an easy job. She'd wanted to be *good*, and BennCorp was the best. James Bennett was the captain of his ship. He'd gone through a football team's worth of assistants before Lauren, and she'd survived Devil-Wears-Prada-style, only for a guy at a media conglomerate, instead of Meryl Streep at a fashion magazine. That was a shame too. She'd have enjoyed working for Meryl.

"I tried…" Lauren rubbed a hand over her face. *Just say it. Stalling isn't going to make the shit tastier.* "His wife, Caroline, took an interest in me. She'd come by the office frequently to see James, unannounced and usually in a snit over some problem only one percenters would care about. I ended up talking to her quite a bit because my job was to keep the-chill-on-my-champagne-flute-isn't-cold-enough-darling pestering out of my boss's hair. That was my job." Lauren had already said that. She'd just been doing her job. But people tended to miss that part.

Emma nodded, stroking Lauren's fingers one at a time with her thumb. She just listened, her eyes never leaving Lauren's face. For some reason, Emma's steady eye contact settled her. Emma so rarely looked her dead in the eyes and that she was now meant more than words.

"Unfortunately, I was good enough that Caroline spent most of her time trying to get around *me* and not with James. Real people, people whose blood isn't bluer than an August sky, don't tend to get noticed by the Carolines of the world. We're below their attention, glorified servants. But apparently finding a decent assistant is second to gold, and James had said something to her at some point, about me, and how I was good at what I did. He'd made some crack about how well I *handled* her, and that'd hurt her feelings. I didn't know that then, of course. Caroline Bennett doesn't appreciate being handled and doesn't appreciate that her husband was grateful for this hard-to-define-on-a-résumé skillset. I was being set up right from the start, and I didn't know it."

They said pain faded over time, but for Lauren this memory only grew heavier. Regret and injustice like a barbell dropped on her chest, the weight stacked to breaking point.

"Another of the seventy-two billion things I didn't know was that James and Caroline were having marriage problems." Lauren shrugged. "He's not an easy man, and it didn't seem strange that he treated his wife with the same I'm-surrounded-by-idiots attitude that he treated everyone else. I'd only worked for him a year. I hadn't seen them during the good times."

Emma stroked soothingly over her wrist. "Tell me what happened."

She was stalling. Giving too much context. But the context mattered. The context was what a suspiciously in focus video in a dimly lit bar hadn't shown. "She didn't like me, and so she used me to get back at her husband. She wanted to make him jealous or piss him off or just hurt him, I guess. She knew I was gay because it was one of the things James liked about me. I wouldn't be at risk of misunderstanding a situation and initiating any of those unfortunate #metoo debacles. His words. I didn't think anything of it. I was just happy my boss wasn't a homophobe, even if he was a misogynist."

"That's hardly an improvement," Emma said dryly.

Lauren shrugged. "James wanted out of the marriage, and Caroline was pissed. She'd signed a prenup and would only get millions, the poor thing. She decided if she couldn't screw James for more money, she'd impugn his manhood instead, and she used me to do it. Caroline started getting friendlier and dropping by more frequently, giving me little gifts. A scented candle here, a cashmere sweater there. I took them so I didn't offend her, but I never used them. I stashed them in my desk draw like contraband."

"She was interested in you romantically?" Emma asked.

Lauren laughed, the sound simultaneously harsh and vulnerable, as raw as a scraped knee. "She was interested in me thinking she was. I didn't play her little game. I never flirted back.

Never gave her one iota of encouragement, not even friendship. She was my boss's pain in the ass wife, with terrible boundaries to boot. She didn't like that either."

"How did every media outlet in the country end up with that video?" Emma asked.

Lauren hesitated. God. She'd only answered this question a hundred thousand times. It should've rolled off the tongue by now. But she cared what Emma thought of her. And that video had been worth not only a thousand words, but hundreds of thousands of dollars.

Emma was tracing circles in her palm, her slender fingers in constant movement on Lauren's.

"You're going to think less of me," Lauren said.

Emma frowned at her. "Why would you think that?"

"Because *everyone* thinks less of me?"

"Well, excuse me if I'm not everyone." Emma stared past Lauren's shoulder for a few seconds, then did that direct eye contact thing again. "Here's what I know. I like you. I trust that you're a good person. I trust that this attraction between us is mutual. I appreciate your willingness to do things my way so that I'm comfortable. I'm *not* everyone, Lauren. I don't want to know what happened to stem my curiosity. I want to know because it's a big fucking deal and it happened to someone I care about."

Someone I care about. That had Lauren's heart in error mode, stuck between rising with hope and sinking with, well, the truth. Emma shouldn't care about her. This was supposed to be a fun diversion. Can't-stop-the-rush pleasure. Only they hadn't even had sex and the rush was turning into something a lot more dangerous. Lauren pushed all that aside. Now wasn't the time to be obsessing about it. She'd kept Emma in suspense long enough.

"I was at the bar of my own accord. That much is true."

"Kink's." Emma stumbled on the word. "A fetish bar."

Lauren nodded.

"That's something we should discuss for later, if kink is your thing."

This wasn't really about the kink bar. At least, that'd only been one element. "Caroline came in. God only knows how she'd found me. She was drunk. Started rambling on about how James didn't love her anymore, and how girls do it better."

"It?" Emma asked.

Lauren waved a hand vaguely. "It. Sex."

"Right," Emma said.

"She was completely plastered, but I couldn't call security, couldn't flag the bartender, couldn't get help from anyone. This was *Caroline Bennett*. I was trying to protect her reputation. I was an idiot."

"You were doing your job," Emma said simply.

Lauren's shoulders sagged. She hadn't realized how tense she'd been until it seeped out of her. *She'd been doing her damn fucking job.* "I put my arm around her to lead her outside, get an Uber. The more I insisted we go outside, the more hysterical she got. Falling down drunk and leaning on me. People were staring. I was terrified someone would recognize her. Eventually, she says, 'Take me back to your place, that's the only way I'll leave.'"

"God." Emma squeezed Lauren's hand.

"Yeah. I played right into her hands. Obviously, I had no intention of taking her home, but my priority was to get her outside and away from anyone with an iPhone, ironic as that sounds now. So, I said yes. We left the bar, and she miraculously sobered up and got placidly into a cab. My party mood had evaporated by then, so I went home too." Lauren shook her head. "I should've gone back inside. If I had, people wouldn't have assumed we'd left together."

"You couldn't have known," Emma said gently. "She set all this up then?"

"Yup." Lauren paused as the waiter reappeared with their steaks. When they were alone again she said, "She had a camera crew there. Micro cams or something, I don't know. But they had sound and audio and caught everything. Superior editing made it look as if I was coming on to her and we'd left together."

"But *why?*" Emma said.

"She wanted to embarrass him. It's one thing to suggest your husband's mediocre in bed. It's another to suggest he's so bad that you can get better with a woman. For all his business acumen, James is a misogynistic dickwad, and she used that against him. She sent the video anonymously to all his competitors, and they were obviously only too happy to run with it for a very long time. Caroline knew she was done. She wanted to go out with a splash, and she wanted to teach us both a lesson. No one *handles* her. She sent me a nice little note to that effect the day the press ran the story. I'd annoyed her, so making me collateral damage in her marital dispute wasn't something she lost sleep over."

Emma's brown eyes were wide. She had held her hand as a gesture of support, but she was practically breaking Lauren's fingers with the strength of her grip. "I'm so sorry. What a *bitch*."

The barbell lifted from her chest and she breathed deep for the first time in forever. Emma believed her. There'd been other people who'd believed her side of things too—her mom, anyone who really knew Caroline. James. James had believed her. He'd apologized to her. Then he summarily fired her ass into next Tuesday and spun the story to his advantage, casting himself as the brokenhearted business tycoon who'd been duped by the women in his life. He'd looked like a bit of a mush bucket, but the stock price hadn't taken a hit, and that's all James had ever really cared about anyway. She couldn't even muster up any enthusiasm to blame him. He couldn't be seen as condoning a situation like that. Appearances mattered more than the truth to people like James and Caroline.

She wondered if appearances mattered to Emma.

"There you have it. The real story behind the raunchy lesbian scandal of Caroline Bennett hooking up with her husband's secretary in a kink club. Sorry it lacks the salaciousness that sold it to Fox News."

Emma frowned. "Don't be a jerk. You think I *wanted* it to be salacious? That I wanted it to be exactly as the media presented it? Trust me, I didn't."

Well, there was her answer. Appearances mattered to Emma, too.

Lauren sighed. "We probably shouldn't have come to a restaurant for dinner. I can make a decent stir-fry. I could've cooked for you at home."

"Why?" Emma asked.

"People might start thinking you're a kinky slut too. That's not a good look for the town librarian, no matter what claims the porn industry may make to the contrary."

Emma sat back in her seat as if a strong wind had blown her back there. Lauren wasn't sure if it was the implication that Emma ought to be embarrassed to be seen with her, or her comment about librarians in porn that'd done it. Emma Prescott didn't seem like the kind of girl who had a Pornhub subscription. "Wow. That's real nice of you to be so concerned about my reputation."

Wasn't it a *good* thing she wanted to protect Emma from being associated with her not-quite-blown-over-yet scandal? Geez. "You know people are going to start talking." Lauren did her best not to sound like she was sulking. She couldn't even knock on Emma's front door without copping an earful. Sunrise Falls, where being a busybody was a side hustle because no one's body was busy having an actual life in this one traffic light town.

Emma reached for her wineglass and downed half of the mid-priced cabernet in two swallows. "I'm going to give you a pass because I appreciate that this is a very difficult situation, and you've earned the right to be sensitive about it. But let's get one thing straight before we take this shindig any further."

Lauren fought a smile at Emma's use of the word *shindig* to portray their relationship. No, not a relationship. Not a date either. It was…Lauren had no fucking clue what it was, so she supposed shindig was just as apt as any other descriptor. "I'm listening."

"I don't believe you were the girl they made you out to be. That girl wouldn't have kissed me like you did. She wouldn't be sitting here eating a steak she doesn't really want and talking about a night she'd rather forget. But if you had gone out of your way to seduce a rich married woman, I'd still want to sleep with you."

It was Lauren's turn to sit back stunned. "You'd have been okay with me being a cheater?"

Emma shook her head. "First, you weren't the one who made promises you couldn't keep, and second, everyone makes mistakes. It's not homo sapiens' most attractive quality, but it's the truth. We fuck up. If you'd fucked up by acting on an attraction when you shouldn't have, I'd say you more than paid for it."

Lauren stared, the air in her lungs rushing out like a deflating balloon. "How did you grow up in this town and turn out so..."

What Emma was defied words. She was too amazingly awesome to be confined to the alphabet. Lauren wanted to curl up inside this bubble of understanding that Emma had created for her and never leave. "Thank you. I mean, I'm really glad that wasn't the case, for my own integrity, but thank you."

"Thank you for telling me the truth. I know it wasn't easy." Emma picked up her knife and cut through her steak. "So, on to the important stuff. Do you have personal experience with librarian porn, or were you just trying to get a rise out of me?"

CHAPTER SEVEN

Emma was going to pass out from sheer anticipation. Lauren had been a superlative dinner companion. After their heart-to-heart, they'd fallen into less daunting conversation. Lauren was charming, with a self-deprecating sense of humor, and Emma had finally been able to relax a little. Enough to appreciate the way Lauren's hair glowed in the dim lighting. The way her fingers wrapped around her wineglass like she was cradling a lover. The deep vee of her shirt that exposed skin so tantalizing Emma was distracted by thoughts of running her tongue over it. That led her to imagining what Lauren's skin would taste like, indulging herself in all the varied possibilities until her mouth had begun to water. The taste of Lauren's skin led her to theorize on the texture, the scent, the shade. Would Lauren flush when she was aroused like Emma did? Or did that only happen to people with pale skin?

She enjoyed herself immensely, even managing, for a short time, to backburner her craving for Lauren to rip her clothes off in favor of basking in her smile, laughing at her jokes, and all-round having fun. But her not-thinking-sex-thoughts came to a screeching halt when Lauren reached for the dessert spoon the waiter had placed in the middle of the table, and she caught the edge of black ink peeking out from under Lauren's shirt. She was an intelligent woman, she had a master's degree to prove it, but knowing that Lauren had ink under her clothes turned the clock in her mind back a billion years to some pre-verbal state where she'd have to resort to crude hand signals to communicate. The tattoo somehow turned Lauren into a rock star heartthrob. Emma basically panted like a thirteen-year-old girl at her first One Direction concert. Or whoever it was thirteen-year-old girls panted about these days.

Riding back to Emma's house in near silence, Lauren tapped her fingers along to some song on the radio and Emma tried not to get a crick in her neck while trying every possible tilt of her head. It was useless though, she couldn't see the tattoo from this angle, so she busied herself by imagining opening Lauren's shirt one button at a time, revealing her tattoo like she was opening her own private Christmas present.

"Here we are." Lauren pulled up in front of Emma's house, then turned off the ignition and shifted to face her. "Did the ride home give you enough time to decide whether this is really something you want to do?"

"Is that what I was supposed to be thinking about?" Emma asked. She'd be getting an F for that assignment.

Lauren studied her. "You've been so quiet I figured that's what you were thinking. I want you to want this, and not just when I'm touching you. Being overcome with passion is sexy sometimes, but it can also lead to regret. I have enough of that already."

Emma wasn't sure what to say to that. In fact, she was a little pissed they were having this conversation at all. She'd admitted her attraction, had already said yes. What did Lauren want? A statement written in blood? A welcome mat with *please fuck me* stenciled on it? Was this a projecting thing? Was Lauren the one who wasn't sure? Her head started to hurt from all the questions bouncing around inside it, so she kept her response simple. "I don't have to think about it because I already know I want this. I'm in, Lauren."

She wasn't sure exactly what she was in *for*, but that was semantics, right?

Lauren frowned so hard it looked as if it hurt her face. "You're sure?"

Emma frowned right back at her. "Are *you* sure?"

"Hell yes."

"Then clue me in as to why we're sitting in the car talking about a non-issue instead of going inside to act out our mutual sureness?"

Lauren sighed. "You're a good, sweet girl."

"Huh?"

"That's what the Cupcake said to me tonight, before you came downstairs. You're good and sweet and I'm not. I don't deserve someone like you, even for a night."

A night. Emma shook that off. She'd fall apart over only having Lauren for a night some other time. "That's bullshit, and you know it. Brenda only sees what she wants to see. You and I know different. Anyway, since when did you start listening to anything the Cupcake said?"

Lauren's shoulders lifted in a shrug too weary to do justice to the name. "She's not the only one. Anyway, she's right about you. You *are* good and sweet."

Emma waved that away. "I'm not that sweet."

"Oh, no?" Lauren grinned at her. "Are you prepared to prove it?"

"Are you prepared to let me?" Emma shot back, sounding a hell of a lot braver than she felt.

Lauren opened the driver's side door. "Let's go find out."

Emma's knees shook as they walked up the path to her front door. Now was so not the time to morph into a trembling, monosyllabic, airhead. She had to keep it together so she could, you know, actually enjoy Lauren West rocking her world. She had no doubt that was exactly what was about to happen. Lauren had promised screaming orgasms, after all.

Lauren waited beside her at the front door, and then Lauren trailed her up the stairs to her bedroom, and then Lauren stood by her bed looking at her like she was the only woman in the room. Of course, she *was* the only woman in the room, but Lauren still managed to make that look feel special.

"So, um, here we are," Emma said. Bonus points for Captain Obvious.

"Any special requests?" Lauren moved in close and ran her fingers through Emma's hair again, pulling it up off the nape of her neck and cradling the weight in her hands.

Emma tensed as a fist of anxiety closed down around her throat at the exact same moment it squeezed all her insides in a vice grip. She could only shake her head. They were really going to do this. Make love.

No.

She mentally punched herself in the nose. Not make love. They were going to have *sex*, probably lots of it, but she shouldn't confuse fantasy and reality. Lauren might respect her enough to buy her a meal before jumping her bones, but this wasn't about love. This was throw her up against a bookcase passion and all Emma's girl parts were totally on board with that plan.

"No requests? That's okay, I much prefer to learn by experience." Lauren dragged Emma against her, catching her mouth in a kiss that had her head spinning and her body going limp with need. How many times had they kissed now? Three? Four? She should be starting to get used to it. But every time, the air around them closed in on her, and she went warm and wet and squirmy. Lauren caressed her throat, along her collarbone, across her shoulders. Touches that should've been simple but were static electricity against her skin.

When they came up for air, they were both gasping.

"I'd say kissing is definitely on the list of things you like. I wonder what else I'll discover." Lauren's tone was all mischief.

Emma's response stalled halfway up her throat as her heartbeat tried to fight its way out of her chest. If Lauren went looking she'd discover a hell of a lot more than she bargained for. A lot more than any one-night stand ever expected. Emma breathed out slowly. She had to keep herself in check. Lauren was just playing, trying to put her at ease.

"I'm not all that difficult to please."

If only Lauren knew just *how* easy she was.

Lauren made a sexy little vibrating sound in the back of her throat as she backed her toward the bed. "I like that. Responsiveness is so underrated."

Emma's stomach dipped. She was responsive all right. To a fault. Her own fault, usually.

Lauren's fingers found the zipper on the side of her dress. "Is this okay?"

She nodded. Her anxiety was a sixteen-year-old, too full of herself to listen to the logic of an older, wiser Emma. But like any rational adult, she gave it her best shot, even though she knew it was useless. Lauren didn't want a Californian Barbie doll princess bikini model and she liked the way Emma looked. If she didn't, then they wouldn't be here, right? Emma could take her clothes off with confidence. She had nothing to worry about. She absolutely, positively, should not inquire as to whether they could have sex fully dressed.

Emma slipped the dress down and let it fall to the floor. She didn't suck her stomach in. She really badly wanted to, but she didn't because Lauren had said she liked her curves. She had plenty of them, and from the look on Lauren's face, she liked them a lot. Emma stepped out of the puddle of silk and crouched to unstrap her heels.

"Oh no." Lauren tugged her back up. "Leave those on."

Emma laughed, the sound so nervous and shaky she winced. "You can't be serious."

"As serious as my tenth-grade math final," Lauren said. "This is much sexier than math, though."

Emma could almost feel Lauren's gaze raking over her skin.

"You're stunning," Lauren said quietly.

No jokes. No teasing. Just truth.

Emma blushed, then groaned, then laughed. "Thank you. Maybe we can even the score though? I'm dying to see what's under your shirt."

"Are you now?"

Emma felt heat rise up her neck. "I mean your tattoo. I got a peek at dinner, and I'm dying to know what it is."

"Ah." Lauren's face did that annoying as hell impassive thing. "It's not all that sexy, I'm afraid."

Emma shook her head and went to work on Lauren's buttons. "Impossible. The tattoo part makes it sexy, whatever it is just adds weight." She parted Lauren's shirt and read out loud the sentence in simple script on the left side of her chest. "What doesn't kill me makes me stronger."

Huh. That's an interesting statement to have tattooed across your heart.

Emma traced the script with a fingertip. "Nietzsche. Impressive."

"It's not. I didn't even know it was that German philosopher guy when I had it done. Then I found out later that he was part of Hitler's inspiration for the Holocaust, so…"

Emma shook her head. "The Bible was used as inspiration for the Crusades, does that make it evil? Tell me about this. Why did you get it?"

Lauren gave her a very slow, very thorough once-over. "I'd really rather be doing something else."

"Talking is my thing. Humor me."

Lauren sighed. "My childhood wasn't easy. Mom is awesome, and she did her best as a single parent, but we scraped by. I felt bad about that for a long time, like I was less than other people. Then I got to San Francisco and realized all that hard stuff had actually really helped me. I was more confident, had more courage, knew myself better, because I didn't have it easy. So, I got this tattoo to remind myself that sometimes hard things can have good results."

Emma traced the word "kill" on Lauren's heart. She had a feeling Lauren had glazed over most of the truth. Lots of people grew up poor and didn't get tattoos to remind themselves they'd survived. But now wasn't the time, and as badly as she wanted to know the answer, Lauren had already revealed so much tonight. Asking her for more felt wrong somehow, like she was seeking a degree of closeness they didn't have.

There were some secrets a one-night stand didn't have a right to know.

"That's very brave and self-aware. Most people run from adversity their whole lives. It takes a special strength to face it and come out stronger."

"Or a special brand of masochism." Lauren shrugged her shirt off. "Now, if you insist on talking, I insist that we change the subject."

Emma hadn't intended on talking. She was more than a little preoccupied drinking in Lauren's small breasts in her simple black bra, her flat stomach with just a hint of muscle, and all that glorious, glorious tan skin that looked oh-so touchable. But now that Lauren had said that, Emma wanted to know what the next conversation would be. "I can agree to that. Do you have something in mind?"

There was a gleam in Lauren's eye that Emma didn't trust one little bit. "I do. This is all about getting to know each other, right? And talking is your thing, but it's time to switch to my way to communicating. Plus, it will help you relax. You're jumpy."

"I'm not," Emma said, even though she totally was. That Lauren had picked up on it was both comforting and annoying. Couldn't Emma at least pretend to be cool? How did Lauren just *know* these things?

"You are. That's okay, but I think some talking might help. Ease us into things. It's an experiment. We're going to trade confessions," Lauren said.

"Confessions?" Emma asked as if she were an echo.

"Yup. So, let's talk. I'll even go first to make it easy on you." Lauren tapped her chin exaggeratedly. "Let's see, I could start by confessing I was late getting up this morning because I was having this amazing fantasy about a certain dark-haired lusciously curved woman above me, rubbing her pussy all over my stomach, her head was thrown back so all her beautiful hair fell down her back. She was having a very, very good time."

"Oh my God." Emma was sure the house was going to burn down because the bedroom was suddenly an inferno. "You can't say stuff like that."

Lauren raised her eyebrows. "Why not?"

"Because…" Because no one ever *admitted* to stuff like that out loud, did they? And certainly not when it involved her. "I don't know."

Lauren took Emma's hands and placed them on her belly. Held them there. "Can you see it? Sliding yourself all over me, getting me all nice and wet?"

Emma's head filled with the image and her face flamed. She couldn't speak. Her vocal cords had been switched off as all the blood rushed between her legs.

"It's natural you know, to imagine it. Now it's your turn."

"My turn?" Oh, this was a bad idea. A very bad idea. She'd skip a turn, thank you very much.

"Yup. Confession time. Did you think about me last night? Maybe this morning?"

Emma twisted her hands in front of her. Ugh. Why was this so embarrassing? Almost everyone masturbated. Lauren was right, it *was* natural. But there was a hell of a big difference between knowing in theory and facing in reality. Especially when the star of your X-rated highlight reel was standing right in front of you. "Last night."

Lauren waited and when Emma didn't say anything else, she laughed. "What's wrong, Ms. Talking Is My Thing? Cat got your tongue?"

"Shut up." Emma tried to shove her, but Lauren caught her and pulled her close. Lauren kissed her, making her melt into a puddle of pleasure goo. Pleasure goo was totally a thing. With Lauren's shirt off and Emma in only her underwear, their skin slid together and she moaned. She ran her hands up and down Lauren's back, luxuriating in the feel of her body. Lauren was so different. Not hard, but taut and firm and toned in a way that Emma just wasn't. She traced the definition in Lauren's shoulders. "You feel so good."

Lauren made an agreeing sound that didn't comprise actual words as she drugged Emma with kisses, trailing those very talented fingers all over her in caresses far too light and oh so tempting. "Don't think you can distract me with your feminine wiles. Tell me about last night."

Emma couldn't look at her, so she stared at the ceiling instead. "I thought about us in the library, what might've happened if we hadn't stopped."

"Oh, so you *are* into librarian porn. Nice." Lauren grinned. "Did you come thinking about us getting down and dirty in the stacks?"

The question cut through her, slicing her open and exposing all the places she kept hidden. "Yes."

"Tell me your fantasy."

"I can't." Emma hauled her eyes from the ceiling to look at Lauren. When Lauren met her gaze, her expression was so warm, Emma wanted to get lost in the maze of her eyes.

"You can. It's easy. Will it help if I tell you that I came thinking about you?"

Emma hissed out a breath. God. Thinking about Lauren coming, coming because of *her*, was too much for her mind to process. She throbbed and ached in places she wouldn't have even known were erogenous zones before tonight. This conversation experiment was making her crazy. "How did you do it?"

Lauren gave her a look. "You know how this works. If I answer that, you'll have to as well."

She bit her lip, considered her options, and weighed her desire to know against her desire to die in embarrassment. "Okay."

Lauren cupped Emma's breasts over her bra and whispered against her ear, "I have a wand vibrator that curves just slightly at the end to hit my G-spot. I used it on myself while I imagined you above me getting off. The vibration was nice, but the look on your face when you came is what really made me explode."

Lauren's voice rushed over her like a stampede of wild horses. She was blown away. Scattered into a million pieces, her thoughts scampering in twenty different directions. "Oh my God."

"Do you like that?"

Emma nodded. It was as if Lauren had described a scene straight out of her own fantasy. A thousand of her fantasies. There was something primal about watching your lover pleasure herself. Somehow both all for you and all for her at the same time. Incredibly satisfying and undeniably frustrating. "I wouldn't mind seeing you touch yourself like that."

"That could be arranged, if it's what you really want. I was kind of hoping you'd want to participate though."

Emma swallowed. She wanted to participate so fucking badly she couldn't breathe. "That could be arranged."

Lauren kissed the curve of her ear, finding a sensitive spot and lingering there. "Your turn."

Time to pay up. She almost didn't even care, hearing Lauren say *the look on your face made me explode* was worth any price. "The library was open and busy. You cornered me in the encyclopedia section no one uses anymore. This time when you kissed me, you slid your hand up my skirt."

Lauren groaned and pulled her in even tighter, crushing their breasts together and caressing down her waist to the small of her back, an inch from her ass. "Fuck. Did anyone catch us?"

She bit her lip. No one had. But that was only because... "You had your hand over my mouth so I couldn't make a sound. You made sure no one heard us."

Lauren's voice was sand mixed with gravel as it rolled over Emma. "Was I rushing? Urgent? We could've been caught at any second."

"You..." The words stalled in her throat, but Lauren was looking at her like this fantasy was the sexiest damn thing she'd ever heard, so Emma mentally shoved past her embarrassment. "You took your time, as if you couldn't care less if we got caught. You stroked my clit over and over. I couldn't help but come, my moans trapped under your palm."

"Couldn't help it?" All teasing was gone from Lauren's tone.

"I had to come. I knew I shouldn't, but you wouldn't stop and I couldn't speak."

Lauren cupped her ass and squeezed, pulling Emma into her body in a way that made her desperately wish Lauren didn't still have her pants on. "Do you often have fantasies like that?"

Lauren's hands on her ass made her knees tremble and all thought blurred for a second. "Huh?"

"Do you like to fantasize about being taken like that?" Lauren asked, an unexpectedly serious note to her voice.

Being taken. A shiver crept down her spine.

More or less, pretty much, exactly on target, complete and total bull's-eye what she liked to fantasize about. But Lauren saying it out loud made it way too real. Admitting it turned her on was one step away from admitting *why* it turned her on. That was a level of fucked up Lauren didn't need to know about. *Nothing to see here. Don't dig any deeper.*

Emma shrugged. "One of many fantasies. It just fit with our kiss in the library."

She wasn't really lying. She didn't exclusively fantasize about being taken, and it *did* fit. Not telling the whole truth wasn't lying, was it? Plus, Lauren had gotten away with explaining her fantasy in a sentence or two. All these questions weren't fair.

Lauren was silent for a beat too long, her expression more intense than it should've been. Then she made that vibrating sound Emma was growing to love. "You have no idea how sexy you are."

Emma let out the mental breath she'd been holding. Lauren was going to let it go. She scoffed. "That's not sexy. Or at least not any sexier than you." Lauren sliding a vibrator inside herself was approximately twenty billion times hotter than her own fantasies.

"Not true. It's incredibly sexy. Did you get yourself off with just your fingers?"

Emma nodded.

"How long did it take you?" Lauren asked.

"You'll think I'm really fucked up," Emma said quickly. If Lauren was expecting the answer to be weird, then maybe it wouldn't be as shocking.

Lauren caught Emma's chin in her hand and tilted her face so she had no choice but to meet her stare. "I'd never think that.

You don't have to tell me if you don't want to. But there's nothing about you that's fucked up."

She sighed. Lauren only thought that because she didn't know the truth. She didn't know the *real* Emma. The raw, dirty, needy Emma who didn't require more than her fingers because the images inside her head were more than enough to send her over. That Emma *was* fucked up. "I haven't timed it. But around five minutes." It was a lie. It'd been less than two because the kiss had her so on edge already she didn't need any warm-up. But five sounded more reasonable. Less like she was a sex addict who got off on a breeze blowing in the right direction.

Lauren closed her eyes and breathed slowly out through her teeth. Emma recognized the move as one she practiced daily. Was she okay? Oh God. She'd freaked her out. "I'm sorry. I can last longer, really. As long as you need. You know, as long as normal people do and everything." The floor could open up and swallow her now. Really. The timing was perfect.

Lauren opened her eyes. "Emma." The word was guttural. Like Lauren had found it buried deep inside herself and dragged it all the way through her body and out her mouth.

Emma blinked. "What?"

"Don't ever say that again. You're not abnormal. You're driving me out of my mind you're so sexy."

"I am?" *She was?*

The pure bafflement in Emma's tone made Lauren lose it. She didn't know how to explain with words that Emma being so hot that she got herself off in a couple of minutes with only her fingers and her thoughts was the hottest damn thing Lauren had ever had inside her head. Not to mention getting off on *that* fantasy. She couldn't say that. So instead she used surprise to her advantage and gave Emma a gentle shove, tipping her backward onto the bed. It was high time they both stopped talking. She was going to show Emma exactly how turn-her-legs-to-jelly sexy she was. "Look at you, all gorgeous and spread out for me. I'm going to make you come."

Emma's quick breaths were making her chest heave in the most delicious way. Lauren reached behind her to unhook her bra, exposing her breasts. "God, you're beautiful."

"The most beautiful girl you've ever had, I'm sure," Emma said sardonically.

She leaned over her to brush her lips against Emma's. "The sweetest."

She kissed between her brows. "The sexiest."

She kissed the tip of her chin. "The beautifulest."

She avoided Emma's eyes and busied herself stripping off what remained of her own clothes. She ignored the warning bells clanging insistently at the back of her brain. Emma *was* beautiful. It didn't really mean anything. It was just the kind of sweet talk people said to each other in bed when rational thought had been usurped by desire. It was all in fun. It wasn't as if she actually *meant* Emma was sexier than any other woman she'd ever known.

"Wow," Emma breathed when Lauren turned to face her, completely nude.

Lauren laughed. "You're good for my ego."

"I have no idea why you'd ever need an ego boost with a body like that," Emma said, her mouth slightly open and her eyes glazed.

Lauren shrugged. She looked okay she supposed, in a lanky, straight up and down kind of way. But Emma was gazing at her like she should be on the cover of *Maxim*. Not that she was upset that Emma thought she was hot, but the girl really had it all wrong when it came to what kind of figure was sexy. Emma, lying on her bed in nothing but blue lace panties and strappy heels, her skin flushed pink and inviting, was so fucking hot Lauren had to do multiplication tables in her head to distract her hormones. Add to that that Emma was as responsive as hell and more enthusiastic than every woman she'd ever been with combined, and "sexiest" was an understatement.

Damn. She had meant it after all.

She stretched out beside Emma on the bed. "I'm hoping that if I strip naked and snuggle up beside you, you'll take pity on me and kiss me senseless."

Emma raised her eyebrows. "You want *me* to kiss *you*?"

"I do," Lauren said. "You're very good at it, and I'm terribly impatient."

"I did notice that about you." Emma pressed her lips to Lauren's.

Lauren held still. She wanted Emma to go for it. For Emma to *act* as well as talk. She wanted Emma to own all that desire simmering beneath the surface of the good girl she presented to the world.

Emma frowned. She shifted closer, her breasts brushing Lauren's, and kissed her again, longer this time, parting her lips and stroking her tongue over Lauren's nice and slow. Anticipation circled giddily in her belly like a dog chasing its tail. Emma tasted like red wine and smelled like fruit and flowers, probably some specific scent she'd spent an hour choosing in the store. Lavender frosted coconut blossoms, or tea-rose infused frangipani petals. Possibly, pink peppercorn melded with sweet pineapple sorbet. Lauren was a girl, but she wasn't the kind of girl who went for heels and lipstick and scents. She was the kind of girl who appreciated them greatly on a very sexy woman, though. Especially when said woman was whimpering little sounds into her mouth.

She threaded her fingers into Emma's hair and crushed Emma to her, too far gone to keep thinking or talking or teasing. She needed to fucking come, and more than that, she needed to make Emma come.

Lauren was done holding back.

Chapter Eight

God. Emma was going to be the death of her, but it was a hell of a way to go.

Lauren wasn't going to deny that she liked being on top, liked to take control. Yeah, okay, sometimes the view was pretty damn amazing from the bottom looking up, but it wasn't worth the sacrifice in power play. When Emma was pinned under her, the view couldn't have been better. Emma's hair fanned out against the pillow, her arms above her head, and the shyest smile on her face. Perfection.

Lauren kissed her again, sweet and slow and sensual. She parted Emma's lips and languorously explored her mouth. She kissed her the way she intended to explore every inch of Emma's body. Carefully, and with the detailed precision of a neurosurgeon. She intended to discover exactly what made Emma tick, what turned her on, what made her sigh, what made her wet, what her deepest, most secret, most intimate fantasies were. She had a feeling that the library was only the tip of the iceberg and Emma was hiding a compendium of erotic imaginings in that gorgeous head of hers. Lauren was going to take it slow, to give Emma all the pleasure in the world, but slow had never really been her forte. She tried for slow, but all too soon the warmth of their kisses heated to the boiling point.

Emma broke away, gasping. "If kissing you is this good, I can't begin to imagine what sex is going to be like."

Lauren pressed her thigh between Emma's until she could feel the lace of Emma's panties. "I thought you'd already imagined it."

"I'm hoping you exceed even my wildest imagination."

Lauren laughed. "That's a tall order."

Emma squirmed against her thigh, her eyes fluttering closed. "Not really. You're halfway there already."

Lauren bit back a groan, giving in to temptation and kissing her way down Emma's body. *Emma needs you to take your time with her. Don't rush this.* She found the curve of Emma's neck right under her jaw, the delicate hollow of her throat, the perfect outline of her collarbones accenting her unbelievably amazing breasts—heavy enough to be full and perfectly shaped, each topped with a gorgeous pink nipple.

Emma was *built*.

Lauren rained kisses all over her breasts, relishing the softness against her lips. When she licked one of Emma's nipples she almost missed Emma's quiet gasp. She didn't miss the way Emma's hips rose or the way her fingers clenched around the sheet she'd grabbed.

That Emma was so damn hot, so damn responsive and on edge from so little contact made Lauren more than a bit crazy. Emma's receptiveness had Lauren wanting to push her boundaries. She wanted to shove Emma's knees up to her chest and fuck her, fuck her until she knew just how far, just how fast, she could push until Emma came screaming. She wanted Emma screaming. Emma begging for it. Emma so out of her mind she forgot all about her nerves. Emma's body melting and electrifying and shattering like a triple-edged blade skittering down her spine.

She wanted all that with Emma, and just how much scared the bejeezus right out of her.

She took a long breath and reined herself in. Now was not the time to be thinking about hardcore fucking. Down and dirty don't-know-which-way-is-up fucking. No. Now was the time for sweet and gentle. The kind of sex that lead to nice orgasms that were satisfying in that way of a cork popping from a bottle of champagne. Not the kind of orgasms that ravished you like you'd just stepped off Temptation Island. Not the kind that made you deaf and blind and stopped your heart. Lauren was no sexpert, but she knew enough not to just blindly fuck one-night stands. Especially not ones like Emma who insisted on being wined and dined, who wanted an emotional connection, even if it wasn't the happily ever after kind. Lauren didn't fault her for it. Some girls just couldn't do strangers. That didn't mean they'd be all up in your business wanting to be your girlfriend.

The person she didn't trust was herself, and that wasn't something she was used to handling. Emma's shyness pushed all her buttons in just the right ways. She wanted to be the one to make Emma forget her reticence. She wanted to show Emma the side of herself that would go to a bar like Kink's, that liked power and dirty sex that was so far from making love they didn't even exist on the same continent. She wanted to show Emma just what did it for her the most in bed. But Emma was already so jumpy that bringing up kink seemed like a really bad idea. *Hey there, pretty lady, I know you were brave to admit to being anxious and shy and nervous, but would you mind terribly if I tied you up and blindfolded you? It gets me hot.* Lauren could come just fine without kink, but orgasms existed on a sliding scale of intensity. Passion was a spectrum, not a fixed state, and Kink's had shown her the outer limits of her hunger.

If by some miracle, Emma did understand, then Lauren would've opened Pandora's box and *just once* sex wouldn't be enough. She'd be left wanting. Left wondering what else hid behind Emma Prescott's facade of the good girl librarian. Lauren wanted to be the one to show that girl just how good bad could feel. Just how good *dirty* could feel. She'd never be satisfied with just once if she went there, so Lauren kissed Emma's breasts gently, licking her nipples and tugging with her teeth until they hardened and Emma moaned, her hips rising again.

Lauren's blood moved like warm honey through her veins, making it hard to think as her slow and sensuous assault on Emma's breasts echoed in her own body. All Emma had to do was moan and part her knees, and Lauren was wet and ready. She moved down her body, kissing down her stomach before dipping her tongue into Emma's navel and making her laugh. Laughing was good. No one ever laughed when Lauren took what she really wanted. Laughing made it playful. Casual. Not at all the rip-roaring need that usually caught her during sex. There was nothing funny about losing your mind, and she didn't have the strength to lose her mind with Emma and then put it safely back into place.

Lauren moved lower until her mouth was level with the waistband on Emma's panties. "These are very pretty. Did you pick them out for me?"

Emma propped herself up on her elbows. "Of course not. They just happened to be on top of the pile in my closet."

Lauren snorted. Emma's panties were as tiny as they were lacy. No way were they not chosen specifically with sex in mind. But if Emma wanted to pretend she wasn't doing everything possible to be sexy as fuck, that was fine with her. She liked a challenge. She kissed the tiny satin bow on the front. Kissed her way lower until her mouth was directly over Emma's clit. "Why do women's panties have bows? Don't you think that's weird?"

Emma didn't respond. Lauren glanced up to find her lying very still, her eyes squeezed shut and her fingers clutching the comforter so hard her knuckles were white. She frowned. Either Emma was three seconds from coming and trying not to, which seemed unlikely. Lauren wasn't *that* good. Or she wasn't having a very good time.

"Emma?"

"Hmm?" Emma murmured, not opening her eyes.

"How're you doing? Still with me?"

Emma pried her eyes open and looked down at Lauren. Lauren nestled between her legs, her mouth an inch from her pussy. Emma snapped her eyes shut again as every cell in her body screamed *yes please* at the top of its lungs. "I'm fine, please don't stop."

She held her breath, but Lauren didn't kiss her again, didn't slide her panties to the side, didn't peel them off, didn't drag her fingers or her tongue down the places Emma rather desperately wanted to be touched. No. Of course she didn't. Lauren wasn't going to let her get away with an eyes-squeezed-shut orgasm. Not the Lauren who was constantly asking her to reveal all her deepest secrets. Reluctantly, she peeked out through half-closed lids.

Lauren rewarded her with fingertips pressed against her opening, pushing the lace inside just a little. A shudder of pleasure whipped up her spine.

Ohpleasemore.

She wanted Lauren to fuck her. Or to at least touch her. Stroke her. Taste her. All this teasing had to stop or she'd go insane from need and have to be committed to an asylum for the perverted.

"Please," was all she could say, just that one word. A string of pleas, of dirty, helpless words built inside her mouth, but she kept them there. One was enough.

Lauren traced up and down Emma's panties, pressing and stroking and rubbing her through the lace until Emma was sure she'd soaked right through them and Lauren's fingers were damp. Why didn't she take them off?

"Mmm. So sexy. You're so wet," Lauren said.

Emma wanted to shut her eyes again, to shut Lauren out, to not focus on how wet she was, how badly she needed to come. If she did, Lauren would stop again. She didn't want her to check out, and Emma couldn't blame her. But if Lauren didn't do something other than torture her, she was going to cry.

Taking matters into her own hands, Emma lifted her ass, tucked her thumbs into her panties and slid them down until she could kick them off. Her plan seemed to be working because Lauren stared at her pussy like it was the Hope Diamond. Or was she staring because Emma's wet and swollen pussy was the kind of bad you couldn't look away from? A three-car pileup that kept you awake at night praying for the people inside.

Ugh. She really had to get out of her own damn head already, or even her heat seeking missile ability to orgasm would fail her.

"Please," Emma said again. Two pleases didn't officially constitute begging, right? No. You needed at least three for begging, four for pleading, and six for beseeching. Two was okay, but she couldn't be allowed a third.

Lauren swirled between her folds, running fingertips across the sensitive skin. Emma moaned. Her pussy clenched, needing something inside, needing more. She bit her lip and held back every sound on the tip of her tongue. She couldn't help wanting, but Lauren didn't need to know just how badly. No one did. Not ever again.

Lauren brushed back and forth against her entrance, dipping and circling and stroking until Emma wanted to wring her beautiful neck. "Isn't there something in the Geneva Convention that makes this illegal?"

"While I enjoy envisioning a bunch of snooty suits debating the ethics of sexual arousal, why should it be illegal?" Lauren traced a wide circle around her clit, sliding fingers up either side but not nearly close enough.

"The senseless torture of innocents should always be illegal." Emma wriggled her hips to try to force Lauren's fingers closer to her clit, but Lauren just moved with her in a way that meant her fingers didn't move at all.

"You're hardly an innocent right now, are you," Lauren said teasingly. "This isn't torture. Doesn't it feel good?"

Not just good. Too good. Emma closed her eyes again and focused on the dark landscape behind her eyelids. She was so attuned to Lauren's touch that she could almost see her. Almost as if someone had scribbled the image of Lauren stroking her pussy on the inside of Emma's eyelids so she'd never be able to escape it. She didn't want to forget, but she had to find a way to distract herself from the pleasure sparking in her pussy and churning in her belly. Need and lust twisting and twining and snaking into every pore of her skin. Lauren hadn't even touched her clit yet, and Emma could already feel the orgasm building.

"Emma," Lauren said in a playful warning.

"No," Emma whispered, then, "please…yes…please."

Emma winced at how pitiful she sounded. Needy and contradictory and definitely, positively, unquestionably in begging territory now.

Lauren's fingers stilled, and the texture of the air changed, frozen and wary. "Talk to me," Lauren said, not moving away but not plowing ahead either.

Code yellow. Proceed with caution.

"I just need to focus on…" *Not focusing.*

Emma couldn't say that. Lauren would think she was ridiculous. What kind of lifetime member of sexaholics anonymous had to close their eyes and think of their disapproving grandmother to keep from orgasming before a woman even touched their clit? It wasn't *normal,* and all Emma wanted in this moment was to be normal. To feel the pleasure without the anxiety. To just get through these first few minutes so that when enough time had passed, she could stop thinking, stop holding back, let go and give herself up to the blinding release of the orgasm she knew would be amazing. An orgasm that would make her scream.

"Emma," Lauren said again, her fingers on Emma's cheek now.

Emma opened her eyes. Lauren leaned over her staring into her eyes. Lauren was always staring into her eyes, looking and seeing and observing her in a way no one else ever had. In a way no one else had ever wanted to. Her heart squeezed in her chest, but right now, sweet tender Lauren was the last thing she needed.

"Please. I don't want to talk."

Lauren shook her head. "I'm sorry. I don't want to push you, but I'm going to need a little more than that because you don't look like you want this, even though you're saying you do. Can you tell me what's going on?"

Lauren traced the curve of her cheek again and tucked a strand of hair behind Emma's ear as tears tracked down Emma's cheeks. Her throat swelled and her bottom lip trembled. She was going to lose it. She had the sexiest, most gorgeous woman in the entire world wanting nothing more than to stroke her pussy, and she was ruining it.

"I'm sorry." The apology came out as a whisper. So inadequate, so insubstantial a reflection of the giant boulder lodged in her chest. She wasn't even sure who she was apologizing to—Lauren for ruining their night when she'd had been so open and honest with her, or herself for allowing reality to forever shatter the illusion of what could've been between them. She should've let it remain a fantasy. Emma was a freak when it came to sex, and just because Lauren made her wish that wasn't true, didn't actually make it so.

Lauren made a sound that was impossible to describe, but she scooped Emma into her arms. Holding her tight, she tucked Emma's head under her chin and pulled Emma half on top of her. "Whatever it is, you can tell me."

"You'll think I'm a freak," Emma mumbled, ridiculously embarrassed but glad Lauren hadn't just rolled her eyes, then rolled out of bed and left. Lauren was still here. Lauren was still asking her to reveal all her secrets. Lauren was still doing everything Emma had asked her for and plenty that Emma hadn't.

"You do remember I'm tabloid fodder, don't you?" Lauren said. "Trust me, I, of all people, am not going to judge you."

"That wasn't your fault." Emma pressed her mouth to Lauren's neck.

"And whatever's going on for you, was that your fault?"

Emma nodded. Shook her head. "I don't know."

"Maybe I can help you figure it out." Lauren tilted Emma's face to hers, kissing her.

Emma wanted to shoot herself. Okay, that was overly dramatic. Not actually *shoot* herself, she was anti-gun and everything, but she wanted to make a statement. That statement being that she was a freaking dumbass letting some decade old, long forgotten drama interfere with the very sexy here and now. She was alone in her bedroom with her biggest crush, and she was bombing worse than a *Survivor* contestant voted off the island on the first day. "It's nothing. More kissing, please."

Lauren's mouth moved down her throat, and Emma tried to stop thinking. She sank into the sensation of soft lips against her skin, until Lauren said, "Remember your epiphany? Touch is my language, and everything about this is telling me you're freaking out and trying not to. I'm going to believe you when you say it's not because you don't want me. But I'm also going to need to know why you look so afraid. Non-consent isn't sexy."

Lauren was doing her dead-on eye contact thing again, and Emma gulped. "God, Lauren. No. I mean, of course I consent. I told you, I just get nervous."

Lauren shook her head. "This isn't nerves. This isn't shyness. It's apprehension and worry and just a little bit of fear."

Why did Lauren have to be so damn perceptive? Emma tried for a smile. "You got all that from me closing my eyes?"

"I got all that from caring about you." Lauren didn't return her smile.

Emma's breath stopped dead somewhere in the no man's land between her lungs and her mouth. Lauren cared about her. Lauren was stopping, asking, checking, because she cared. Emma's fingers trembled as she brushed the hair out of her eyes, buying herself three seconds to think past the rush of *she likes me* that was making her just a bit dizzy. Now was the worst possible time to be getting all misty-eyed over a statement as simple as "I care about you."

Lauren might've somehow landed herself with a shady past, but she was turning out to be exactly the dream girl that Emma had always hoped for. Lauren didn't know that Emma wasn't anyone's idea of a dream girl, though. She was an anti-dream girl. She should have her own action figure: Nightmare Girl.

Chapter Nine

That adage about the thing you most admire being the very thing that drives you insane two decades later was showing up to haunt Emma. Only two decades was more like two hours. She'd never met anyone like Lauren before. Someone who could read a touch, or translate a kiss, like it was a conversation rather than foreplay. Someone who paid so much attention they knew things about her before she did. Hell, she felt fortunate when a woman looked at her during sex. Lauren studied her like she was the most fascinating woman on the planet. Lauren *focused.*

"I'm not afraid, not really. I'm just…"

"Really worried," Lauren supplied for her when she trailed off.

Emma nodded. She wasn't sure what it said about her performance that she had given the impression of "really worried," but she couldn't deny the truth.

"I'm developing my skills in bilingual communication. Let's talk and touch. Tell me what's going on," Lauren said. "Why are you so worried?"

Emma closed her eyes. Somehow it was easier to tell Lauren what'd happened without looking at her. She had to do it. Lauren had revealed her history and Emma owed her the same honesty. The only difference was, Lauren's problems were actual problems, complete with a villain who was legitimately out to get her.

Emma's problem was ridiculous hurt from a thousand years ago, and her villain was a blond cheerleader.

Except, that's not exactly accurate is it? The real villain is me.

"It's silly," Emma said.

"If it's bothering you, I promise it's not silly."

Emma wrapped an arm around Lauren's waist, wanting to slide her hand lower but not having the guts. "You know that game, seven minutes in heaven?"

"Where you go into a closet and make out?" Lauren traced lazy circles across Emma's back.

Emma nodded against her shoulder, losing the battle with her curiosity and not so accidentally brushing a fingertip along the outer curve of Lauren's breast. "When I was sixteen I was invited to my first party. I had my first drink. I played my first game of seven minutes in heaven."

Lauren tightened her hold and shifted, giving Emma unencumbered access to her breasts. The move was intentional. Lauren had done it to distract her, to make it easier to talk. Feeling Lauren up while she explained "the catalyst for her clinical anxiety" according to her far too perky-in-the-face-of-insurmountable-odds therapist should've been weird. But somehow touch was just the perfect thing to ground her in the present so that the past could stay a memory to be retold, and not a moment to be relived.

"That's quite the introduction to the joys of being a teenager," Lauren said.

"You're telling me." Going with the tacit permission, Emma stroked Lauren's breasts and had to hold back a whimper. Lauren was just as soft and firm and smooth and sexy as she'd imagined, her breasts small and perfectly proportionate to her slender frame. "I was really nervous to play. I knew I wasn't very attracted to boys, even then, and the idea of being alone with one made me cringe, but I didn't want to look like a loser."

Lauren squeezed her shoulder.

"Fortunately, or unfortunately, depending on your perspective, there wasn't an equal gender split, and I was the last person the spun bottled pointed to."

Lauren rubbed up and down Emma's arm, playing her fingers along the bones in her elbow. "Who was the second to last person? A girl I'm assuming."

"It was Jessica Norman." Just saying the name out loud made Emma sick.

Lauren muttered a string of curses that began with crap and ended in motherfucker.

"I mean, at the time I couldn't believe my luck. Even if we didn't *do* anything, and I assumed we wouldn't, I'd still get to talk to her. I'd still be the girl who got to play seven minutes in heaven with the head cheerleader and the prettiest senior in school."

"Hmm." Lauren was clearly unwilling to commit to an opinion on that.

"There wasn't an actual closet, so we used a bedroom, closed the door and turned the lights off. It was summer and not all that late so even with the blinds closed I could still see her. I was so awkward for a few seconds, until she said, 'Have you ever made it with a girl before?' I about lost my mind. To my sixteen-year-old hormones, the way she phrased it implied that she *had* made it with a girl and was offering me a gilded invitation. I told her no, and she stepped closer and asked me if I'd ever thought about it. If, maybe, I'd end up with some crazy stories to tell my boyfriend one day. Maybe that would get him off. I didn't have a boyfriend. I wasn't connecting the dots because my head was rushing and my heart was pounding and Jessica Norman was about to kiss me…"

She paused to take a breath, the memory of that kiss flooding her senses, working its way under her skin and into her blood. A kiss that had shown her who she was and then destroyed her.

"Did she kiss you?" Lauren asked.

"She did. She made the first move. There's no way I could've done it because my feet where cemented to the floor and my hands glued to my sides. She kissed me."

"To make her boyfriend hot."

Lauren was already putting it together. Somehow that made Emma feel like even more of an idiot. She should've known.

"Yup. What I didn't know was that the other kids had turned off the lights in the hallway and cracked open the door. They were watching."

Lauren cradled her so closely Emma was cocooned, the physical closeness managing to wrap itself around her emotions too. "Oh. I'm so sorry."

"I don't think they did it to be mean. It's just teenagers, you know? They don't think with their heads when two girls are possibly going to make out."

"That's no excuse," Lauren said.

"Jessica was kissing me and…" Emma's words petered out, no match for the memory that was far too close to the surface. She stopped talking and cupped Lauren's breast, marveling at the curve that fit so perfectly into her palm it seemed to have been made for just that purpose. Emma didn't know if she believed that God was a man, but God sure had a thing for breasts to have made Lauren's so utterly perfect.

"What happened next?" Lauren stroked up and down her arm

"I lost all reason. I don't even remember most of it, honestly. Just the hot rush of *ohpleaseyes* and kissing her back. Amping everything up. Sliding my tongue into her mouth. She made a sound, probably shock, but I took it as encouragement. God. It's so embarrassing to admit, but I was having my first lesbian kiss, and I thought it was the most fantastic thing in the entire world. I wanted to kiss her forever, and if the wetness in my panties was any indication, I wanted a hell of a lot more. I didn't know any better. I didn't know I was supposed to go slow, or ask for consent, or not act so desperate. I'm pretty sure I climbed her like a tree. We ended up on the bed, maybe because I dragged her there, or maybe because she wanted to make it look good for her friends, I don't know. When the seven minutes were up, I was gasping and so hot I could've come in my jeans."

Emma was surprised she'd managed to tell the story without tears. The wound was old, and she was fresh out of waterworks. But the pain that leaked into her brain, into her body, into her desire, remained. Now every time she felt that way again, turned on, needy, wanting to be touched, the pain found her and reminded her of all the ways need could get you in trouble. Get you ridiculed. Hurt someone you maybe could've liked.

"When it was over, I wasn't any the wiser. I had no idea everyone had seen or that I had done anything wrong, until an hour later when I went looking for Jessica. To ask her if she *had* ever made it with a girl. If maybe she'd consider making it with me. She was in the middle of a group telling the most hilarious story, waving her arms while everyone fell all over themselves laughing. The time wasn't right for a serious conversation, so I stayed back. But I couldn't help overhearing what she said. Overhear her tell everyone I was a nympho. I'd attacked her. I'd moaned like I was cheap and desperate, and wasn't it all just *so funny*? Could they believe I was such a slut that I went around begging for it from straight girls?

"I just ran. I ran and ran and ran until I was home and then I cried myself to sleep and didn't go to another party until prom."

"Emma. I'm so sorry." Lauren said her name as if she were in prayer, holding her and stroking her back.

"I'm a freak," Emma said softly. "You don't understand. I go from zero to six billion faster than the blink of an eye. I want so much that I can't stop, can't help myself. I don't ask. I don't consider the possible outcomes. I just want and want until the other person has nothing left to give." Emma let go of Lauren's breast, her gaze glued to the corner of the nightstand where she wouldn't have to look into Lauren's eyes and see the judgment she knew would be reflected there. "When you were touching me just now, I had to close my eyes. I had to tense up and try to think of something else, so I didn't come too soon."

"Emma." Lauren tilted Emma's chin so their eyes met. "There's absolutely nothing freakish or fucked up about wanting someone or needing to come."

Emma's stomach twisted like a pretzel. Lauren wasn't just looking at her to drive her point home. The intensity in her eyes communicated all the things they'd left unsaid. All the things they didn't say because they didn't even know each other that well, and this couldn't be anything more than a one-night stand.

Let go with me.

I need you too.

You're safe here.

She didn't know how to handle all that. Couldn't process what it might mean. Everything was too close. It was only supposed to be one night, but Emma's heart didn't know that, and she had to protect it the way a mother protects a child whose boundless enthusiasm makes them run into a busy intersection. When you were a heart at risk of being broken, you had to be stopped for your own good.

Emma shrugged. She wasn't proud of it. It was an insult in the face of Lauren's heartfelt expression. Not that it really mattered in the long run. They might be talking about it, but sex wasn't even in the same zip code as this conversation. No one was getting laid tonight, and the disappointment floated down to settle itself on top of all her other emotions, blanketing them in sadness. With nothing left to lose, she didn't bother to sugarcoat the truth. "It's wrong to get so lost in your own needs that you're not aware of the other person's. To lose sense of time and place and reality. To be selfish. That's wrong."

"Is that what you think? That giving in to your desire is selfish?" Lauren asked like it wasn't as obvious as the sky being blue.

Emma scoffed. "Isn't it? Just look at the difference between us. You've bent over backward to give me everything I've asked for. You've been open and honest when you didn't really want to be, just so I'd feel comfortable. You kissed me when I asked you, you talked me through our confessions to give me a chance to adjust, and then, the moment I got too far inside my own head, you were considerate enough to back off, to make sure I was okay, and to ask that we talk about it, even when I lied and said I was fine."

Emma ran out of breath as the words tumbled out of her mouth, crashing into each other like marbles rolling downhill. "*You* are always aware of me. Hell, you seem to know what I'm feeling even before I do half the time. You always know what's going on around you, and what I need. But I'm so wrapped up in what *I* feel that I all but forget the other person has feelings. That's the epitome of selfish."

"Emma." Lauren cradled Emma's cheeks in her palms. "You're an idiot sometimes. A sexy idiot, but still." With that, she captured Emma's mouth in a slow, coaxing kiss.

When their tongues touched, Emma gasped, but unlike all the other times they'd kissed, she wasn't struck by overwhelming arousal. No. This kiss wasn't sexy in an allow-me-to-demonstrate-just-how-talented-I-am-with-my-tongue kind of way, though Lauren would earn a five-star review. This kiss was physical and intimate and powerful, but at the same time it didn't feel like sex. It felt like...Emma didn't know exactly. A single word couldn't do it justice. Like Lauren was reaching inside her to unlock all the doors she kept shut tight, flooding them with light. Like Lauren was wrapping all her insides in a tight hug. Even now, with the shadow of her past looming over them, she wanted Lauren to touch her and never stop. She wanted the comfort and the desire she knew Lauren would deliver in spades.

"Listen to me," Lauren said against her lips. "I want you. I want to bring you pleasure. I want to make you come. Do you understand? When you're with someone you trust, with someone you're sure wants you, it's okay to let go. It's okay to indulge in the pleasure for no other reason than how good it feels. Who I am, and what I want, *does* matter to you, Emma. You know it does, because who I am is the difference between right now and the way Jessica fucking Norman abused the trust of a younger, naive kid. What she did made it not safe."

Emma looked away. Lauren was trying to make her feel better by blaming it all on Jessica. Sweet of her, but what Emma had done made it not safe too.

As if reading her mind, Lauren continued. "Should you have clued in that she didn't intend for it to go so far? Should you have checked before hitting the bed? If you'd known you were supposed to do that, then yes—knowing what's right and choosing not to do it, makes it wrong. *Not* knowing means you learn and don't make the same mistake. You were sixteen, and it was your first kiss. It wasn't perfect for so many completely fucked up reasons, but none of that is on you. You learned the hardest way possible to make sure that everyone is on the same page when it comes to intimacy. That it hurt you so badly, that you're so worried it will happen again, tells me that you've *never* let it happen again. That you're not selfish, and you wouldn't override someone else's feelings for your own pleasure. You didn't know because you were innocent. You know now. That's enough."

"Wow," Emma said, "that's some speech."

Like a speech that could change my life.

"Am I wrong? Being unreasonable?" Lauren refused to allow her to lighten the moment.

"Wrong? No. I suppose not. Not when you lay it out logically like that. But the way I felt when Jessica touched me, the way I feel when you do, it's not logical. I don't have the mental bandwidth to rationalize it. I just don't think."

Lauren leaned back and gave her a long, silent look Emma wasn't sure how to decipher, though she didn't have to wait long for clarification.

"That's the biggest load of bullshit I've ever heard," Lauren said.

Emma pushed up. "What?"

"Bullshit," Lauren repeated. "You don't *think*? Is that what you're asking me to buy? That you just lose it and don't think?"

Lauren shoved a hand through her hair. It was too long for her to reach the ends, so half got messed up while the rest lay flat, giving her the bed-head, she should've gotten from rolling around, not having this conversation while stark naked. Lauren either didn't notice or didn't care.

"All you do is think. Overthinking, holding back, wishing and stopping and wanting, but not allowing yourself to let go. It's all thinking."

Lauren sat up too and tapped two fingers to Emma's temple. "It's all up here," she said, softer now, "when it should be down here." Lauren placed her hand flat against Emma's pelvis. "Emma, you're so consumed with some ridiculous definition of normal that Jessica put in your head, you can't get past an innocent teenage mistake. You think you're fucked up because you get aroused and need to be touched? Well, allow me to be the one to tell you, that's normal. Hell, baby, when a woman is holding you, kissing you, naked with you, that's the damn *point*. That my touching you makes you need to come is the best compliment I could've received. Knowing I make you hot makes me feel like the sexiest, most desirable woman in the world. It feels *good* for me when you get hot. It's going to feel even better when I can make you come, because the thing you're so afraid of is the very thing that makes sex intimate. You're vulnerable getting naked with someone, when you need something from them, and don't want to stop, when you let go and show that person a side of yourself not many see. That vulnerability makes sex hot, not the friction."

Emma swallowed, but the knot in her throat didn't budge. She stared down at her hands, at Lauren's hand still pressed against her. Lauren made sense, Emma knew that, but she was wrong. Vulnerability might be hot for the person you were in bed with, but for her, being vulnerable, being exposed in a way that went deeper than skin, deeper even than every molecule she had, deeper in that way of getting inside your head and twisting you up, wasn't hot at all. For her that kind of vulnerability was terrifying. More terrifying than boogeymen and vampires and the Cupcake in a bikini put together.

Emma bit her lip. "Can you tell me about the kink club?" She was as surprised as Lauren appeared to be when the question popped out of her mouth, but the idea had intrigued the hell out of her ever since she'd read a stupid article someone had forwarded her about Lauren and Caroline at Kink's. Maybe she'd be more comfortable with this idea of sexual vulnerability if it went both ways. If Lauren could be vulnerable, too.

All the expression on Lauren's face slammed shut like she'd swung a door to block it out. "This isn't about kink."

"Oh." Of course Lauren didn't want to talk to her about kink. She couldn't even have a damn orgasm without falling to pieces first. Why would Lauren believe she could handle kink?

Lauren stroked her hand across Emma's pelvis. "It's not the right time for that conversation."

"We're naked in bed. Is there a better time for kink?" Emma smiled but the joke fell flat when Lauren didn't smile back.

"That stuff is a lot to take in. You've had a difficult night already. I want to make this easy for you, not harder."

"I could say the same for you. Sharing your story wasn't easy, but you still managed to listen to mine. It wasn't too much for you," Emma said.

"I don't want to freak you out, not when you're already struggling with how you feel."

"That's a cop-out," Emma said. "You've managed to turn me on sixty-seven times tonight, I'm getting used to it, and it feels pretty damn awesome. But you're asking me to be vulnerable with you. To give in and let go. That's what vulnerability is, right? Is it so wrong that I want you to be vulnerable with me too?"

Lauren hesitated. "What would you say if I said your nervousness turns me on?"

"I…" Emma had no idea what to say next. She didn't have to come up with anything though because Lauren took over.

"I'm not saying that I *want* you to be anxious. I don't. And nervous is different from worry and pain. I absolutely don't want you to feel that way. But that you're so responsive when I touch you, that part of you tries to hold back… It turns me on. I know that eventually you won't be able to help yourself. Eventually, you'll come, and that you started by holding back, makes coming a surrender."

Emma's head spun, her thoughts grappling with each other and climbing up the inside of her head, so jumbled she could only echo. "You like it when I fight the way I feel."

That sure as hell needed some explaining.

Lauren shook her head as if annoyed she wasn't being clear. "Not fight like it's a bad thing. You being shy and nervous, it turns me on because I want to be the one who earns your trust. I want to be the one who shows you how amazing you are when you let go. In the same way that sex isn't as good if it's just friction, sex isn't as good, for me at least, if it's easy and simple and uncomplicated. I want..."

Lauren trailed off, and for the first time, Emma was able to supply a word Lauren couldn't muster.

"Vulnerability. You want me to be vulnerable, and that I get nervous and hold back makes you hot." How was that at all fair? She'd asked Lauren about Kink's to share the vulnerability and it turned out Lauren's kink *was* vulnerability.

Lauren rubbed a hand across her face. "It's not the struggle that makes it hot. It's the surrender. It's being the one you surrender to."

Emma got off the bed, walked to the window, and stared across her backyard, patchy with snow and ice. Lauren wanted her to be submissive. But no, that wasn't the word Lauren had used, was it? Not submissive. Not happily kneeling at the feet of the one in control, knowing that it settled a place deep inside to be exactly there. No. Submissive would've been easier. If submissive felt anything like being crowded against the door of a bar, against a bookcase in the library, against her kitchen sink, then submissive was the best thing ever. But Lauren hadn't said submissive. She'd said *surrender*. No matter how Lauren phrased it, surrender implied a battle, a fight, opposite sides and opposing goals. Lauren got off on Emma's shyness and nervousness because they were the obstacles that she had to overcome to win her surrender.

Emma turned from the window. "Why'd you stop, just now? You had everything you wanted. If you just let me keep my eyes closed I would've come. We both know it. I'd have tried to hold back and been unable to, which is exactly what you're telling me you want. So why did you stop?"

Lauren sat on the side of the bed, her hands braced at her sides like she was stopping herself from jumping up and running over to Emma. The moonlight filtering through the window highlighted all the angles and planes of Lauren's face, giving her a ghostly appearance that was no less sexy.

"Because you weren't enjoying yourself."

Lauren's words were flat, like she was disappointed that she had to explain. "Do you think wanting your surrender is the same thing as wanting to watch you suffer? It's not. If it hurts you, if it's not consensual, then we stop, always. Surrender is sexy only because we both know you *do* want it."

Emma leaned against the window, the frigid glass chilling her all over. What Lauren didn't seem to get was that she wanted an orgasm, she wanted to be touched, but forever hoped it would somehow get easier. That she wouldn't need to surrender because she'd never have to fight.

She took a deep breath and realized that she hadn't had to focus on her breathing once since Lauren touched her. That was odd, especially given the direction the night had turned. If anything was going to make her anxious it should've been this conversation. "I'm having trouble reconciling *enjoying* and *surrender* the way you do. It's not hot for me."

Lauren slowly came over to her, not touching her but vibrating with so much passion Emma felt as if she were. "That's a lie. It's a comforting lie right now, I understand that. But, still, you're not being honest with yourself."

Emma's heart began to pound. Who the hell did Lauren think she was, anyway? No one had the right to tell her how she felt. The whole conversation was insufferable. "I know my own mind, Lauren."

Lauren's smile seemed more sad than happy. "You do know your mind, but do you know your body? Didn't you tell me tonight that you liked it when I took control, because you didn't have to think? That not having to make decisions made it easier for you? More pleasurable, perhaps? That being able to let go and lose yourself in that kiss was only possible because I made it seem like you had no choice? Is that not surrender?"

"I..." Emma felt like she'd been drugged and didn't know which way was up. "That was different."

"It was different. It takes trust to let someone kiss you. To allow her to control the kiss, to take responsibility for it so you don't have to. But not as much trust as sex does, not as much as being shy and nervous and still surrendering to your orgasm with your eyes open."

"It's not easy for me to trust like that," Emma whispered.

"I know. But I can't seem to not care that you won't look at me. I know it's not easy, but I want you to trust me."

Emma couldn't stand the intensity in Lauren's eyes. Her expression was so open, so raw and honest, and, yes, so vulnerable. Emma had asked for her vulnerability, and Lauren had given it to her freely. She'd asked Emma for something that wasn't easy to ask for. Lauren *needed*, and just because Lauren's need was different didn't make it any less powerful. But what Lauren needed wasn't something she had left to give.

Emma turned her back to Lauren and stared out at her empty flowerbeds. How could she trust Lauren with the very thing that caused so much pain? She'd trusted once, and that had landed her with a goddamn *clinical* condition that she battled every day. She might've revealed her past, but she'd resolutely blocked all of Lauren's attempts to persuade her from what she knew was true. More than knew, *felt* was true. That mortifying disaster had been her fault. She wasn't normal. How could Lauren want her trust when Emma had ignored the emotion in her eyes and the promise of her words? How could Emma trust her when Lauren had told her she wanted the very thing Emma had had ripped away from her?

Lauren needed something that was already broken. Already gone. Dead long before tonight.

Emma began to count the branches on the old oak by her garden shed, wishing she could block out her thoughts. Lauren had said sex wasn't as satisfying without vulnerability. Emma didn't want to be vulnerable ever again. She didn't want to struggle either. How could the Lauren who'd done everything in her power to make tonight easy on her, also be the same person who got off on how nervous she always was? It didn't make any sense. Except, that maybe it did. Considering the one thing Lauren had said that Emma didn't want to hear.

I want to be the one who earns your trust.

The jury was still out on whether or not being vulnerable in bed made sex hotter. But being vulnerable standing naked in her heels by her bedroom window was close enough, thank you very much.

"You should go," Emma said to Lauren without turning around.

CHAPTER TEN

Friends were as important as family, but Lauren had the right to reverse her opinion when friendship involved hauling a fifty-pound barrel of sloshing hot chocolate five thousand treacherous miles from the car to the tiny-ass tent they'd be huddling under while filling five million Dixie cups with the brew. Also, it was snowing. Of course it was. Main Street was fully decked out with Christmas decorations and refreshment tents. That Christmas was already in the rearview mirror wasn't a problem for anyone but her.

It looked as if the entire town had abandoned their La-Z-Boys, warm fires, and Saturday night television to jostle for prime sidewalk real estate. And for what exactly? To watch a bunch of tractors they got stuck behind on country roads every day covered in cheap plastic lights? To listen to police sirens as if that wasn't usually a reason to slam on your brakes and curse the gods for getting caught driving over the limit on roads that had no traffic anyway? Really, was a parade all that exciting? Small towns like Sunrise Falls had so little going for them, people *did* think parades were worth leaving their house for.

"I hate you." Lauren caught the toe of her boot on a tent peg and almost landed on her face.

Roxie had a bag of cups and napkins slung over her shoulder like she was Santa's employee of the month and took the insult with a smile. "No, you don't. You just hate winter. And Sunrise Falls. And the Christmas parade."

"And yet you're forcing me to participate in all of the above."

They finally reached their tent, and Lauren carefully settled the thermos on the table provided while Roxie got busy setting out the cups.

"I'm sorry, but have you seen me? I couldn't carry that thing if I lifted weights every day for a million years," Roxie said.

Unfortunately, she had a point. Rox wouldn't be winning the Ultraman marathon anytime soon. She didn't have a small frame like Emma, but she was definitely more bone than muscle.

Stop thinking about Emma. Thinking about Emma will get you nowhere. You know this because you spent half the night and most of the morning thinking about Emma and getting, exactly, precisely, specifically, no-fucking-where.

Lauren tugged her hat firmly down, hopefully saving herself from the stabby pain she always got when the wind whipped around her ears. Had she mentioned in the last half a second that winter sucked? It bore repeating. Repeatedly.

They'd only just managed to set everything up when Doug and not-hers Gayle strolled up to the tent, hand in hand, looking exactly like a couple off the cover of a stuck-in-a-snow-covered-cabin-whatever-shall-we-do romance novel. Lauren sighed the kind of long-suffering sigh usually reserved for mothers of two-year-old triplets. "Hi there."

Gayle's smile was perfect. "Lauren! How are you?"

Gayle made Lauren feel bad about herself. Not because she did anything to cause this reaction, but because her innate *goodness* shined all over Lauren and lit up all the petty, mean, lazy, judgmental, and just downright dickish things she'd ever thought, said, or done. Gayle asked her how she was with a smile on her face and zero mention of the elephant in the room, because she genuinely wanted to know. That's how nice she was. If Lauren told her the truth—that everything sucked because the whole world thought she was a home wrecker, and she was maybe, kind of, sort of, falling for the local librarian who currently wanted absolutely nothing to do with her, not to mention that she lived in a town that was the last exit before Hell—Gayle would listen. She'd give her a big hug and impart mature and well researched advice that would be authentic instead of preachy. Gayle wasn't just out of her league when it came to romance, she was out of Lauren's league when it came to being a human. She was better than Lauren in every way that better was possible.

"I'm fine, thanks. How are you?" Lauren smiled at Doug and experienced the odd sensation of not wanting to throat-punch him.

Gayle's smile kicked up from pretty to knockout. She all but danced on the spot. "My mom is going to *kill* me for not telling her first, but I can't keep it to myself. Doug just proposed. We're getting married." Gayle said *married* as if the word contained approximately thirty thousand *i*'s.

"Wow. Congratulations." Lauren waited for the hopelessness. The longing and regret that usually gave her nausea. Gayle hadn't just moved on with Doug, she'd gotten freaking engaged to him. Trampoline bouncing, sophomore year royalty, diamond-present-giving Doug, was going to be her husband and Gayle Wentworth was forevermore off the market. Lauren waited, bracing herself for the let's-just-die-now feelings. They never came.

"Thank you. We're so excited, aren't we, babe?"

Clearly just as besotted, and who could blame him, Doug wrapped an arm around Gayle's shoulders. "So excited." They grinned all matchy-happy, and Lauren had to work extra hard to shove aside the wave of jealousy that only served to prove her point. Their happy faces made her feel like crap, but not for the reason she'd expected. She just didn't want to be around happy in love people because she wasn't. Looking at Gayle, the woman she would've given her little toe to have been with only last week, made her think of Emma, and if that wasn't the most fucked up thing ever, she didn't know what was.

She poured them cups of hot chocolate and launched a conversation about honeymoon destinations. Hawaii was awesome, but so expensive, so even though it was farther away, maybe Bali was better. Marriage decisions required fiscal responsibility after all. They chatted until Doug and Gayle had to hurry home and tell their folks the good news with thirty thousand i's.

She and Roxie watched them walk away, still wrapped up in each other and still laughing at things that weren't even funny.

"I hate the Christmas parade, too." Roxie slung an arm around Lauren's shoulders and gave her a tight side hug.

"It's okay." Lauren actually meant it for once. It *was* okay that Doug and Gayle were getting married, because Doug made Gayle happy. Lauren might not be the world's best human, but she was good enough to recognize that Gayle had made the right choice. Maybe someday she'd look back on last night in Emma's bedroom and hindsight would show her that Emma, too, had made the right choice by asking her to leave. She couldn't imagine it. Couldn't imagine anything but emptiness.

"Look!" Roxie pointed to a horse drawn carriage someone had decorated with a giant wreath. "We should go for a ride later. Wouldn't that be awesome, with the snow falling softly like this? It's almost a postcard."

"Hmm." Lauren knew it was better not to say anything than to vomit her bad mood all over Roxie's optimism. She grimace-smiled at a family with twin babies and poured them cups of hot chocolate, marveling that the biological imperative of procreation compelled otherwise sane people to have children, then to bundle them up in so many layers you could've rolled them downhill without a scratch, and bring them to a parade in the middle of a snowstorm.

Sorry. *Postcard* snowstorm.

"Okay, whatever you have stuck up your ass needs to be removed immediately, and don't tell me this is about Gayle. You were pissy before she stopped by."

Lauren almost choked on her fake smile as she watched the family walk away, cups in hand. "What?"

Roxie glared, hands on her hips. "You heard me."

Lauren took a long, cold breath and mustered a little patience. "I can say with complete authority that I currently don't have anything up my ass, stuck or otherwise."

"Really? I'm surprised, because I can't imagine what the hell else would give you a scowl so permanently ingrained."

She didn't even bother denying it. She felt like a scowl, so it probably was on her face. "Sorry."

Roxie filled cups of hot chocolate for more of the townsfolk before turning back to Lauren. "Don't be sorry. Tell me what's wrong."

"Nothing." Lauren ignored the pointing and laughter coming from a group of teenage boys, ridiculously relieved when they were hurried along by their parents. Why the hell was she standing here feeling threatened by a group of teenagers who were ten feet away?

"Is it Emma?"

Lauren poured hot chocolate directly onto her hand and jumped back yelping. "Damn it, Roxie!"

"Let me see." Roxie took a cursory glance at Lauren's hand, then bent down to scoop up a handful of snow and dumped it in her palm. "There you go. All better."

"You're a saint. Thanks." Lauren was fairly certain she was scowling again.

"So? Is this about so-hot-Emma?"

"No. Yes. I... Yes." Lauren was thankful the parade had started and most of the people milling about had converged on the sidewalks for a good view of the action. The noise level increased as cheers rose for the start of the parade, providing some small semblance of privacy.

"So, your totally-a-date-even-though-it-wasn't thing didn't go well then?" Roxie asked.

"That part was fine. Better than fine. It was great." So great she'd told Emma about Caroline. A story she hadn't even told Roxie yet. She couldn't remember the last time she'd felt so understood, had lost track of time, had wanted to make a woman smile or laugh—not because it got her anything in return—but because happy looked so damn beautiful on Emma. She had a face made for happy.

"So?"

"The sex didn't go well." Lauren bent down for more snow to ice her hand rather than look at Roxie.

"Huh," Roxie said in a musing tone. "That's surprising."

Lauren tried to think of a way to explain that wouldn't break Emma's confidence. "Something happened to her as a teenager, and she experiences some anxiety when it comes to sex."

Roxie covered her mouth and said through her fingers, "Was she..."

"No," Lauren said. "Not abuse. Just a really very hurtful teenage thing." She couldn't say *what* it was, not without Emma's permission, but dancing around the topic, calling it hurtful when what it was was soul destroying, just didn't feel right. "It was bad, Rox, what happened to her. I tried to help her see that it wasn't her fault, that sometimes kids make mistakes, and sometimes other kids are just downright mean. But she wasn't hearing it. Then I topped everything off by saying what I think now was maybe the worst possible thing."

Roxie frowned. "What did you say to her?"

Lauren leaned against the table, suddenly too weary to bear her own weight. "She gets shy and nervous and kind of lost in her own head, which makes it hard for her to relax and enjoy being touched. I was trying to explain that it was okay to be nervous, that it didn't bother me, you know? But what I actually said was that her nervousness turns me on."

Lauren risked a glance at Roxie and the expression on her face confirmed that yes, she had said exactly the wrong thing. Apocalypse, doomsday, axe murderer with a grudge kind of wrong.

"You told a woman who had endured a hurtful sexual experience, and was brave enough to tell you about it, that you got turned on by her nervousness?"

"I…" Lauren's eyes stung, but that was the cold. Just another stupid side effect of winter. "I was trying to show her that she didn't have to worry so much, that I wanted her just as she was, that I wanted to be the person she could let go with. Is that so bad?"

"Look at me." Roxie's voice was principal's office quiet.

Lauren looked.

"I don't know Emma. I can't speak for her. But if she reacted badly, then maybe that's because you told her the thing she doesn't like about sex, that it makes her nervous, was the thing that turned you on."

"I didn't mean it like that," Lauren said. "You know I didn't."

Roxie rolled her eyes. "Give me a break, Lauren. You did mean it. It's unfortunate that Emma's nervousness comes from a bad experience. I know you didn't mean to upset her, but don't kid yourself that you weren't really honest about what makes you hot. You can't just go around acting out your little role-plays with any old woman. You can't ask that of people who aren't walking into it with their eyes open, and you definitely can't ask it of Emma, when she reveals what sounds like might've been honest-to-God trauma. Please tell me that you didn't tell her what you do at Kink's. Tell me you had the brains not to bring that up at least."

How was it possible to actually still be alive and breathing when you wanted the earth to swallow you as badly as Lauren did right that second. "I didn't tell her. I honestly didn't mean to freak her out. I didn't tell her anything like what happens at Kink's."

"What happened next?" Roxie sounded thoroughly unimpressed.

"I tried to explain, as best I could. Like, that I wanted her to be vulnerable and surrender because those things meant she trusted me."

Roxie let out a windy sigh that was lost instantly to the swirl of the weather. "You guys really suck at first dates."

"I know." Lauren didn't mention that she'd told Emma her sordid history, or that Emma had been nothing but supportive.

She didn't tell Roxie that Emma had asked her about Kink's, or that Lauren had told her the reason she'd gotten her tattoo, or that every time she looked into Emma's endless brown eyes she never wanted to look away. All of that was heavy, and none of it spelled first date.

"You can't tell her, you know." Roxie put a hand on Lauren's shoulder and squeezed. "I know you like this girl. I can see it all over your face. But so-hot-Emma has been through something, something real, and you can't ask her to role-play with you. It sounds like regular vanilla sex costs her. What you want is a price too high for her to pay. You know that, right?"

Nodding, Lauren turned away from Roxie and stared out across the town. All the falling-down houses full of falling-down people. The whispers, the jokes, the death stares that would've killed her seventy times over if the pain they'd inflicted was physical. She hardly saw any of it. Instead there was Emma's bare back, turned away from her, distant and cold and unwilling to accept what Lauren needed. Unwilling even to accept what she needed herself.

Unwilling to surrender.

"What are you going to do?" Roxie asked.

Lauren watched as a group of women in pastel puffer jackets and fur-lined duck boots approached the table. Odd that they weren't watching the parade. "No idea. Nothing I guess. It's not like it was going anywhere anyway."

Yeah, right. Keep telling yourself that. It could have gone a lot of places if you hadn't fucked it up.

"Well, look who it is, Lauren West, front-page scandal in the flesh. You look better with your clothes on. The getup you wore to that slut club was so trashy."

Lauren barely registered what Jessica Norman had said. All she could see when she looked at her was the way a teenage Jessica had laughed at and belittled Emma. Emma who'd done nothing wrong but be genuinely attracted to her. She wanted to wring Jessica's scrawny neck so badly she didn't trust herself to speak.

Jessica Norman, the quintessential mean girl, reigned supreme as the biggest fish in the smallest pond.

Jessica raised her eyebrows and laughed. "What? No pithy response? I suppose I shouldn't be surprised. You had nothing to say when you destroyed a Christian marriage for your perverted sex games. Why should you start defending yourself now? You can't, can you? You did everything they say. Did she pay you? Was that what it was about? Did Caroline Bennett pay you to whip her, or something equally disgusting?"

"Why don't you shut the fuck up?" Roxie stood shoulder to shoulder with Lauren and stared the group down.

"I'm just saying what everyone is thinking," Jessica said.

"Not everyone thinks that," Roxie said. "Some of us believe that other people's personal lives are just that, their business."

Jessica laughed again. "Seriously? It's none of my business, even though it's been in the news for months? The whole world not only knows Lauren's business, but now they know what I've always known." She turned to Lauren and said without a second's hesitation, "You're nothing but white trash. You think getting a college degree and moving to a big city made you better than the rest of us? It didn't. You're still making trouble. You're a joke and still the laughing stock of this town."

"Why don't you go the hell home," Roxie said, fighting a losing battle. No way Roxie was going to outwit Jessica, not with so much ammunition on the wrong side. Lauren knew she should say something, if not to defend herself then to make Jessica go away, but her throat had closed up and her stomach was seizing.

You're nothing but white trash.

Intellectually, she knew it wasn't true. No human being was trash and that Jessica thought so said more about her than it did about Lauren. Her brain knew this. But the soft mush of her insides where her heart lived was too busy battling a lifetime of shame to give a damn what her head thought.

Garbage. Waste. Rubbish. White trash.

"Oh damn," said a friendly voice from behind Jessica. Emma casually walked around the group, a candy cane in hand and a Santa hat perched jauntily on her head. She circuited the refreshment table until she was standing by Lauren's side. Looking at Jessica, she said, "And here I thought *I* was your best joke. Or was that just in high school? It's so hard to keep up with all the things you find funny."

Jessica's mouth snapped shut for a moment, her eyes going wide. "Stay out of this, Emma. It has nothing to do with you."

Emma brushed Lauren's thigh before finding her hand and squeezing, her trembling fingers and too-tight grip the only sign she was nervous. Emma smiled at Jessica the way a serial killer might smile at their victim before making them very dead. "It has about as much to do with me as it does with you. More, actually, seeing as how Lauren and I went on a date last night. She wore the trashy getup." Emma made a show of fanning herself and smiled her killer smile.

Some people went red when they were mad. Others got kind of pale. Jessica, though, her skin went a really interesting shade of blotchy purple. "You went on a date with *her*?"

Jessica actually pointed at Lauren, like she just had to be as rude as humanly possible.

"Sure did. Then we had amazing kinky sex, and she whipped me until I begged her to let me come." Emma stuck her candy cane in her mouth and bit off a chunk, concealing the way her breath rushed out of her. "You should give it a go, Jess. You don't know what you're missing. I think I see Dan over there by McFarland's farm stand. You should ask him to come on over. We'd be happy to give him some pointers. You need a pro like Lauren around when you do the whipping thing for the first time."

"That's *disgusting*," Jessica all but hissed, glancing warily at her husband to make sure he hadn't overheard Emma's suggestion.

Emma just shrugged. "Well, I am desperate, so it's not that much of a surprise, is it? Where do nymphos go for a good time except to kinky home wreckers? It's a small town."

Lauren heard Roxie snicker next to her.

"Bye-bye," Emma said, waving them off as if they'd already decided to leave.

Jessica turned on her heel and stalked away, nose in the air, her entourage trailing behind her.

"Holy flying monkey dicks. You're my hero." Roxie burst out laughing. "That was brilliant."

"Thanks. Wow. Did I actually do that? I can't believe I really did that. Can I have one of those?" Emma said in a rush.

"Sure." Roxie poured Emma a cup of hot chocolate and looked at Lauren as if realizing she hadn't said anything at all. Nothing to defend herself and nothing to Emma. Roxie paused a beat, giving Lauren a you're-failing-as-a-human-right-now look, before saying what Lauren should've said herself. "Thanks. That was really awesome of you to come to Lauren's rescue like that."

Emma smiled a smile that fell off her face before the corners of her mouth had even finished lifting. "It's no big deal. Jessica isn't my favorite person."

Roxie nodded. "I picked up on that. Desperate nympho, are you?"

"According to Jessica. Quite a reputation to have at sixteen."

Roxie looked at Lauren again, clearly putting two and two together faster than Lauren would've liked. *A hurtful teenage thing* hadn't been vague enough apparently.

"She's such a bitch," Roxie said.

Since none of them could argue the point, silence fell. Roxie stared such intense holes into Lauren she expected to find them carved into her face when she got home. "I'm going to start packing up." Roxie tied a plastic black trash bag and shoved it at Lauren. "Walk Emma to her car and take this with you."

Lauren wanted to glare right back. Best friends had an annoying habit of never being able to mind their own business. But she didn't want to be rude in front of Emma. Emma who'd come to her rescue by standing up to her teenage tormentor in epic fashion. Did she have to be so damn brave all the time? It would've been easier to put last night behind her, to let's face it, start what was sure to be the long and arduous process of getting over Emma, if Emma would stop being amazing. Stop showing up looking so adorable in a Santa hat and skinny jeans and an ugly Christmas sweater under a classic black coat. Couldn't Emma just do her a favor and be mean and horrible for five minutes so she could pretend she didn't have feelings for her? Confusing, contradictory, warm and gooey, smile-for-no-reason-at-all type feelings. It sucked.

"I parked around the back," Emma said pointedly.

"Sure. Come on." Lauren turned and started walking. Walking away from Emma was becoming a habit.

Emma caught up to her and put a hand on her arm. "Hey, I'm sorry that happened. I believed you when you said people were gossiping, but I had no idea it was so nasty."

When had this town ever not been nasty? But someone like Emma, someone people liked and respected, someone who wasn't *trash*, would never understand what it was like to be treated as less than human. Lauren shrugged. "Don't worry about it. It's not your responsibility."

Emma walked around in front of her, forcing Lauren to stop or risk flattening her. "That's unfair. I know last night didn't go as planned, but that doesn't mean I don't care."

Lauren maneuvered past Emma and dumped the trash bag into a dumpster. "You shouldn't have said all that to Jessica. Now the whole town is going to be talking about you, too."

Emma laughed. "No, they're not. No one would believe I'd actually want to be whipped in bed."

Then, as if realizing what she just said, she closed her eyes and winced.

Well, there you go. If she'd needed confirmation that Emma wasn't into anything kinky, she had it. By the way her hands were shaking and bile rose to her throat, she had needed it confirmed.

Read the damn memo. She doesn't want you.

"That came out wrong," Emma said.

"Wrong as in being whipped in bed is indeed disgusting and perverted, and of course no one would believe that sweet and innocent librarian Emma would engage in such a disgraceful activity? Is that what came out wrong?"

Emma sighed. "That would be what came out wrong. I'm sorry."

"Don't worry." Lauren stomped toward the deserted back lot. "I'm well aware you're not into anything kinky."

"Because I said I didn't want to *surrender* to you I'm not into kinky?" Emma's voice was a hiss as she attempted to speak quietly and yell at the same time.

"Don't even try to convince me you'd get off on being dominant," Lauren said. "Not after the way you melted against me when I was on top of you."

God. Why had she brought that up? Emma all lush and supple and pliant against her was the last thing she needed to be thinking about right now. Or ever again.

"I'm not trying to convince you of anything. I just think it's rude to categorically assume that I wouldn't be into kink because I have a problem with the idea of surrender."

Lauren considered this. "Fine. Fair enough. You could still be kinky, and to assume that you're not was wrong. But let's be real here, you're not, and telling Jessica that you are was stupid and is only going to create rumors about you. About you and me together."

"Oh dear." Emma's voice dripped sarcasm. "People talking about you and me together, that sounds terrible."

"*God.* I'm trying to protect you. Being gossiped about isn't fun. You want people to start calling you trashy, too? Why are you insinuating yourself into all this?"

"If you have to ask that," Emma said, each word a verbal punch, "then I definitely shouldn't bother. And screw you for thinking I don't know what it's like to be called names that don't apply—names that should never apply to anyone."

Lauren walked faster, wanting nothing more than to leave this conversation, this ache in her damn heart behind her. Emma yanked on her shoulder, and she spun around to save herself from falling.

"Why are you so angry?" Emma's eyes blazed.

She was none too calm herself.

Because you're so brave and beautiful. Because I want to touch you so badly I can hardly breathe. Because you make me want things I can't have. Because you don't want me the way I am.

"I'm not angry."

Emma stepped closer to her, getting up in her space, until she was forced to take a step back, and then another and another until her back hit the door of Emma's car, and she had nowhere to go. "Why are you so angry?" Emma asked again, standing so close they breathed the same breath.

Snow fell onto Emma's eyelashes, and Lauren had to mentally restrain herself from kissing it away. "I'm angry at myself, for saying what I said to you last night. I didn't realize I was being insensitive. I'm angry at you for not being able to forgive yourself. I'm angry that we're arguing over all the names that Jessica Norman has called us. I'm angry that we have this…connection… that's only going to hurt us."

"It's already hurting us," Emma whispered, a war raging in her eyes, too many emotions battling each other for Lauren to decipher them all. She knew exactly how that felt.

"Why are you angry?" Lauren asked, unable to stop herself from running her fingers through Emma's hair, damp from snow.

"You hurt me."

Lauren's breath stopped as if she'd flicked a switch to turn it off. How could such simple words have so much impact? She'd hurt Emma. She understood now, why. Emma fought against her nerves and anxiety on a daily basis, maybe even hourly. In many crucial ways, they defined her life. That Lauren found her shyness sexy, that her heart raced just a little faster when Emma got nervous, minimized the painful experience at the heart of Emma's anxiety.

Lauren rested her forehead against Emma's and breathed in the pine needle scent of her shampoo. She didn't want to have hurt her. She'd much rather bask in her righteous indignation. She'd rather focus on Emma asking her to be vulnerable and then telling her to leave when she dared try. That she'd been as honest as she could be and Emma hadn't even met her halfway. Anger was so much easier than hurt. Hurt meant you cared. Hurt meant this wasn't about sex. This wasn't a one-night stand gone wrong. This wasn't casual. Hurt meant that feelings were involved.

Hurt was all that mattered because it confirmed she wasn't the only one feeling stripped and vulnerable. Her heart wasn't the only one on the line. She didn't want to have hurt Emma, and she'd take it back if she could, but knowing she wasn't alone in her hurt, in her feelings, settled her deep down inside.

They were in this together.

Lauren kissed her.

Chapter Eleven

Impulse sucker punched Lauren's better judgment, leaving it flat on its back with no hope for a second round. The air seemed to spit and spark like flames around them, as if the touch of their bodies had created energy all of its own. Lauren dragged her tongue along Emma's lips, need flaring to an ache in the pit of her stomach when Emma moaned and twined her arms around Lauren's neck. No matter how much they sniped at each other, neither of them could deny or resist the desire that was always there, just under the surface, rising to crash over them. Lauren kissed her slow and coaxing, teasing and tasting, tugging at Emma's bottom lip and then sliding inside when she gasped. The heat of Emma's mouth was a lightning strike to Lauren's system. Everything short-circuited. Emma tasted like mint and Christmas and the heady unmistakable flavor of desire.

"This is insanity." Emma pulled back, panting. "Didn't we just agree that we don't want the same thing in bed?"

Blood was rushing in twenty-seven different directions in Lauren's brain, making it hard to think. "Did we? Good thing we aren't in bed then." Lauren slid a leg between Emma's thighs until her head tipped back, her Santa hat falling to the ground.

"It feels so good when you do that."

"Think how much better my hand would be. My mouth. Don't you want my tongue on your clit?" Lauren ground her thigh shamelessly against Emma, knowing that under a thin layer of clothes was wet need. Need that was all for her. It was high time Emma stopped being ashamed of it.

"Lauren." Her name on Emma's lips, the *want* in it, made her shudder. Screw what she wanted, she would give Emma whatever she asked for, however she wanted it, if only she'd say her name again in just that way. If only she wouldn't close her eyes.

"Tell me what you want."

When Emma didn't reply Lauren trailed kisses along her jawline and down her throat. "Tell me. We both know we can't stop what we feel. Anything you want."

Emma remained silent and Lauren almost let her go. Almost walked away despite the way Emma had moaned and melted and rocked against her. But then she had an idea that just might work. If she could do it. If she could trust Emma the way she had asked that Emma trust her. If she had the guts to show her how it was done. They were in this together.

All the moisture evaporated from her mouth until she was sure her throat would crack in two if she dared swallow. Still, she had to go for it. The alternative was unthinkable. "Maybe you'd like it if I was the one to surrender. Would that turn you on?"

Emma went still. "What?"

"Maybe, what you want, at least for now, is for me to surrender to you. To show you what it means to be vulnerable. To trust you like I asked you to trust me."

"Would you?" Emma's question sounded more skeptical than eager, but the look she gave Lauren burned from the inside out.

"Yes." For Emma she'd be willing to do just about anything. Emma thought that surrender took something away from you, that it made you less. That it made you what *Jessica* thought it did. Desperate and needy and out of control. But Emma didn't realize there was power in surrender, too. Power in desperation and need and not being in control. That letting go could be the very thing that saved you. It might be the thing that saved them, if Lauren led the way.

"Come with me." Lauren tugged Emma along behind her until she found what she was looking for—a snow-encrusted alley between the bookstore and the café. At close to five, the night was already near black, the moon rising to take its place in the sky, darkness spilling into the light. Darkness was exactly what she wanted.

Halfway down the tight walkway, she pressed her back to the brick wall. Her blood beating in her veins made her skin feel too tight. On a deep breath, she said what she'd never thought she'd have any reason to say. "If you want my surrender, you're going to have to take me."

"Here? Right now?" Emma twisted her hands in front of her, glancing up and down the alley.

Lauren could tell Emma's breath was seizing from the way her chest rose and fell. "Please don't make me wait. If we wait, we'll rationalize this. We'll figure out that it's a terrible idea and we'll convince ourselves not to do it. Please."

She'd thought it would cost her to be the one with nowhere to go, to be the one who begged, but she'd been wrong. It hadn't cost her a thing. Strangely, it felt right. Not because she found it all that sexy to say "please," but because she really did want this. If it made Emma hot, if it got Emma to trust her, then she wanted it more than she wanted her next breath.

"We're outside, in public, in a dirty alley." Emma stated the obvious like she was ticking things off a list. She licked her lips, twisted her hands, stared at Lauren as if doing so would make Lauren change her mind.

"We are." Lauren stared right back. She pressed her hands to the wall to prevent herself from hauling Emma into her arms and making her forget her anxiety. "But it's dark. No one can see us. You can do whatever you want."

We're in this together.

Emma stepped closer and fingered the collar of Lauren's shirt, dipping her fingers inside. "The possibility of having sex in a semi-public place makes me nervous."

"I know. It's a risk. But it's also just a little bit thrilling, isn't it? My heart's pounding and my breath's unsteady. I'm so wet."

"God." Emma breathed the word into her neck. "When you say things like that everything inside me goes desperate. I'm not sure I can do this."

Lauren pushed off the wall, but Emma held her back with a hand on her shoulder. "Stay there."

"Okay."

Emma worried her lip between her teeth until Lauren thought she'd bite right through it. "I'm not going to take my clothes off and neither are you. We'll get hypothermia."

"Okay." Emma Prescott, prim and proper librarian, laying down her terms for fucking outside, in public, in the middle of winter, was ridiculously hot.

"And you're going to have to keep quiet. I don't want anyone rushing up here, so no screaming."

Lauren's knees went a little weak. "Okay."

Emma pressed her body against Lauren's and whispered against her ear, "And you can't touch me."

Lauren groaned, her fingers digging into the mortar between a row of bricks as Emma shifted against her, pressing their breasts together. The back of Lauren's head tapped the wall as she moaned. "No fair."

Emma's lips on her ear felt like a smile. "Do you think I'm stupid? That I don't know what you're doing? That I don't know why we're in this far-too-dirty-for-me-to-be-thinking-about-right-now alley instead of in a nice comfortable bed?"

"Because you said we don't want the same thing there?" Lauren said hopefully. She was too preoccupied with the way Emma was moving like liquid heat against her to be having this conversation. God, she hoped Emma would touch her soon. Surrendering was killing her. She wasn't scared of the fall, but the *wait* was crazy-making.

"No," Emma said. "You know as well as I do that having sex when there's a possibility of getting caught takes trust. That it pushes boundaries." Emma kissed her way down Lauren's neck, opened her coat, and unbuttoned the first few buttons on her shirt. She slid her hands under the collar and cupped Lauren's shoulders to hold her in place.

"That's a total coincidence," Lauren said with approximately zero conviction.

"I bet." Emma stroked her shoulders, managing to open the last few buttons.

The freezing night air hit Lauren's bare skin, doing absolutely nothing to cool her raging need.

"Is this what you do at Kink's? Do you push people's boundaries? Do you earn their trust?" Emma asked.

"Yes." Lauren tilted her hips into Emma's. So hopelessly wet, she almost reached for Emma, more than prepared to beg shamelessly. Only Emma's command not to touch her kept her in place. "Though usually from where you're standing."

"Mmm." Emma slid a palm down her belly and cupped Lauren's pussy through her jeans. "You like to be in control."

"Usually." The night was starting to fade. The scrape of the brick against her back, the chill of the air, the faint glow of a streetlight, all being slowly but surely obliterated by the pleasure that arced through her. Emma's touch ignited a wet need that she had no hope of containing. "Right now, I don't seem to mind you being in charge."

"Am I really in charge?"

Lauren tried to rein in her rampaging heartbeat and ragged breathing. This was too important to fuck up by getting so turned on she couldn't think. So fucking desperate to come the answer to every question was "yes." That's what *she* wanted from Emma, but Emma wanted to talk it through. Just because she had her back to the wall didn't mean she wasn't trying to pull Emma's strings just a little. This was about trust, and it was time she showed up for it. "There's only one way to find out. Take me however you want."

Emma's eyes were just a little glazed as she rubbed her palm against Lauren until the seam of her jeans pressed against her clit and Lauren groaned. "Do you trust me?" Emma asked.

"Yes." The word was a gasp, Lauren had no air for words, only for soft throaty noises and fighting the desire to come in her pants.

"Are you ready to surrender?"

"Yes." She'd had never been readier for anything in her life. Ready for this woman, this moment, this trust. "Please."

"Turn around."

Willing to do anything, Lauren faced the wall. Emma reached around her to unbutton her jeans and slid them and her underwear down only far enough to ease a hand between her legs. When Emma found her clit, Lauren whimpered and thrust into her fingers.

Emma pressed along her back, pushing Lauren against the wall and preventing her from getting what she was sure would've been a very embarrassing case of butt frostbite. Lauren's cheek hit the brick, her bare belly meeting the rough surface, as Emma crowded her from behind, cupping her pussy and discovering just how very, very turned on she was.

"Oh," Emma said. "Look how wet you are. You like this."

The unmistakable confidence in Emma's voice, sent desire snaking in Lauren's belly. Emma's nervousness still showed in the stiffness of her body, but she wasn't unsure, she wasn't scared. She was in control.

Lauren's thoughts tripped over themselves as her brain went into emergency shutdown mode. "I didn't expect you to do it like this."

"You mean that you didn't expect that I'd want you turned away from me, shoved up against a wall in this alley you're making me fuck you in?"

Colors swirled behind her closed eyes as Emma's words hit her like a punch to the solar plexus. She'd add talking dirty to the list of things Emma was goddamn brilliant at. "Yes."

"But you still did it." Emma's voice held a note of amazement riding on the edge of wonder. This was new for her. Emma wasn't used to putting her faith in the unexpected. She didn't leap into the unknown.

"I trust you." Unable to help herself, Lauren ground into Emma's palm. The heat of Emma along her back was seeping into her even through her coat, the unyielding freezing roughness in front of her almost painful. Everything inside coalesced into a well of need so deep she worried that if she jumped, she'd never stop falling. "Please."

"Please, what?" Emma stroked her folds, pushing inside her and then backing off, pressing a finger to her clit and letting go. Torturing her with infinite patience and maddening gentleness.

"Please. I need you to make me come."

"We're in this gross alley because you need to come? Because you couldn't wait until we got home?"

"No." Lauren whimpered. The word sounded wrong when every circuit she had was flashing yes signals.

"Please what, Lauren?" Emma pressed the tips of her fingers inside her. "What do you need?"

"I need you." The truth of her words nearly stopped her heart, but she had no time to think about it because Emma thrust inside her.

"So wet and ready for me, aren't you? So hot you're going to come all over yourself."

Emma fucked her, rocking against Lauren's ass. "You're very good at being in control, but I'm in charge now. You're going to surrender. You're going to come."

Lauren rode the wave of sensation that skated across her skin and filtered into her bones. She was losing it. She rocked into Emma's thrusts with an abandon straight out of her most private fantasies. Desire filled her head, wrapped around her body, bled through her veins until her belly quivered. "Oh God. Yes. Please."

"Go over for me. Give it to me," Emma ordered against her back, thrusting in and out of her with sure, steady strokes, propelling and curling and pumping her fingers just right. Not hard or urgent, but strong and commanding. Emma fucked her with no fanfare. She fucked as if she knew she didn't need to go deep, to go hard, to make Lauren come. She just needed to never stop. Never never never stop.

Emma hit that perfect place inside her for the last time, and Lauren splintered into a million pieces, breaking her promise to be quiet and crying out her pleasure. Her cries didn't even sound human, completely foreign to her ears. Reckless and heedless and just a little bit wrecked. She was achy and needy and throbbing. Falling into the well. Falling so fast that landing was all but impossible.

She'd led them to the dirty alley no way good enough for Emma, to earn trust, to break apart and come together and finally, *finally* sate the need that had her by the throat. She'd agreed to surrender. She'd wanted Emma to take her for all the things it would show Emma, for all the ways it would build a bridge between them.

Oh God, had Emma delivered. She'd faced her anxiety and won the battle. She'd plowed ahead when she wasn't sure she could. She'd accepted Lauren's trust and honored it by delivering an orgasm that just about blew her head off.

Lauren stayed pressed against the wall as her heartbeat slowed and her breath returned. Eyes closed, she focused on the pleasure still throbbing in her pussy, on Emma's fingers still inside her. "That was amazing."

Emma made an appreciative noise behind her. "You're amazing. Thank you."

Lauren didn't turn around when Emma pulled out. She didn't drag Emma into her arms and kiss her the way every fiber of her being was screaming at her to. She didn't tell Emma that she'd never done this before, never given herself over to a woman, never wanted to the way Emma made her want.

She focused on pleasure and struggled to ignore the truth that lurked at the edges of her brain. Emma had accepted her trust. Emma'd been brave. But Emma hadn't looked at her. She'd turned Lauren to face the wall. She'd commanded Lauren not to touch her, and given herself a way to hide, behind Lauren's shoulder. Just as she'd hidden behind her closed eyes, behind her anxiety.

Emma had taken one step, and Lauren had fallen.

They weren't really in this together.

Chapter Twelve

At noon on Sunday, Emma pushed open the door of the Grumpy Goat and stopped just beyond the threshold. Funny how you could live in the same place your entire life, drive on the same roads, walk down the same streets, eat at the same restaurants, and you just took it all for granted until something special happened and everything came alive. Until *someone* special imbued a place with racing hearts and trembling hands and that wonderful, indescribable feeling of being singled out, of being chosen.

That place was this place, right inside the door of Grumpy's where she'd almost fallen and Lauren had caught her, where she'd talked to Lauren for the first time ever, where Lauren had called her beautiful and asked her to dance. This spot right here. Their spot. Where special had happened.

"Hey, it's the nerdy book lady." Doug French picked her up and spun her in a circle before depositing her back on her feet, effectively ending Emma's daydreaming. "Thanks for coming. I know all this was last minute."

"Hey yourself, recently engaged dude." Emma smiled. "I'm always up for celebrating happiness. How's the whole stupid in love thing working out for you so far?"

Doug rolled his eyes, but even that looked cheerful. "Susan's already sent me five links to venues, three for caterers, and we absolutely *must* have the flowers done by Holly Thomas because she really is the very best in the business, and her little girl deserves the best on her big day." Doug shook his head. "Let me ask you, do you know any guy who gives a fuck about flowers?"

Emma laughed. "You should've told Susan that her little girl *is* getting the best because there's no better guy than you."

Doug managed a scoff, but he looked pleased. "Says the lesbian who wouldn't go out with me in middle school."

"That only means I'm objective. I can say you're good without being blindsided by those contractor muscles of yours."

"Speaking of being blindsided." Doug took her arm and led her away from the crowd that had gathered to celebrate his engagement. "I wanted to catch you before anyone else did." His blue eyes turned serious and the smile faded from his face. "What's going on with you and Lauren?"

Oh boy, that was a loaded question. Did he want to know how every time Lauren looked at her she felt seen in a way she'd never before experienced? Or maybe Doug was asking if she was possibly, maybe entertaining the idea of asking Lauren over for dinner tomorrow night so she could cook for her. Or, hell, maybe Doug wanted to know how incredibly sexy Lauren had sounded last night when she came all over her. How Lauren's pussy had pulsed and tightened around her fingers, how wet Lauren had been. How wet *she* had been. With so many possibilities the question needed clarifying.

"What do you mean?"

"Are you dating her?" Doug asked.

"I'm…" Were they dating? Not really. Dating was plural, and they'd had exactly one not-a-date. "Yes, we're dating."

She was clearly delusional and should probably run that statement by Lauren before she started advertising it to the whole world, but she'd deal with her masochistic streak later.

"Emma."

His tone was so world-weary her back was instantly up.

"What? Please don't tell me you're going to scold me because of what's been reported in the media. I'm an adult. And anyway, you know Lauren. She's not who they say she is."

Doug's concerned expression didn't waver. "I used to know her. Once upon a time. But she changed in middle school, Em. She's guarded and has a chip on her shoulder the size of Texas."

Emma flashed to last night in the alley—Lauren pressed against the wall like it was doing all the work of holding her up, admitting that she needed her, that she wanted Emma to take her. Emma remembered tracing Lauren's tattoo and wondering what it was that hadn't killed her. If Lauren had changed in middle school, Emma had no doubt there was a very good reason. "She isn't guarded with me. She's the opposite."

Doug shoved a hand through his blondish-brown Ken doll hair. "She's not right for you."

"Didn't she have that whole thing with Gayle a bunch of years back?" Emma's near obsessive interest in everything-Lauren was about to come in handy. Normally, Emma wouldn't have brought it up. Ancient history tended to be buried for a reason, but Doug was starting to piss her off. "Perhaps your judgment is clouded because your fiancée and Lauren got hot and heavy?"

Doug laughed. "It was one kiss. Plus, I'm a guy. Hot girls kissing is, well, hot."

She couldn't argue that point, so she raised her eyebrows and gave disbelieving her best shot. "Sure this isn't all because you're worried Gayle might still hold a torch?"

"I'm not worried. I have something Lauren doesn't." Doug tapped his belt buckle and winked.

It took Emma a second, but when she got it, she wrinkled her nose and shoved him. "That's gross."

Doug grinned. "That's not what Gayle says. I'm not worried about her. I'm worried about you." Before Emma could point out that it was none of Doug's business, he got there first. "I know you're a grown woman who can make her own choices, and normally I wouldn't interfere even if I thought you were wrong.

But Jessica is spreading this rumor that you and Lauren are having BDSM sex." Before Emma could reply, Doug put a hand on her shoulder and squeezed. "Also, none of my business. But it's getting around. People are talking. The town council is talking."

"The council is talking about my *sex life*?" All the blood drained from Emma's head until the room began to sway. The mental picture of six council members convening in the Cupcake's fussily decorated living room, sipping flowery tea and discussing her sexual proclivities made Emma want to laugh, puke, and run away all at the same time. God. Lauren had been dealing with exactly this kind of thing for weeks. Lauren had warned her that exactly this was bound to happen. How had she survived?

Doug nodded. "I'm sorry. It's just a rumor at this point, and it will die down if you don't do anything to keep it going. But the kink thing is an obvious target for gossip, and with Lauren's history…"

Doug let that last part hang and Emma's desire to disappear was only outweighed by her anger. "It was a joke. Jessica was giving Lauren a hard time, and I made a joke. It's not true, and even if it was, it's no one's business but mine."

"I know," Doug said earnestly. "No judgment, I promise. I just thought you should know."

Emma stared at Doug helplessly, her heart sinking. Both of them thinking what neither of them had to say. Doug's father had been chairman of the council the year Emma had graduated high school. The same year her mom decided that Emma was now a fully-fledged adult and up and moved to Florida without warning. Emma had been valedictorian, but she couldn't even afford a loaf of bread let alone college. She didn't blame her mom for doing what she'd needed to, but she'd had no one. The council stepped in to fund a scholarship that paid for college in exchange for her working in the library after graduation. That scholarship had set her future. It had saved her life.

She *owed* this town. She owed the council. Not just her job as librarian, but because in all the ways that included *caring* about her future, the ragtag crew of octogenarians comprising the council, who were so often a pain in Emma's ass, were also her family. They'd been there for her. They'd made a concession and given her hope. That council, and this town, was a part of her. Because of the chance they'd given her, she'd become strong and independent and able to handle anything life threw at her. Well, almost anything. Brenda Baker picturing her naked, tied up, and whipped, that she was pretty sure she couldn't handle. The laugh-puke-run combo was an attractive option right about now.

Emma rubbed a hand over her face. "Okay. So that's not exactly good. But also, so what, right? I can handle a little embarrassment."

That was a bold statement she was none too sure she could actually live up to. But Lauren had survived much worse already, and Emma wasn't going to leave her alone to endure more. Especially not when it had been Emma's angry comeback to Jessica that had caused all the trouble.

Doug leaned against the wall with his gaze on the floor. "I heard from Dad, who still has contacts on the council, they denied funding for the e-book lending program. They're going to tell you tomorrow."

A boulder the size of a small island in the South Pacific lodged in Emma's stomach. "What? You can't be serious. My proposal was flawless. That program is going to increase circulation tenfold. We'll be able to offer thousands—"

"I know. But they denied it." He shrugged, but there was nothing dismissive in the gesture. "If you ask, I'm sure they'll say that your sex life is none of their business and that wasn't why the program was denied, but we both know it's a lie."

Emma's legs had turned to jelly. The peanut butter sandwich she'd had for lunch was going to end up all over the floor. "That's discrimination."

"Sure it is, but what are you going to do? Sue the people who sign your paycheck? Sue the reason you even have that paycheck?"

"This is ridiculous," Emma snapped. "It hurts the library, not me."

Doug gave her a soft look. "You don't have to be brave with me. We both know it hurts you, Em. It's a warning shot. If you keep seeing Lauren, who knows what they'll do next. It won't just be the library that suffers. If they find a reason to fire you, you'll have to pay back the tuition money."

She shallowed hard and willed herself not to cry. "They wouldn't do that."

Doug pulled Emma into his arms and rubbed her back briskly. "Probably not. But some people in this town are none too fond of Lauren and her mother. You don't want to be caught up in all their drama. Why risk it? Sex isn't worth your job. Isn't worth the whispers and the stares. Just stay out of her way until she goes back to San Francisco, okay?"

Emma pulled back to look up into Doug's face, biting the inside of her cheek hard when she felt her eyes well. "What about Lauren? She hasn't done anything wrong. What am I supposed to do, ghost her like she means nothing to me?"

Doug's hands moved to Emma's shoulders and he gripped them hard. "Emma. You're not in love with her, are you? Damn it, she's never going to stay in this town. She ran away from here like her ass was on fire and everyone was glad to see her leave."

Emma's anger surged again, burning away the tears. "You sound like you agree with them."

"Some people cause trouble wherever they go and never take responsibility for it, even when they're the common denominator. I don't know if Lauren's mom did what people say she did. I don't know if Lauren did what the media claims she did. But it's mighty coincidental, don't you think?"

Emma waved a hand at him. "Why does it matter? Whether or not her mom took money for sex, or Lauren got it on in some kink club with a married woman. Does that make either of them so bad the town should treat them like lepers?"

Doug looked exasperated. "You're really gone over her to be asking a question like that. Prostitution is illegal in New York. Sleeping with a married woman, kink or not, isn't okay."

"But ostracizing them and gossiping about them is when no one knows the truth," Emma shot back, completely fed up with this conversation.

"Hey!" Doug threw up his hands like Emma's words had come to life and were about to smack him in the face. "I'm not doing either of those things. I don't care about Lauren. I care about you."

Emma looked at her friend, the boy who'd been nice to her when he didn't have to be. The boy who'd stood up for her against bullies and listened when she'd prattled on about literature like the characters in a book were real life friends. That boy was eons apart from this man. A man who couldn't see how a simple comment like "I don't care" spoke louder than any hateful action or hissed gossip. Indifference was worse than hate. To hate, you had to care. No wonder Lauren didn't want her mixed up in this. But like it or not, she was thoroughly mixed, and she had a choice to make.

Stand up or back down.

Fight for Lauren or walk away.

Be brave or give in.

"I care about Lauren," Emma said quietly. "What I said about whipping wasn't true and if you want to filter that through the town gossip channels, I'd appreciate it, but I'm not going to stop seeing Lauren, not even if it costs me my job."

Doug stared. "You love her."

Emma just stared back. She had no idea if she loved Lauren. It was too soon. They had too much to figure out. They weren't even officially dating, and the absurdity of losing her job over something that might end up being nothing, the insanity of coming to the defense of someone who would probably just break her heart didn't escape her. Lauren would likely leave town in another week or two, and she would spend the next forever picking up the pieces. But some things were worth the risk. Some things were bigger even than love. Emma was going to stand up to this, for Lauren.

But mostly for herself.

"I don't know if we're ready for love. But I do know that blackballing me because of who I date, or what I may do in bed, is wrong. I don't agree with it and I'm not going to stop seeing Lauren. I'm not going to join the seemingly endless procession of people who've treated her as if she's expendable. As if she doesn't matter. She *does* matter. She's a good person, and she needs someone to be there for her, to be on her side." Emma sealed her lips shut. She'd said too much, but Doug hadn't seen Lauren's face when Jessica called her trash. Doug hadn't seen the way Lauren had just checked out, gone blank, fuzzy static where her personality should've been. Emma knew trauma. Hers had been swift and cutting, the deep wound of a blade slicing through her life in one definitive swipe. Lauren's trauma was different. Slower, and in many ways more insidious. If Emma's world had been sliced in two one fateful night when she was sixteen, Lauren's world was death by a thousand cuts. Shallow maybe, but enough to make her suffer. Emma couldn't stand to watch her bleed.

Doug pulled her in for another long hug. "You're stubborn and entirely inflexible. I hope Lauren knows what she's found in you. She'd better treat you right, or I'll have a reason to believe what people say about her."

Emma hugged him back. Dread an anchor gluing her to the spot. Lauren wanted to know her, wanted to know her with an intensity that blew her away. But for Lauren it was all in fun, just a diversion before going back to San Francisco. Even if it wasn't, even if there was nothing tying Lauren to the West Coast any longer, Emma couldn't ask her to stay here. Not when this town had done everything to make her feel unwelcome. It wasn't just the current spectacle and the gossip it generated that made Lauren hate Sunrise Falls, but years of gossip, of snide comments and casual snubs, because of how her mother had paid the bills as a single parent, because Lauren had been an angry and rebellious teenager, because if you were different in a small town, there was nowhere to hide.

No. She couldn't ask Lauren to stay, but she could stand up for her. She'd been a disaster around Lauren so far—not able to let go, not able to be vulnerable. But what she lacked in vulnerability she made up for in strength. Lauren's story could've been her story. Change a few facts and shake well. It could've been her. Instead, Emma knew what it was to be alone in the world and have a community you could count on. She'd had people to support her and give her a home. Lauren hadn't had that, maybe not ever. Could anyone blame her for being angry?

Starting right now, Lauren had Emma, a community of two. She was going to stand for her, for them, for what was happening between them that just maybe, might be, falling in love.

CHAPTER THIRTEEN

The red brick library dated back to the 1800s, as old as Sunrise Falls itself. The town spent a small fortune repairing and maintaining this building and others just like it. Lauren didn't get it. It would've been cheaper to knock it down and build something new. Something a little more durable, with a play area for kids, and a Wi-Fi connection that didn't disintegrate the second you stepped too far to the left. Something that might actually serve the needs of the community. But history was the only feather in Sunrise Falls' cap. When you had an aging population stuck in its ways, advancing into the future wasn't an option. History was all you'd ever be remembered for. So, half the money her mom paid in town taxes went to fixing broken things that'd just break again soon enough.

It wasn't quite five, but the windows were dark and the wheelie cart full of discount books that usually sat by the entrance was nowhere in sight. She checked her texts again, rereading the one from Emma.

Meet me at the library at five. I have something for you.

Of course Emma texted in full sentences, complete with punctuation. She'd even spelled out "five" which was probably grammatically correct according to some rulebook she'd never heard of. Emma was like that, precise and orderly and just a little bit old-fashioned. She didn't do one-night stands, she wanted a date, she was above fucking in an alley. Lauren grinned. She might've relented on the first two, but Emma'd fucked her in that alley just fine. So fine in fact, she couldn't stop thinking about it.

Before her palms had time to get sweaty and her skin began to tingle, she jumped out of the car. She barely had the willpower not to sprint toward the library as if she were mainlining liquid caffeine. She'd been surprised, and okay, why not admit it, elated when Emma had texted her. The way they'd left things had been stilted. Not awkward enough to be embarrassing, but not exactly brimming with closeness either. The sex had been just as phenomenal as she'd anticipated. Emma had done just what she'd asked. Emma'd been brave and faced her anxiety. Emma had taken her. She'd embraced the experience wholeheartedly, even talking dirty, her words like strokes against Lauren's clit, turning her on and making her desperate to come. Even though her orgasm had been amazing, she'd enjoyed watching Emma come alive even more. Emma had fucked her with a confidence that made her want to grin from ear to ear. Yet the very thing that made her so happy was exactly the problem. She cared about Emma more than she cared about sex. She had right from the first moment with her arm around Emma's waist and the certainty that she wouldn't need a bet to seduce this woman ringing in her ears.

But under the warm fuzzies, under and around and between the cracks, were all the things they hadn't done. Emma still hadn't looked at her during sex. Emma hadn't come. Emma wasn't any closer to surrendering. And deeper still were all the things they hadn't said. *I want to take you out on a real date. I want to stay and figure this out. I want you and I choose you and I need you.* Lauren had only been back in town a week. It didn't rate as the worst week of her life, not by a long shot. But it'd kind of sucked, until Emma had made all the difference.

Lauren tried the door to the library and found it unlocked despite the closed sign hanging in the window. She pushed it open and stepped inside. "Emma?"

"Back here. Lock the door, will you?"

She turned the notch on the doorknob, then secured the deadbolt and followed the sound of Emma's voice. She entered the main section of the library and stopped dead. All thoughts of what stood between them and where this was headed were eclipsed by the sight of Emma sitting very tall and straight on the circulation desk, one knee crossed over the other and her hands clasped on her knee like a devotee at church.

"Well, hello there." It was a stupid line, sounding about as lecherous as she felt, but all her brain cells where currently occupied with the task of picking her jaw up off the floor so she didn't trip over it when she inevitably lost all her willpower and ran at Emma. Here was the thing: Emma was naked. Not artfully arranged trench coat concealing her glorious skin naked. Not sexy lingerie hinting at those mouth-watering curves naked. *Naked* naked. Totally bare. Totally fucking sexy. Just her silky hair, her drive-me-crazy blush, and so much naked that Lauren's heart hammered.

Emma's smile looked as if it took some work to achieve. "Hi."

She took a careful step, and then another and another, until she was standing in front of Emma. She touched her cheek with fingers that tingled from all the adrenaline coursing through her. "This is a nice surprise."

"I decided to be brave." Emma sounded anything but.

"This is jumping in the deep end of the brave pool." She wasn't sure *she'd* be brave enough to strip naked and wait for a lover in the place she worked every day. *In the place she'd fantasized about coming with my hand over her mouth.* Emma had chosen this time, this place, for a reason. Did she want to act out her fantasy? Lauren took a breath, held it, and let it out slowly. Emma had a talent for snatching the air from her lungs. "I thought you didn't like to push boundaries."

Emma tugged her closer and played with the top button of her shirt, sliding it free and dipping her fingers inside. "I had this really hot woman show me that pushing boundaries can be fun if you let it be."

"Did you have fun?" The question was so simple and the answer anything but. Fun was such an inadequate word for all the pheromones zigzagging between them, pinging off each other and making her dizzy.

Emma nodded, then shook her head, summing up Lauren's feelings exactly.

She waited but Emma didn't say more. She was starting to understand Emma Prescott. Bravery came in different forms, and Emma wasn't nearly as shy as she appeared. In fact, she was excellent at making moves. At getting Lauren to ask her out, at getting her in bed, at making her want so damn much she gave more of herself than she'd thought she'd had in her to give in the first place. Emma made her want, and then Emma wanted her to push. To pick up where she left off and drive her to that next boundary, that next peak, that next discovery. Emma had come this far, but how far they went from here was up to Lauren.

She made an obvious display of sizing Emma up, letting her gaze linger on all the bare skin on display. She allowed her eyes to drop from Emma's face, to her breasts, to her waist, and then to the place between her legs that Emma managed to conceal with crossed knees. She didn't bother to hide her perusal. She wanted Emma to see. She wanted Emma to know how sexy she found her. Her fantasies about Emma over the past few days were hot enough to make a hooker blush, but Emma sitting naked on the circulation desk, the *reality* of it, had the blood pumping through her so hard she was sure Emma could see her pulse beating.

Emma had made the move.

Now it was time to see how far she'd trust.

Emma might think that vulnerability, that *intimacy,* was about sex, as if the brush of two bodies together was what made total exposure so uniquely terrifying, but she had it all wrong. Intimacy was about absolute trust, about showing up and revealing all the things that made up who you really were when no one was watching, most of them not entirely honorable.

"Spread your legs."

Emma's blush went from a tinge of pink to a second-degree burn. "What?"

"Spread your legs." Lauren enunciated every word precisely, her eyes locked on Emma's.

Emma squirmed, and then slowly, as if not quite believing herself capable, spread her legs.

Every so often life hands you a moment. The kind of moment where even in the midst of enjoying whatever splendor is before you, whatever emotions in your body, you're compelled to stop and notice the significance of *this* moment and remind yourself not to forget it. This was one of those moments. Lauren took her time perusing Emma's pussy, etching the memory of every detail. With one hand, she held Emma's knee when she tried to cover up again. "Are you going to deny that this turns you on?" She knew it did, but she also knew the question, or rather, having to answer the question, would arouse Emma.

"I…" Emma just looked at Lauren helplessly.

She slid her hand from Emma's knee up her thigh. "If you're going to cover up, if you're going to deny that you like it when I look at you naked, then you won't be wet when I touch you. I very badly want to find out what makes you hot and wet. I want to discover all the things that make you moan, if you hide from me, I won't be able to."

"Please, I…" Emma focused on her breathing, grappling with a storm cloud of conflicting and confusing desires that were turning her stomach into a watery churning mess. She wanted this. God, how very fucking badly she wanted this. But it was hard not to be nervous when there was so much riding on it. On her ability to show up and be the lover Lauren needed her to be.

She huffed out her breath. Wow, lie to herself much? Sure, Lauren did need this from her, but she needed it from herself too. She needed to know she could. She needed to put the past behind her. She needed to be brave, not because it would make Lauren happy, but because she wasn't the person she'd been last week. Lauren's stoic resolve no matter how bad things got, her compassion and sincerity when she had every reason to be hard and jaded, her willingness to give Emma everything she wanted, and all the things she needed and didn't know how to ask for—they had changed her and she couldn't *not* face this. She couldn't *not* try.

But despite herself, the words, barely loud enough to earn the name, that she actually said out loud were, "I can't."

"You can't, what?" Lauren cupped Emma's pussy and the heat of her palm seared. Emma whimpered as her need built, clawing and churning and rushing everywhere all at once. Need had compelled her to text Lauren. Need made her strip in the library and expose herself in the most wanton way possible. Need that made her want to surrender.

Like hell. Perhaps it had a little something to do with Lauren pressed against a brick wall trusting you. Perhaps realizing you'd rather lose your job than lose a chance to be with her even if this goes nowhere. None of this is about sexual arousal. Except that it kind of, actually, really really *was* as Lauren slid her palm up and down her pussy, dragging her fingers lightly over her clit, pressing the heel of her hand at Emma's opening.

Oh yeah, this was most definitely all about sexual arousal.

"Oh God. Please." Emma grabbed the desk behind for support before she fell and gave herself a concussion. The longer Lauren touched her the more her anxiety moved to the back of her consciousness, floating behind her like a gauze curtain, shoved aside by her wet, swollen need pulsing impatiently against Lauren's hand.

"You can't what?" Lauren asked again. "You can't enjoy this? You can't want this? You can't admit that you need me to make you come?"

Emma was experiencing prolonged tachycardia. Her heart wouldn't stop racing and her mind couldn't keep up. "Please."

Lauren shook her head slowly. "Which is it, Emma? You can't or please?"

"Please." It was the only word there was to say. She hadn't even realized she'd closed her eyes until Lauren made a cranky sound in the back of her throat and gripped the back of her neck in a hold gentle enough to be comfortable but strong enough to get her attention. Her eyes sprang open and Lauren's look-at-me-damn-it gaze radiated through every cell in her body.

"You're not going to close your eyes. You don't have to watch what I'm doing to you if it's too much. But you have to be here. Be present. No checking out. Do you understand?"

She swallowed. *This* was the side of Lauren that had been lurking just beneath the surface whenever Lauren had kissed her, backed her up against a bookcase or a counter or a bed and took over. The Lauren who got off on being in charge.

But, no, this was more than that. Lauren's gray eyes, usually so soft, were swirling with something she couldn't describe. Lauren looked calm, relaxed even, but it was a deception. Like the eerie quiet before a tornado. Underneath was the fierce intensity of the dominant, ready to rip her world apart.

That word, *dominant,* had hot ribbons of need twisting and twining over her skin. She wasn't even close to understanding what it all meant. But she didn't want to analyze it. She didn't want to have to explain it even to herself. Lauren's precisely measured tone, her clipped words, the way Lauren's eyes were boring into her, it was doing it for her in crazy mind-melting, going-to-come-so-so-soon ways. Lauren's fingers brushed her clit and she made a sound like the squeal of tires.

"Oh God. Your hand should be considered a lethal weapon."

"Lethal to all those thoughts I can see swirling in your head. Are you ready to let it all go?" Lauren asked.

"Yes," Emma said, her voice sounding rusty even to her own ears. Lauren's gaze never left hers, as if she was searching her brain and plucking out her thoughts.

"I'm going to make you come," Lauren said. "You're going to surrender. You're going to trust me enough to be vulnerable. Just as hot and needy and crazy as you were at sixteen. That's what I want. So fucking turned on you don't know your own name."

Short and sharp, Lauren's words were a command.

"I know," Emma whispered, hardly able to breathe around the lump in her throat.

"I want that to be what you want too."

"I want you."

Lauren frowned. "It's not going to work if you're only saying yes because you want to please me."

She touched the tips of her fingers to the frown lines on Lauren's face. "I very much want to please you. I want to submit to you. I'm not sure I would've used that language exactly, if kink wasn't a factor for you, but I can't deny that it makes me hot when you take charge. I can't deny that I've had fantasies about being tied up. Being blindfolded. Being ordered to kneel or bend over. Fantasies about being teased mercilessly but denied orgasm. Fantasies about being controlled. Fantasies about you and about this. About us."

Lauren's breath hissed out of her. "Fuck. You're really very good at that."

"Good at what?" Emma asked.

"Talking dirty. You're a natural. It's driving me crazy."

"Oh." Emma blushed. "Well...I...okay, then."

Lauren laughed. "Okay, then."

Lauren tugged her closer and kissed her. The touch of her lips was brief and so gentle Emma's heart swooned. She held on to the moment, just one small moment, just one simple kiss, that acknowledged the wobbly, fragile, near-translucent faith they were putting in each other.

"You'll need a safe word," Lauren said.

Emma tensed. Fuck. A safe word. She hadn't thought of that. With all the rumors flying around about her kinky night of whipping with Lauren, she'd actually managed to forget that pain was a pretty significant component of kink. Double fuck.

"I don't want one." Emma could hear the tinny sound of her own unease coating her words and cursed herself. She didn't want Lauren to feel bad if giving pain turned her on, but she'd been right the first time—being whipped wasn't Emma's thing. Pain and passion were fine for other people, but just didn't do it for her, even in theory. Why had she made that stupid joke and put the idea in both their heads? *Thank you, brain, for being so incredibly unhelpful.*

Lauren took Emma's face in her hands and held her still, forcing her to focus on only Lauren. "A safe word is mandatory. You need to be able to call a halt at any time if you're uncomfortable. We're going to push limits and if we go too far, we both need a way to communicate."

She bit her lip, wanting badly to wring her hands, but they were trapped between her body and Lauren's. "I don't want it to hurt. I don't think I'd like that."

Lauren's expression didn't change. "Okay. That's no problem. Do you have any other limits?"

Did she? How was she supposed to know? She wasn't experienced outside of her own head. "Is that…" she took a breath, "is that a sacrifice for you?"

Lauren shook her head. "Being in control isn't about being a sadist, at least not for me. It's a psychological rush I get from having you surrender to me. Having you *want* me to be in control. Having you like it. It's not about pain unless you like pain. It's not about bondage unless you like bondage. My dominance is only possible through your submission, so if it doesn't turn you on, it's not going to turn me on either."

The relief that rushed through her made her just a bit dizzy. She should've known all of this. Lauren might be dominant in the bedroom, or the *library*, but she was still Lauren. "I definitely want to try the bondage thing some time. But I don't get why we need the safe word. Why can't I just say no or stop or something? Why does it have to be watermelon or ballerina or red?"

Lauren hesitated, her face shutting down in that supremely annoying way she had.

Emma flicked her on the shoulder. "Don't do that. Don't back off just because I asked a question. I'm here. I'm naked. I want to try this."

"It's just that the answer might freak you out."

Emma lifted her chin. "You won't know until you tell me."

Lauren stroked down Emma's arm, the palm of her other hand moving against Emma's pussy in a way that had her instantly clenching and needy. She tried to hold back the whimper. This was important, and Lauren was better at saying important things when she was touching her. Emma wanted to give her that, if Lauren didn't drive her out of her mind first.

"No can be a safe word if you want, but sometimes, during role-play or other kinky activities, words like 'stop' and 'no' are part of the scene."

Emma frowned. "That doesn't make any sense. Why would someone say no if it's consensual?"

"Because it's not real when you're role-playing. It's intentionally and consensually a fantasy." Lauren's voice was calm and steady. "There's freedom in not having to admit what you really want. Pretending it's not something you choose, that you're being coerced or persuaded frees you to indulge in desires that would otherwise be illicit. By pretending not to want what you want, you're free to have it without embarrassment."

Emma processed the information, and processed the fact that Lauren seemed to know a hell of a lot about it. "But doesn't that just circumvent the real issue of feeling guilty for your desires? Shouldn't that be what you work on?"

Lauren tapped her lightly on the nose. "You tell me."

She smiled, silently acknowledging that she had more than a little guilt about her own needs. "Fair point."

"There are a lot of ways to work through things, and this kind of role-play is more common than you think. It's not real, and it's completely safe. If it makes you or me or anyone else hot as a fantasy, I don't think there's anything wrong with that."

Emma chewed her bottom lip. Could she really role-play being coerced? *For real?*

"I don't know if it's really okay to pretend."

Lauren ran a hand through Emma's hair and tugged on the ends playfully. "You've already pretended. Up here." She tapped Emma on the temple. "Remember your fantasy, right here in the library? It's not so different from being trapped against a bookcase. The fear of getting caught heightening your excitement. My hand covering your mouth so you can't object. You imagined me not stopping, not letting up, until you had no choice but to come."

No choice. Not stopping. Forced to come.

Emma nodded slowly. Lauren was right. More than that, *being taken*, was her number one, without fail, always-did-it-for-her, fantasy. The dirtiest of all the dirt piled high in her imagination. The fantasy that made losing control not her fault, the fantasy that made her abandon sexy. How had Lauren seen so clearly when she'd barely recognized it for herself?

While they were on the subject, why did the idea turn her on so much? Lauren's hand still cupped her pussy, applying just the right amount of pressure to make her squirm. But if she was being honest, really, really, no-one-ever-has-to-know kind of honest, the wetness coating Lauren's palm wasn't just from the pressure. The image of being trapped under Lauren, tied up, saying no, saying stop, and getting wetter and wetter when Lauren ignored her was making her crazy hot. Lauren telling her she had to take it. Telling her she'd never stop. Lauren forcing her to orgasm, forcing her to find pleasure in it, because Emma couldn't stop her. She could finally let go by pretending not to like the very thing she craved.

"So, I need a safe word then," Emma said.

I'll need a safe word because I'll want to say no when I really mean yes.

"Anything you like," Lauren said.

Emma eventually came up with, "Filet mignon."

Lauren laughed, and the tension in the air broke like the snap of a branch. "Good choice."

"It's ironic that I don't want to admit, that I don't want to admit what I want in bed."

"Makes perfect sense," Lauren said gently.

Emma looked at the water stains on the ceiling, at the stack of returns she had yet to process piled precariously high on a chair, and over Lauren's shoulder toward the library entrance that was more appealing as an exit right now. But that's what she'd done before. Run. She'd let Jessica mock her. She'd run and run, and it'd been the worst night of her life. It was time to stop running, stop hiding. It was time to be really truly naked.

"Did you bring this up because it's your *thing*?" Emma asked.

Lauren's expression turned puzzled. "My thing?"

"You know, the thing you like to do most at Kink's. Is this your favorite role-play?"

Lauren rocked back on her heels and regarded her cautiously. "It depends on the other person and what works between us. When you told me your fantasy, I thought perhaps taking it a step further, getting out of your head with a partner might appeal to you."

"Does it appeal to you?"

"It's an option." There was so much casual in Lauren's voice she could've been selling flip-flops by the beach.

Emma's heart wrote a big fat red F on top of that answer.

"Trust has to go both ways," she said. "If I'm going to trust you with thoughts and desires I've only ever explored in private, then you have to meet me halfway. Be honest, otherwise, what are we even doing here?"

Lauren shoved a hand through her hair and had the decency to look a bit sheepish. "Okay, Ms. Talking Is My Thing. Yes, it appeals to me too."

She waited, but apparently that's all Lauren had to say about that.

Emma sighed. "But what about what you want?"

Lauren looked confused.

"Are you going to deny that this turns you on?" Emma asked with just a hint of bite, using Lauren's own phrase. Once she started, the questions tumbled out of her. "Are you not going to admit you'll enjoy this? That you want this? That it will make you need to come? Are you going to hide behind your rationale and not admit that having me under you, nervous and battling, turns you on? Are you going to deny that you want me to say no just as much as I want to say it?"

Lauren pressed her palm hard into Emma's pussy, making them both groan. "Fuck." She let her forehead rest against Emma's. "Really really good at talking dirty."

"Okay, then," Emma quipped, smiling despite the seriousness of the conversation.

"Okay, then—It's been a fantasy running on repeat all week, but that night, when you couldn't surrender, I worried that what I wanted, that *this*, wouldn't work for you up here." Lauren tapped Emma lightly on the temple again. "Even though I suspected that it would work for you down here." Lauren brushed a fingertip lightly over Emma's clit.

Emma swallowed, trying not to grind herself into Lauren's palm. She knew better than anyone that some passions just didn't make sense, that the very inexplicableness was what made them hot. She also knew, deep down under the surface of things, that Lauren was right. This was a choice and nothing like being assaulted. Finding a *fantasy* arousing wasn't wrong, neither was acting it out with someone she trusted. Her body screamed too loud to be ignored, even if her brain was still catching up. She'd denied herself too long not to act on what would push every button she had.

She'd said it herself, trust had to go both ways.

"I want to do this." Emma heard her own words and smiled. Not a single quaver.

Lauren moaned, long and low, like it'd been trapped inside and was finally being freed. She sagged against Emma as if every bone in her body instantly liquified. Resting her forehead to Emma's, she murmured, "God. Yes. Fuck."

Emma wrapped Lauren in her arms and held her, biting her lip to hold back tears that were suddenly stinging her eyes. This wasn't just casual sexy times. This specific brand of pleasure was who Lauren *was,* and holding back because Emma wasn't ready had cost Lauren a lot more than Emma realized.

"I want this," Emma whispered in her ear again, wanting to say it again and again. She'd needed time, and she wasn't sorry for taking it, but Lauren's moan when she'd finally said yes made her realize just how *essential* this was.

Lauren cupped Emma's cheek, brushing her thumb back and forth gently like Emma was a priceless heirloom. "I have one more question."

Emma leaned into the touch, blinking hard and swallowing past the emotion expanding in her throat. "What's that?"

"How will I know you're having a good time?"

Were her senses in a jumble and somehow her watery eyes had affected her hearing?

"Didn't we just go over the safe word stuff? If I'm uncomfortable, I'll use it," Emma said.

"It's important you feel comfortable using your safe word, so I'm very glad to hear this." Lauren stroked her cheek, her hair, across her brow, and down the bridge of her nose in tender sensual caresses. Caresses that, if Emma thought too hard about it, she'd have said were loving. "But how will I know you're experiencing *pleasure* when you may choose to behave as if you're not enjoying things. Consent isn't just defining boundaries. It's not just agreeing. Consent isn't limited to a single 'yes.' It's an ongoing process of checking in, connecting, and making sure your partner is experiencing pleasure throughout."

Emma pulled back and stared at Lauren. If she were a cartoon character her head would be exploding in puffy animated smoke clouds. Her mind was blown. Her body was blown. Her heart was blown. Whatever else existed within her to be rocked to the core, it was all fucking blown. "You're amazing."

Lauren frowned. "Of course I'm not. Anyone would ask."

"No, they wouldn't. You're amazing." She brushed her lips against Lauren's. "You'll know because I'll be wet."

Lauren squeezed her pussy. "Wet. Got it. What else?"

Emma shifted, heat on her cheeks a constant warmth. "Even if I say no, or stop, or don't, if I'm experiencing pleasure, I won't be able to be quiet."

A smile curved Lauren's mouth. "What does that mean?"

Emma poked her. "You know exactly what it means. You just like me to say dirty things out loud."

"Guilty. Say dirty things out loud, please."

Emma squirmed, but had to smile. Lauren made her want to be all kinds of dirty. "Moaning and gasping and cursing and possibly the screaming you keep promising me."

Lauren's fingers clenched around her pussy and Emma gasped, punctuating her point perfectly. "Not quiet sounds deliciously sexy. So, if you're wet and swearing like a sailor, I'll know you're turned on and fully present?"

Emma nodded. Gratitude and wonder and a little bit of something scarier closing her throat. Of course Lauren would seek specific cues to be sure she consented when they role-played. She should have expected it—Lauren was just being Lauren—an experienced and caring dominant. Natural for Lauren, maybe. But for her? Nothing short of a revelation. Not just because she'd failed to do any of this during her first sexual encounter, but because *no one* ever had. Sure, everyone knew you asked for consent. You got the standard yes before stripping down and going for it. But it was rare for a lover to check in mid-romp and no one had ever asked about her experience of pleasure before. *No one* had ever cared about the signs and the signals and making sure she was pleasured and connected *throughout* the experience.

Lauren was eleventy million different kinds of amazing and each one was sexy as hell. She pulled Lauren closer. She wanted nothing between them now—not even air. "I want this. I want you. Please."

Lauren kissed her. "Remember your safe word and close your eyes."

Chapter Fourteen

Emma closed her eyes. She was ready for whatever Lauren asked her to do. Hell, Lauren would likely know her limits before she did, and if she didn't, well, there was the safe word.

Lauren pulled her closer, her breasts pressed against Lauren's shirt, her legs spread to accommodate Lauren's thighs, and her pussy hostage to Lauren's hand.

Lauren leaned down and whispered directly into her ear. "I'm going to tell you my fantasy. Let's see if you like it as much as I do."

Lauren's whisper was on loudspeaker, reverberating in Emma's brain. They'd agreed to do this, but the shock that Lauren was willing to share *this* fantasy with her was a punch in the gut that burned all the way down to her clit. Darts of pleasure pinballed through her, and she prayed to all the gods that Lauren would stroke her while she talked. Getting naked in front of someone wasn't easy, sex always took trust. But fantasy? That was the ultimate gateway into what *really* turned you on.

No rules.

No boundaries.

No judgment.

All the things that make you come.

"You're driving some tiny tin can girly car on a deserted country road in the middle of nowhere. It's bucketing down rain, visibility is zero and you don't see the giant pothole until you slam right into it. You're going too fast and get a flat, forcing you to pull to the side of the road. You don't start to panic until you realize there's no cell service on this empty stretch of bumfuck nowhere. You have no idea how to change a tire, and even if you did, you don't actually have a spare, let alone a jack. You flunked Girl Scouts. Your AAA membership is worthless. There's no way to contact anyone. No one's expecting you at home. You could be stuck here all night."

Emma's breath hitched as the images flashed behind her eyes. The truth was, she actually didn't know how to change a tire and could totally see this happening to her.

"You hear a distant rumble. It gets closer and closer, and when you see headlights, you realize it's a truck about to pass you on the road. Before you can think better of it, you jump out of the useless car and flag it down. Your T-shirt and jeans are instantly drenched and you're shivering. You have no choice but to hope the driver can help you. It's a risk you have to take."

Emma's fingers curled into Lauren's shirt. She knew where this story was heading, it shouldn't be arousing, and yet...

Remember Lauren's words. *You choose the no, Emma.*

"I pull the truck off the road and jump out. The glare of the truck's headlights cast my face in shadow, making it hard to tell in the rain if I'm a man or a woman. I ask what's wrong and you try to explain your predicament, but the rain is roaring down making it difficult to hear. I motion to the cab of the truck. You hesitate. You don't want to follow me inside. Every instinct tells you it's beyond stupid to get into a stranger's car, but what choice do you have? Even now, before I lay a single finger on you, I have all the power."

Emma didn't think she was breathing. Part of her knew she was siting naked on the circulation desk with Lauren whispering in her ear, but her senses were fragmented—distant and yet so fucking present. So attuned to the sound of Lauren's voice, she didn't dare move and risk breaking the spell.

"You get in the back of the cab, expecting me to get in the front. You jolt when I slide in beside you. You sit on your hands so I can't see them shaking. Why didn't I get in the front? Was it just an innocent assumption that conversation would be easier like this? Or are my intentions darker? Your heart starts pounding so hard you're sure I can see it beating in your chest. I control everything now, even the beat of your heart.

"I'm soaked too, my shirt plastered to my chest, my hair dripping water. I smile, but the look isn't friendly. It takes about half a second for you to settle on calculating, and your stomach roils. Panic fogs your brain. You grab for the door handle and pull, only to find it child locked.

"You have to fight your way past me and back to your car. But I haven't *done* anything. You tell yourself you're overreacting. Anyway, where are you going to go? You're at least five miles from the closest town. You shrink back in the seat. I haven't laid a finger on you and already you're trembling. I lay out my terms for giving you a lift.

"You'll be a good girl won't you, and say thank you? It's not every day I happen upon such a pretty helpless little thing. I'll be your knight as long as you show your appreciation. As long as you keep paying when the price goes up. You have to admit, I'm a Good Samaritan helping you out like this. Without me you'd be stuck here all night, cold and alone. All I'm asking for is a little gratitude. That's hardly unreasonable, is it?

"You could start by stripping off that wet T-shirt. The heat's on and you'll warm up faster without it. Take it off so you don't catch a cold. I only want to see your breasts. Just take off your shirt and then I'll drive you anywhere you want to go."

The only sound in the library were the shallow gasps slicing from Emma's throat.

"What do you say to me, Emma?" Lauren asked.

Somehow, she found her voice, "Just my shirt, right? Then you'll help me?"

"You take off your shirt and I stare at your tits like a hunter stares at prey. I'm sure your bra was modest in a past life, but wet with rain, it clings to your curves, not concealing as much as enhancing them. You stare at me insolently, trying to be brave, but your bottom lip won't stop trembling.

"I ask you to take off your bra and you shake your head. I'd promised you just the T-shirt, hadn't I? Sorry, beautiful, inflation's a bitch. Lose the bra before I lose my patience, or you'll be on your own. You strip it off, your face flaming, and I cup your breasts and run my thumbs across your nipples. I'm too close now, crowding you, my breath against your cheek, my thigh hot on yours. So close that I could do anything I wanted."

Emma made a choked sound, like a sob being squeezed out a small hole. Her belly dipped. No matter how much she inhaled, she couldn't manage to catch her breath. Her brain was alive, like Lauren had chopped through a bunch of live wires in her head and now everything was charged, spitting and sparking and burning inside her. "No. Stop. Don't. You're not being fair." *Please. Please. Yes.*

"Oh, come on, beautiful. It's not as if I'm hurting you. It's not my fault your nipples are hard and begging to be touched. You can tell yourself it's the cold, if it makes you feel better, but we both knew what would happen when you got in the truck. Why play coy now?"

"I didn't know," Emma protested, her words breathless, with a trace of *I'm so turned on* belying her statement. "Please. Can't you just drive me to the closest gas station?"

"I lower my head to suck your nipples while I consider your request. Of course, I *could* drive you anywhere you wanted to go. But I'm having too much fun to stop now. You're squirming and pretending you want to get away, but your nipples are so hard under my tongue and you can't stop gasping.

"Almost casually, I push you horizontal on the bench of the cab and pin your arms over your head. I'm lying on top of you, holding you down, enjoying the way you struggle and beg me to stop."

Lauren wrapped her fingers around Emma's chin, so their eyes met and locked in a connection so potent she felt the sizzle all the way to her toes.

She shook her head. "No. Please. If you stop now I promise I won't tell anyone. Just let me go and I won't tell a soul."

Lauren swirled her fingers in the ridiculous amount of wetness between Emma's thighs. "No, and please, and please no. You make denying sound so much like begging, beautiful. No one would blame me for misunderstanding you."

Emma let her head tip back as Lauren stroked her clit, capturing it between her fingers, teasing and caressing. The pleasure, the sheer enormity of how goddamn good it felt, had Emma arching back. She stared at the ceiling as Lauren worked her. Her head, her body, every bit of her whirled and seized and flew off to distant corners of the room—all of it building and building inside her, sensation layered on top of sensation, stacking until she was sure she'd burst from all the pent up...everything.

"You're trapped under me. I've unbuttoned your pants and I'm three seconds from discovering just how wet and hot you are. You shove the thought away, unable to face it. You try to kick me, but the leverage is all wrong and you barely make impact with my shin. I laugh, my grin mocking as the truth that you can't stop me settles into your brain. This is going to happen. There's nothing you can do to prevent it. You'll struggle, but you're too weak to do much more than squirm. Squirming just turns me on.

"I lean my weight fully onto you, pinning you down, and you close your eyes and tell yourself that you'll just check out. That's what you do when things get too much, isn't it, beautiful? You can pretend to be somewhere else as I tug off your jeans and slide your panties down to your knees. My pants are rough against your bare skin and you whimper. I stroke your hair and tell you to hush, there's no need to fight how much you want it. Underneath the good manners, at the very core of who you are, we both know you crave being fucked.

"You want to be held down so you can convince yourself you had no choice.

"You want me to cover your mouth, so you don't have to hear your own moans.

"You want my hand around your throat, as the ultimate sign of my control.

"But primarily, predominantly, more than *anything*, you want me to fuck you. Fuck you, and fuck you, and fuck you until you come so hard you pass out. Until you're absolutely wrecked with no hope of being put back together. Knowing how much you need it makes me want to fuck you even harder."

Emma groaned softly as Lauren swirled fingers around her opening, gathering up the evidence of her arousal. "Oh God, please...I need..."

"Begging for it already? You're supposed to be fighting me."

"Then stop being so gentle." Emma's nerves stood no chance against the fantasy Lauren had created. No longer censoring her emotions, her *desire*, she was right there, spread out under Lauren in the back of the truck, Lauren's hips pinning hers, Lauren's hand scrunched in her hair, or ripping at her shirt, or around her throat. Lauren was fucking her hard, pounding into her relentlessly, taking and taking and... Stroking her pussy far too softly.

It was everything and too much and not enough all at once.

"Please, Lauren." What did she care if she was begging now? She was too far gone.

"Emma." Lauren ground out her name like it was nails in her throat, raw and painful. She opened her eyes. God, she was so turned on she didn't know which way was up, let alone have the sense to ask for what she needed. What they both needed. But Lauren was holding back, and the time for tiptoeing around each other had passed. Lauren wanted vulnerability? Emma was there. She was so there she was basically the blue dot on the GPS map. She was ready to trust, and damn if she was going to let Lauren use kid gloves.

Lauren had made her helpless, made her powerless, made her so fucking wet and now she needed to follow that up with some action, damnit. "Fuck me. Show me exactly what you plan to take from me. We both know I want this."

"It can be intense." Worry was a living thing in Lauren's eyes.

Emma was done asking. She thrust her fingers into Lauren's hair and kissed her hard and urgent. Kissed her until Lauren surrendered in her own way groaning and clamping her hand around Emma's pussy, her grip stronger now. Surer. Harder. Just a little bit mean.

"I force your legs open with my knee, and you know I'm about to start fucking you. You're going to spread your legs like you're begging for it. Your head starts to whip back and forth and tears sparkle in your eyes. 'No,' you tell me over and over again like a benediction. 'No, no, no.' I ignore you and thrust inside you so hard you can't breathe for a second. Just for a second it hurts, one brilliant flash of pain before all you feel is pleasure. Exposed and helplessly wet under me with tears tracking down your cheeks. You tell yourself you're crying because you don't want this, but the truth is just the opposite. You're so hot. So ready to come you feel depraved and perverted. You can't control the way I'm making you enjoy it, can you? It's not your fault that I'm making you want it. I smirk at how wet you are. I could tell just from looking at you that a woman as needy as you would want to be fucked relentlessly. I like that you proved me right."

Lauren gave her no further warning, just grabbed Emma's hips to position her on the circulation desk and thrust inside her hard. Emma's groan started in her belly and gained intensity as it gathered in her throat.

She really, really didn't want to come. Not yet. Not until it was no longer just a story. The time for stories had ended. She wanted the real role-play.

"What do you think you're doing?" She bit back a moan as Lauren began to move inside her, fucking her slowly, letting her adjust, her fingers driving so deep Emma wished she had a strap-on. Swelled with need for it. "You're not going to get away with this. I'll report you. You'll go to prison."

Lauren's laugh was half a sneer. "You think so? Who's going to believe a woman did this to another woman? Not the cops."

"Fuck you." Lauren was right. There was no one to help her.

"Already doing that. Quite effectively from the way you're clenching around me. So wet already, aren't you? Are you going to tell the cops how you came so pretty all over me, beautiful? Will they be adding that to their official report? Reading it out at the morning briefing so all their buddies can laugh?"

Emma sucked in a breath, more a shudder than air, and blew through the need that wanted to send her spiraling into the stratosphere. *Hold on just a little longer.*

"You say no, but you mean yes. So, I tell you all the things I plan to do to you as I fuck you, pumping my hips into yours, relishing the slap of skin, the gasp of your breath, the grimace of pleasure on your face as you close your eyes and try to block me out. Block out how fucking good this feels, that I'm the best you've ever had. That all those namby-pamby equal-opportunity chicks you've slept with in the past have never rocked your world this hard. That this is what you've always wanted. Fear and pleasure spin inside you, twirling around each other, until you can't tell one from the other.

"I drag your panties all the way off your legs and get comfortable. If you don't stop protesting, I'm going to shove them in your mouth and tape it shut. It would get me off to know you can taste the evidence as I fuck you. To see you shake your head and pretend you weren't into it with your mouth stuffed full of your own desire. But a bigger part of me wants to hear you scream when you come."

Lauren's words had lost their measured quality, that faint cadence of storytelling. Her speech turned raspy and uneven. With Lauren's eyes ferocious, sweat coating her brow, a hard line to her jaw, she looked as if she could devour Emma alive. Lauren's whole body taut with passion was the sexiest thing Emma had ever seen. She was losing it, but Emma was already so far past lost. She needed Lauren to be right there with her so they could find each other.

"Please." Emma tilted her hips up into Lauren's palm. "I'm so close. I might actually fucking die if you stop."

Lauren groaned. "I'm going to make you come. It's a point of pride. A statement. I know that forcing you to come like this when you don't want to, when you shouldn't like it, will mean stripping your ego. Too bad for you that you're a terrible actress."

Lauren pulled her fingers all the way out of her, and Emma glanced down. Lauren's entire hand was soaked and slippery. Emma was so wet she knew it had to be all over her thighs. She didn't care. All she cared about was coming. That's what Lauren had reduced her to. A base version of herself, an animal with no control over her own instincts. No control over all the things Lauren was forcing her to feel, to want, to crave. "Please."

"Please what?" Lauren rasped.

No longer able to say no, to deny she needed Lauren back inside her, Emma gave in and begged just as passionately as she'd struggled. "Please. I need to be fucked. I have to come. I can't wait."

"Look how wild you are," Lauren whispered in her ear, her fingers hovering at Emma's entrance. "You want this bad, don't you? You can't help it."

"Please," Emma begged again, spreading her legs wide and tilting her hips up shamelessly. "Please."

Lauren clamped one hand around the back of Emma's neck, holding her in place with a grip almost strong enough to bruise. With the other she thrust inside Emma. No finesse this time, just long hard thrusts, over and over and over again. Hard, then harder, then just shy of ruthless.

Emma fell into sensation as if nothing else existed. She made dirty, gritty sounds she'd have been embarrassed about if any part of her brain had still been working and let her head tip back in Lauren's hold. Fuck yes. This. Only this. Always this.

"You're going to come," Lauren said. So sure. So fucking certain. "I'm going to make you come."

When the palm of Lauren's hand hit her clit, Emma exploded. Light ignited behind her eyes, and she came on a scream. Everything inside her trembled and spun. Twisting and turning, knotting and unraveling, seizing and releasing, until her breath came in parched wheezes and her bones were jelly.

She kept her eyes open, kept her gaze on Lauren as Lauren penetrated her, Lauren's look as deep as her buried fingers. She didn't want to be anything, or anywhere, but exactly where she was—with Lauren—surrendering to her with her eyes wide open.

Lauren wrapped her arms around her, hooking Emma's legs around her waist and Emma clung to her. Wrapped around Lauren, dizzy from an orgasm so intense her pussy wouldn't stop clenching, the moment was unspeakably intimate. Tears flooded her eyes and she buried her face in Lauren's neck, fighting back a sob. Lauren stroked her hair and started to pull out, and Emma grabbed her wrist.

"No. Stay. Can you stay inside for a little while? I can't…" She couldn't what? Bear to be empty after having been so completely filled? Bear not to be as close as possible to Lauren right now? She craved physical closeness, but what she really needed after an orgasm like that was emotional closeness.

She buried her face in Lauren's neck and held on as tightly as she could.

Goddamn. How had she ever lived without this? Without exactly this? She *needed* it. The absolute certainty hit her like a sledgehammer. Things that had always been asymmetrical suddenly clicked into place. This was her. Needy. Helpless. Begging to stop. Begging for more. Begging for things she'd never even known she could beg for.

For Lauren, this was about surrender that went so deep it was bottomless. Lauren wanted her to try to resist. Not just physically, not just as she lay under her struggling like a fish on a line. Lauren didn't want to force her. She wanted to force her to like it, force her to come, force her to experience the overwhelming all-consuming destroying pleasure of being entirely out of control. Boy, had she succeeded. Gold star and first place medal.

Everything came down to control. Having it. Clinging to it. Losing it. Wanting it. Then goddamn reveling in the moment when you have no say at all. Not in whether or not you're fucked. Not in the hand around your throat or the things whispered in your ear.

Not even in the words you say or the pleasure you feel. Having no control at all made her hotter than she'd ever imagined possible.

She'd never been comfortable with the way her arousal had overwhelmed her senses, her common sense, her ability for reason. It made her feel crazy, and crazy scared her. But with Lauren she didn't need reason. Her inability to contain her own passion was exactly what Lauren craved. Lauren had forced her to let go, to give up, to be overtaken by the rush of her own need.

Emma's need had always made her vulnerable, and that had never felt safe. With Lauren it wasn't just okay, she wasn't simply accepted for exactly who she was. Who she was, and what she needed, was exactly what Lauren needed too. It was Lauren's fantasy they were wrapped in. Lauren had asked for this and it turned out to be exactly what Emma needed. Finally.

Somehow in the last twenty minutes, without her ever having decided it, she'd fallen in love. Falling was a stupid word for it. It wasn't a graceful head over heels, romantic comedy come to life, emotion.

Love was cocky and overconfident, a skinny actor preening in a superhero suit. Love was narcissistic in the way it invaded her awareness and forced her to care so deeply. Love was arrogant to think it could somehow be the answer to all her problems. Love had her bound and helpless, more of a hostage and ten times as frightening as when Lauren had fucked her.

Emma closed her eyes, breathed in the subtle scent of Lauren, all tangerines and sex, and let her herself relax. Love was a pain in her ass, but it was here, and now she had to deal with it.

Chapter Fifteen

"Did you know that orgasms are good for cognitive health?" Lauren stroked the long delicate line of Emma's spine as she gently pulled out of her.

Emma snuggled close. "That can't possibly be true. My brain's fried worse than a funnel cake at the fair."

Lauren tipped Emma's face to hers and kissed her forehead. "Funny, I was just thinking that you pull all the ragged edges of my mind back into place."

As soon as the words were out, Lauren wanted to snatch them out of the air and shove them back inside her mouth. Emma needed time. She'd *just* gotten to the point of trusting Lauren enough to orgasm in front of her, and Lauren had no business saying something like that, especially when she had no idea what the hell she was going to do about any of it. That Emma had surrendered, cocooned inside a fantasy that would give any rational person pause, was nothing short of a miracle. The last thing either of them needed was her making grand declarations in the heat of the moment that she couldn't deliver on later.

To cover the sheer awkwardness of her way-too-much honesty, Lauren changed the subject. "Do you have a kitchen here?"

Emma gestured vaguely behind her, and Lauren scooted around the circulation desk and through a door marked for the staff. She was back with a chipped blue Star Wars mug full of tap water as fast as possible. "Drink this. It's important you stay hydrated."

Emma blinked at her with eyes just a bit blurry. She took the mug and a couple of careful sips. "You made me scream."

"I heard." Lauren smiled. The sound of Emma coming for her was music she wouldn't soon forget. She steadied the mug as Emma took another sip. "You were amazing. Absolutely perfect. How're you feeling? You're going to be sore tomorrow. That's normal. If it's uncomfortable try some Motrin. But any stinging or sharp pain and you tell me immediately, okay?"

The soft dreaminess of Emma's face morphed slowly into horror. "If I have to go to the hospital with a broken vagina, I'll never forgive you. Never."

Lauren grinned. "Not loving small town life now, are you? Don't worry, with only my fingers inside you it's very unlikely, but everyone is different, so you'll tell me, okay? Worst-case scenario, I'll drive you to Albany so we don't run into anyone you know while they patch up your broken vagina."

Emma searched Lauren's face for further confirmation before nodding seriously. "Have you taken someone to the hospital before?"

She tried not to interpret the question as, "Have you hurt anyone before?" but it was difficult. "Yes. But a friend, not a lover. The person she was with fucked her with a wine bottle a little too vigorously, and she had some internal bruising. Glass isn't a great choice at the best of times, and fucking someone with something that has no give is an amateur move."

"And you're not an amateur."

"No, I'm not." Lauren held her breath.

"Lucky for me then."

Lucky. She let her breath out slowly. She took the empty mug from Emma and put it on a nearby stack of books. "How do you feel otherwise?"

Emma pulled her back in for more cuddles. "Kind of floaty. It's nice."

Lauren had to bite the inside of her cheek to stop herself from moaning out loud. Emma didn't know, but no other answer could've been as perfect. Not every submissive experienced the contented floating feeling after an intense scene, but it was common enough to be a pattern. That Emma did calmed Lauren more than any words of reassurance could've. Emma had enjoyed what they did. Not just because it was sex, but because she had gotten off on, gotten *into,* the surrender. Emma liked it. It wasn't some monumental favor she'd given Lauren out of the kindness of her heart. Thank God.

She hadn't really let herself believe they could maybe make this work, that her feelings for Emma weren't going to end in a series of frustrating encounters that ultimately satisfied neither of them, until Emma had begged her to fuck her and had come in screaming gasps around her fingers. Sex wasn't everything. Not even the most important thing. But for her, someone with particular tastes who needed a particular kind of partner to satisfy them, sex wasn't inconsequential either. She couldn't brush it aside and pretend it wasn't important. She hadn't realized how heavy the weight of her fears had been until Emma's comment lifted them completely, and she was free.

"That's good to hear." Lauren rubbed slow circles along Emma's spine. "You relax for a few more minutes."

After a moment, Emma said, far too quietly, "That was a very nice thing to say before."

Lauren sighed. Emma hadn't forgotten. Why did she have to go spouting off about her *feelings* and make everything weird? For lack of any better plan, she started babbling to cover the silence. Having experienced the contentment fantastic sex could give you, Emma would understand that sometimes sex made you say things better kept to yourself.

"I'd forgotten how much I like it. It's easy to get jaded. Even before what happened with Caroline, going to a bar every weekend hoping to meet someone who actually gives a damn…it can drain you. But sex, it calms me. It makes the world right again. It's the one place I always feel totally myself. I'd forgotten that."

Where just a moment before Emma had been relaxed and pliant against her, now she tensed, planting a smile on her face that looked as fake as a circus clown's.

"I'm glad you have something that makes you feel that way. That must be very nice." She pushed away from Lauren and hopped off the desk, swaying for just a second before walking around it to find her clothes.

Lauren stared. What had happened? Had she said something wrong? Surely saying she liked sex after making a woman come wasn't completely unwarranted? She knew what to do after an intense scene to care for the person who had gifted her their vulnerability and trusted her to keep them safe. Didn't Emma realize that she was just as vulnerable? Just as stripped, even if she was standing there fully dressed? That her heart was on the line?

Emma couldn't back off now, not after what they'd just experienced together. Emma leaving her arms, putting her clothes back on, felt like abandonment—rational or not. Lauren wanted nothing more than to chase after her and beg her to stay, naked and kind of floaty against her, forever.

Just stay and be here, all hers, for always.

Lauren didn't move. "Are you okay?"

Emma wobbled on one foot as she stuck the other through the waistband of her skirt. "Sure, why wouldn't I be?"

The question mark at the end of that sentence felt less like a desire to know an answer and more like a bomb about to detonate. "You seem annoyed."

Emma zipped up the back of her skirt and shoved her hair out of her eyes. She held Emma's gaze, barely glancing at all the lovely girl parts on display. Something more important than sex was happening.

"Why would I be annoyed when you just qualified a really beautiful statement about *me* with the knowledge that you feel that way every time because really, any willing woman who *gives a damn* will do."

Emma had tugged on her shirt and was doing up the buttons by the time Lauren made it around the circulation desk. "What are you talking about? I didn't say that."

"Sex is the one time you always feel totally yourself? Sex calms you? Puts all the pieces of your mind back together? You couldn't possibly have had all those experiences with me when we've had less sex than you could fit on the back of a postcard."

That last statement stumped Lauren. "Can you fit sex on the back of a postcard?"

Emma let out a sound that was one octave higher than nails on a chalkboard. "That's not the point."

She shoved a hand through her hair so she didn't use it to haul Emma into her arms and show her exactly where they could fit sex. This wasn't fair. She'd just had the best experience of her entire life. The kind of sex that makes you believe there must be a God because simple evolution couldn't possibly have created someone so absolutely, perfectly, earth-shatteringly sexy, and someone so maddeningly, frustratingly, annoyingly obstinate all in the same package. She needed to come so badly she was dizzy with it. She wasn't sure she could get her heart to stop pounding in her ears long enough to hear Emma, let alone have a coherent conversation about some point that made absolutely no sense. It was more than possible the need clawing at her insides was compromising her judgment, but she didn't care. Right this second, with Emma half dressed in front of her, her feet bare and her hair wild, Lauren wanted to howl at the fucking moon.

Why were they having this stupid argument about a history that didn't matter, right after Emma had let down her walls enough to make Lauren say something so personal in the first place? She suspected Emma was looking for a way to put her walls back up, and that just pissed her off. They could go forward as slowly as Emma needed, but hell if she'd let Emma drag them backward.

"You're jealous then? I've had some nice sex with other women, so you're jealous." Lauren crossed her arms and raised her eyebrows. *Really?*

Emma stopped buttoning her buttons as if the sheer preposterousness of the accusation froze her. "Of course not. That's ridiculous."

"I couldn't agree more." She invaded Emma's personal space and began to undo the buttons Emma had abandoned. She didn't touch Emma. She specifically and deliberately did not touch her skin. She didn't quite trust herself.

"What are you...that's not...Lauren, I didn't..."

Emma couldn't seem to finish a sentence, so Lauren just kept going, tugging Emma's shirt off and letting it fall to the floor. Emma's bra came next, whipped from her shoulders before she had a chance to protest.

"Let's set the record straight," Lauren said with a casualness she didn't feel. "I like sex. I like it so much that I seek it out, even when I'm single. Sex makes me feel good about myself. It releases tension. I can express myself in a way that I can't in any other context—"

"By dominating people," Emma cut in, interrupting her.

She let that slide and continued as if Emma hadn't spoken. "But sex with *you*..." She stopped. She'd been all prepared to give a speech, one that might possibly also be considered a lecture, fueled by her righteous indignation at the unfairness of Emma's annoyance. But sex with Emma was...beyond. She didn't know what to make of it herself, let alone explain it to someone else.

"Sex with me, what?" Emma asked.

Lauren hesitated.

Emma took a breath and unzipped the back of her skirt. As it fell to a puddle at her feet, she asked again, "Sex with me, what?"

There Emma went, being brave and leaving her breathless.

"It feels like more." Lauren took Emma's hand to help her step out of the circle of her clothes. Her fingers tingled with the spark of electricity that ignited at the simplest of touches. "You can't tell me that what we just did wasn't more. It doesn't just feel good. It's *emotional*. It fills me up in a place I didn't even know was lacking until I met you." *Don't you see how vulnerable you make me, too?*

Emma tugged at her bottom lip with her teeth. Lauren closed her eyes. For the first time, she understood Emma's desire to hide, to choose not to see, to shut everything out. It was way too soon for revelations like this, and even if miracles existed and Emma was falling for her too, the last thing she needed was Lauren putting more pressure on sex.

"Emotional, like what emotions exactly?" Caution seeped out of Emma's words and ran toward Lauren like water from a tipped glass.

I think I might love you.

It was the *think* and the *might* in that sentence that stopped Lauren from saying the words out loud. Grand passionate declarations didn't include those words. Loving someone shouldn't be laden with maybes. Love was supposed to overcome all obstacles. Love was the emotion to end all emotions. The only thing that mattered. The secret password to a happy life. Love was...everything.

Only, it wasn't. Not really. Not outside of books and movies and country songs where the story ended before people got bored or things got tough. Love was important, sure, but she'd seen enough unhappy marriages, enough divorce, enough love turned to hatred to know that love wasn't some magic elixir.

Love was a start. It was the beginning. The thing that brought two people together and held them there until they either worked out their shit or they didn't. It was a foundation you either built upon or chipped away at. Love wasn't a majestic cure for everything that still needed fixing between them. Love was only a chance, and Lauren didn't know if someone like Emma should take that chance with someone like her. They might've grown up in the same town, but Emma was strong in all the ways she was weak, good in all the ways she was bad, respected in all the ways she was condemned. Love would unite them, and Emma would get the raw end of the deal.

What was Lauren supposed to say to Emma when *emotional* meant "I'm falling in love with you, but I'm not sure that's good."

Instead, she said, "I care."

That sounded pathetic even to her own ears. Caring wasn't even decent enough to be the weak sister of loving. Caring was a third cousin twice removed.

Emma stepped back as if those words now filled the physical space between them. "I see."

How? How could she possibly see? And if she did, then maybe she could explain it for both of them.

Lauren closed the gap and tried again. Tried to put into words what was bouncing around and bursting at the seams of her heart. "Really, that was amazing. The best sex I've ever had. You're incredible."

She shoved a hand through her hair again and wished for the first time ever that she'd had a relationship or two under her belt. Some experience with saying stuff like this so it didn't feel like a foreign language. "I want to see you again. I want more than just once."

Because that's what it came down to in the end. More of this. More of Emma.

Just more.

"Twice," Emma said, "three times if you count the night in my bedroom."

"I want more," Lauren repeated. She was starting to think it wouldn't matter how many times, she'd never get enough.

Emma stuck her hands on her hips and nailed her with a glare she must've practiced at librarian school. "What does that mean, *more*? Sex? You want to spend the week you have left fucking my brains out?"

Lauren held back the "Hell yes" that hovered on her lips. She might not have a lot of experience with this emotion thing, but she knew Emma wasn't really asking about sex. She was asking about a relationship. A commitment. That meant more than a week. That meant going public and facing the consequences. A terrible idea, and not only for her, but for Emma.

"I want us to go out, to see where this goes, to, be girlfriends if everything works out." Jesus. Did she have to be awkward as fuck and sound like a twelve-year-old? *Girlfriends*, really? Emma was sure to want to be with her now. "I know it's a lot, to ask you to visit San Francisco just so we could date."

Say you'll come anyway. Say nothing could stop you. Say you care, too.

Emma looked at her like she'd just said they should fly to the moon on Aladdin's magic carpet. "I can't leave Sunrise Falls. My job…"

And just like that, all the color seeped from the room. All the sounds hollowed into silence. Emma's life. Emma's job. This fucking town. All of it was more important to Emma than she was. The abject disappoint that flooded her veins shouldn't have hurt as much as it did. What had she expected Emma to say? That Lauren was worth a trip across the country? That she cared too? That she fucking *loved* her?

Nope. Not going to be happening. Emma had been vulnerable during sex, during the ten minutes she'd spent coming down from her orgasm, but Lauren was the one with no defenses left.

Emma picked her skirt up off the floor and put it on— again, shimmying her panties underneath. Lauren watched her methodically reverse her skirt-drop bravery, making more of a statement than if Emma had just come right out and said that "I care" wasn't good enough.

And she would've been right. It wasn't. Not for Emma and not for herself either. But it was too soon. She didn't even have a job. The last thing she should be doing was falling in love. The last thing she should be hoping was for the woman who'd just rocked her entire world to move across the country to be with her. But it didn't matter what was reasonable or appropriate. She wanted, and Emma had said no.

Once Emma had her bra on and was doing up the buttons on her shirt, she said, "You know something? It's really annoying when you do that."

Lauren wasn't sure she even cared what Emma found annoying right now. Just something else she could add to her ever-growing list of stuff people in this town hated about her. "What's that?"

"When things get hard you shut down. Your whole face just goes blank, like someone switched it off. Now I have no idea what you're thinking."

Blank. That's what Emma thought. That she just pressed escape to close a program so she wouldn't have to deal. Wouldn't that be nice right about now.

"I just told you I care about you, and you didn't say it back. I asked you out on a real date. I told you I wanted a relationship, and you said no. I'm not sure how you're expecting me to react, but if you're after understanding and compassion, I'm all out. What we just did, what you just gave me, I've never felt that before, and I want more. That's what I'm feeling, Emma, that I want more and that you don't."

Emma's eyes flashed like lighting in a storm. "I didn't say no. Stop putting words in my mouth. I said I can't leave Sunrise Falls. The town council funded my education after Dad died and Mom left. In return, I have to work in the library for six years after graduation. If I quit, if they fire me, that's tens of thousands I have to pay back within sixty days and without a job."

Oh. *Ohhh.*

Why the hell hadn't Emma led with that rather vital piece of information? Of course, it was the town council's fault that Emma couldn't leave. This town had taken everything else from her so why not Emma, too?

"God, I hate this town. That's so typical. They *support* you, but with so many strings you can never get free."

Emma shook her head. "You don't understand. I had nothing. I had to take the deal, and I'm grateful they offered it. It's a *good* deal."

Lauren sighed. What could she say? It was really annoying that she understood what Emma meant. She'd never had anything of consequence in her life until she'd moved to San Francisco and built something from all the nothing, only to lose it. But Emma had had a real family. A dad who'd died suddenly of a heart attack, and a mom who couldn't cope. She'd lost them both. It some ways, she'd had it easier than Emma because she'd never really known what it was like to have. She'd never had the opportunity to take it for granted. When her life had fallen apart, she'd had very little to lose. Emma, though, had had everything and lost everything. So, the offer from the council was more than a business deal to secure a librarian for a small rural town. It was a lifeline. Emma's life.

"I'm sorry. That was a dumb thing to say. I get it. You have to stay."

Emma took Lauren's hand, but her posture was stiff and her muscles tense. When she spoke, her voice was funeral procession subdued. "You could stay, too. Date me here."

From her tone, Emma expected her to say no. No one in their right mind would expect her to stay in a town that wanted to see the door hit her ass on the way out so badly they took turns holding it ajar. She didn't fit. She was an outcast. A kinky homewrecker who belonged in the big city.

But if they wanted a future, staying was the obvious answer. Emma was too diplomatic to mention it, but the fact that Lauren's life in San Francisco was nothing but a pile of ashes made the choice a whole lot easier. She could stay in Sunrise Falls, at least long enough to see where this went, and if it wound up happily ever after, they'd stay long enough for Emma to fulfil her contract with the town. Then they'd leave on a UFO and colonize Mars if that's what it took to see this place in the rearview.

Years of snide remarks and people crossing to the other side of the street when they saw her coming wouldn't be easy, but she didn't feel completely terrible about it. If someone had told her last week that she'd choose to stay in Sunrise Falls, she'd have sworn on her life it'd never happen, and then kicked their ass for good measure. But here she was. Willing to stay for Emma.

She just had to know first.

"You still haven't said it. I'm pretty bad at begging, but you're making me want to."

Emma rolled her eyes, completely unimpressed with Lauren's lame attempt at humor. "You want me to tell you I care about you, too? After what we just did together? After the way you just pulled me apart and touched everything inside me? After the way you lit me up so I'll never be the same again? After you showed me not just what I want, but who I am? Do you want me to say that I care? Is that the big revelation you're holding out for?"

Lauren didn't even try for a smile. Was it so wrong to hope that her feelings were reciprocated? To want Emma to want more, too? "You make all that sound like the worst thing in the world."

Emma just stared at her for one long heated second. The very air around them was so charged, it pulsed like the beat of a heart. Then she launched herself at Lauren, grappling and shoving until Lauren's back hit the circulation desk. All the breath whooshed out of her as Emma tore at her clothes. Buttons went flying and Lauren's pants were halfway to her ankles before she had the sense to put words together.

"Emma. Jesus. What are you doing?" Emma Prescott going bat-out-of-hell-sexy and stripping her naked at a moment like this was unexpected to say the least.

"What am I doing?" Emma panted, her eyes fierce and her voice raw. "I'm going to fucking show you just how much I *don't* care. Just how lame and superficial and not at all satisfying caring is when what I want, what I feel, when *this*, is so much bigger than some damn caring."

Emma collided against her, hot and urgent. Emma's hands were everywhere, clawing at her skin like she wanted to rip it off and reach all the way inside her.

"You want to know how I feel? Well, I'll tell you. I was really happy before I met you." Emma gripped Lauren's shoulders and, reaching up on her toes, kissed her hard, pushing her tongue inside Lauren's mouth and claiming her with lips and teeth until she could barely breathe.

Lauren kissed her back like she was lost at sea, and Emma's mouth her only lifeline. The need went bone deep. Her life. Her heart. Their future. "Oh fuck."

"I was happy before I met you. I have a job I love, friends who support me, and fond memories of you in high school to keep me warm at night. I was content with that. I wasn't looking for anything more."

She held on as Emma divested her of the rest of her clothes. She shuddered when Emma stepped back half an inch to study her, Emma's obvious enjoyment at seeing her naked at odds with what she was saying.

None of it made sense. God, she needed to come. Maybe it would all make more sense if she wasn't losing her damn mind as Emma's eyes bored into her skin. "And now?"

"Now," Emma dropped to her knees in one fluid motion and looked up at Lauren with the sweetest of smiles, like the world's most obedient submissive. "Now you've made me fucking miserable."

She moaned when Emma put her mouth on her. The unsated arousal from earlier roared back to life and amped up a thousand percent. Pleasure shot down her spine like fire toward her clit, toward Emma, ready to consume them both in a white-hot blaze. Her thoughts zoomed from one inconceivable revelation to the next. Emma didn't care. She'd made Emma miserable. But oh God, Emma was licking her, sucking her, stroking her. Emma swirled her tongue from one place to the next in unending, teasing torment. Soft then hard, fast then slow, never staying long enough to make her come but making her near delirious with need.

"I don't want you to be miserable." Lauren gasped the words, her fingers in Emma's hair, guiding her motion, pressing Emma's mouth to her. Sososo good. Just a little more, and she could come.

Emma looked up at her, her mouth shiny with the evidence of Lauren's arousal. "It's too late for that. You made me want more. You made me unsatisfied with a life without you in it. You made caring not nearly enough."

Emma captured Lauren's clit between her lips and sucked. Not teasing now but stroking, dipping and pressing with her mouth and fingers all over Lauren's pussy until the pleasure stampeded inside her, wild and whirling. The need was so strong she thought the orgasm would destroy her before it broke. When she came, the release engulfed her in its fury, roaring through her and leaving nothing in its wake but a cascade of burning embers.

Emma. Emma. Emma.

Her pussy was still pulsing when she somehow found the energy to haul Emma to her feet. "I'm staying. The Cupcake's going to have to live with it."

Chapter Sixteen

Emma slid a crusty loaf of asiago cheese bread out of the oven and placed the tray next to a casserole dish of delicious-smelling homemade lasagna. If Lauren hadn't already been hopelessly in "I don't care either" with her, this would've sealed the deal. Emma had put her hair up in a messy bun with strands falling to frame her face, and she'd changed out of her work clothes into dark skinny jeans and a soft looking sweater. The house smelled like an Italian eatery, and a miniature Christmas tree twinkled merrily next to a roaring fire. Lauren had a glass of cabernet sauvignon, a seat at the kitchen island, and the best view in town. She could get used to all the cozy and homey.

"When do you get vacation time?" Lauren asked.

Emma glanced at her before taking a lethal looking knife from a block and slicing into the bread, releasing an aroma decadent enough to make Lauren's mouth water. "Early February. Only the most diehard bibliophiles use the library in the dead of winter. Why?"

"I was thinking maybe you'd like to come with me back to San Francisco for a week or so." Lauren accepted her plate and pulled out a stool for Emma to slide in next to her. "If you wanted to, we could go to Kink's."

Emma was about to take a heaping mouthful of lasagna only to have it clatter onto her plate when she dropped her fork. "What?"

Emma's complete astonishment made Lauren think back through her comment. But it wasn't any less normal the second time. "We don't have to, obviously. I just thought you might like it. What's wrong?"

Emma picked her fork back up and bit into her food like it was going to come to life and snap at her. She swallowed. "You want to take me to a *sex club*? After today?"

Men were from Mars and women were from Venus, but Emma was from Jupiter. Lauren understood her so little sometimes. "Why not? It's not like we haven't already had sex. Three times, didn't you remind me?"

"Four. I went down on you until you came all over my face." Emma checked her watch. "About an hour ago."

She wanted to laugh at the prim and proper tone Emma used to inform her of this oh-so-sexy fact. "Of course, how could I forget. Four times. By February, I expect that number to be closer to four million. What number would suit you before sex clubs were an appropriate venue?"

Emma bit her lip, then put down her fork, on purpose this time, and faced Lauren. "This is new and neither of us have a ton of experience at dating, but I don't want you to fuck other women. I'm sorry if that makes me an old-fashioned fuddy-duddy and polyamory is the cool new thing. Just, no, okay?"

Lauren put her own fork down. She didn't know whether to kiss Emma or throttle her. "What on earth gave you the idea I wanted to fuck other women?"

Emma waved vaguely at the air. "Sex clubs! That's why you go, isn't it? To find people to fuck?"

Lauren couldn't help herself. She burst out laughing. "Oh, Emma."

Emma's sigh was long and windy as if all the air in the world had been trapped inside her lungs. "It's not very nice to laugh."

Lauren grinned and dragged Emma's stool closer until their knees touched. "I'm not laughing at you, I promise. I'm laughing because what I meant was, we would go together, and have sex together, if you wanted to. They have equipment and toys that I think you'd enjoy. I was thinking about fucking *you*, not someone else."

"Oh." Emma considered this. "You can fuck me here. Why bother going all the way to San Francisco?"

"Because it's fun," Lauren said simply. "Because sometimes a change of environment can be exciting. Because I want to see you trussed up and bound with your arms over your head, and it's easier there than rigging something homemade to do the job."

Emma swallowed and Lauren watched her throat work while she waited for her answer.

"Trussed up and bound, huh?"

It took everything she had not to jump up and down in triumph when a telltale blush spread across Emma's cheeks. "You said you wanted to try bondage."

"Well, yeah, but a sex club seems—"

Emma trailed off, and Lauren cut in gently. "Like a really safe place to try something new for the first time on equipment designed for the exact purpose?"

Emma groaned. "You think I'm freaking out about the sex club, and I am, but not for the reason you assume."

Lauren took her hand and squeezed. She tried her best to morph her expression into something non-judgmental. This was a learning curve for Emma. She had to get used to that. "Then tell me so I don't have to guess."

Emma looked at her plate and shuffled her feet along the rung of the stool. "There will be other people there. You have a lot more experience than I do."

Lauren was about to interrupt, but Emma shook her head vigorously. "I'm not jealous, I promise. I mean, okay, so I don't *love* all the probably Hollywood-attractive women you've made scream, but it's not about that."

"Tell me what it's about."

"You're this uber talented Don Juan type, and I've only just overcome my anxiety enough to orgasm. To be fair, I orgasmed very, very hard, so thank you for that, but still. I have some catching up to do, and I can't promise that I won't still have some issues to sort out. That's going to be hard enough without adding strangers and sex clubs to the mix."

Lauren sat back. Emma made a good point. The last thing she wanted was to make things more difficult. But Emma too often jumped to conclusions about what she liked or wanted without exploring what actually turned her on. "Okay. How about this. You make a list of all the things you've ever fantasized about that you'd like to do, and we'll try some of them here. If it goes well, and it will, because you're sexy as all fuck and I'm Don Juan, then we'll revisit the idea of Kink's."

Emma took a tiny bite of bread and carefully chewed and swallowed before answering. "You're not actually Don Juan. Don't go getting a big head about it just because I compared you to a legendary lothario with the ability to seduce any woman he set his sights on."

"It's a singular talent. I try to be modest."

Emma laughed. "You really want me to make a sex list?"

"An anything Emma wants fantasy buffet come to life list."

"If you're going to insist, then I'll be forced to make the list, won't I? But strange equipment bondage goes somewhere in the middle. I'm putting you fucking me from behind with a strap-on at the top."

Ohfuckgodyes. Now. Now would be perfect.

Lauren took a really big gulp of wine. "Been thinking about that one, have you?"

Emma nodded. "I really enjoy it from behind. The angle is perfect and not having to look someone in the eyes helps."

When Lauren made a choked sound, Emma poked her playfully in the ribs. "Don't you go getting jealous now. I've had some nice sex with some other women too, you know."

"Yeah. Not jealous." Lauren shifted on the stool, suddenly wishing she'd chosen clothes a little looser, so her clit wasn't trapped and pulsing against the seam of her jeans. God. Emma had no idea how hot she was. Or for that matter, how hot she was making Lauren.

Emma picked up their empty plates and put them in the sink. "Sounded like jealousy to me."

"That's a shame because it should've sounded like me getting turned on at the idea of watching someone fucking you from behind. You'd look amazing on your hands and knees with your ass in the air." Lauren drained the rest of her wine in one swallow.

Emma's wineglass almost hit the floor as she fumbled it. It was cute how clumsy she got when she was flustered. Lauren hoped it was more than flustered. Edging into the ballpark of unbearably aroused would put them on an even keel.

"You'd really want to watch someone else fuck me like that?" Emma asked.

Lauren nodded. "Don't get me wrong, I'm still Don Juan. But yeah, it's appealing."

Emma huffed out a breath but failed to stop a smile. "For the last time, you're not *actually* Don Juan."

"If you say so." She winked and took Emma's hand to lead her to the couch. The sofa was draped with knitted throws and ancient looking pillows that just begged someone to sink into them. "It sounds like that would make you uncomfortable, someone else making you come?"

"People. Insecurity. Blah, blah." Emma waved it away as if it didn't matter, and then added, "Getting fucked by a stranger with your ass in the air isn't exactly the best way to feel more secure."

Maybe it was exactly the perfect way to feel more secure for someone like Emma, but Lauren kept that observation to herself. She knew a boundary when she heard one. Boundaries or not though, Emma was all hot and bothered. Her cheeks hadn't cooled, and she kept shifting on the couch like she couldn't quite get comfortable. Emma wasn't ready, but she was sending all kinds of signals.

Lauren took a chance. "Come here."

She threw a few of the throw cushions against the arm of the sofa, put her feet up, and gestured for Emma to settle between her thighs with her ass snugged between Lauren's thighs.

Emma rested her head against Lauren's chest and mumbled, "This is nice."

"It's about to get nicer. Close your eyes."

Emma's eyes drifted shut, and Lauren's heart did a quick tap dance. Questions and conversations were good and important parts of the process, but the easy acceptance of Emma doing exactly what she was told without comment—the trust that took—was its own special pleasure. She eased up the bottom of Emma's sweater, baring her waist and the button on her jeans. "You don't want to go to Kink's yet, and you don't want to let me watch someone fuck you, but maybe you'd like to think about it if we stay right here together and imagine."

Emma groaned, her breath already choppy. "Lauren."

Lauren danced her fingers along the waistband of Emma's jeans, stroking softly. "But you like it when we imagine together, don't you? It makes you come very, very hard."

"I don't want—" Emma began.

"Yes, you do. You know what to say if you don't want it. But you're blushing and fumbling, and you can't catch your breath, can you? I think you want to imagine being at Kink's. I think inside you want me to tell you that you *have* to go... You want me to lead you through the front doors. I have my hand on the small of your back, a clear signal to everyone that you're there with me. Mine to play with. You wore a dress you don't like, so you won't mind if I tear it off you. The little straps holding it up won't take much to snap. I think you chose it on purpose, hoping I'd rip it."

Emma squirmed, her eyelids fluttering and her legs falling open as if by instinct. Her body language was screaming for Lauren to continue, and when Lauren ran her hand down the inside of Emma's thigh, Emma quivered.

"We find seats at the bar to do a little people watching until I decide that I'm ready to fuck you. When *she* walks in, your breath catches and you look away. You shift toward me and put your hand in mine. You don't want to find her attractive. You don't want anyone but me, and yet..."

Emma groaned and Lauren smothered a grin, stroking up and down her thigh. *That's right. All the things you want and don't think you should have are driving you crazy, aren't they?*

"It makes me hot to know you want her. We're here together, but why should that make either of us blind? I check her out, too. She's on the wrong side of the equation to rock your world the way we both know you need. This one's a slave. I can tell from the way she walks and the tilt of her head. Her wrists and neck are bare, and her skin is unmarked for now. Perhaps she'd be interested in doing a favor for a gorgeous woman who lost her breath just looking at her.

"I slide off my stool to talk to her. I ignore your squeak of protest when you reach out to stop me. Sorry. The second you saw her, you gave yourself away and now you don't get to decide. If I want her to make you come, she will. That's why we're here. For whatever I want and all the things you don't have to ask for. I know you want this. Your eyes bore into my back as I cross the room. If your stare could burn, my shirt would be aflame."

"Lauren." The word came out on a whisper. Emma tugged Lauren's hand toward the apex of her thighs

"Not yet," Lauren said. She loved seeing Emma turned on, lost and needy and not fully aware of what she was doing. She loved the Emma who could let go, the Emma who could embrace her sexuality and be true to her desire. How much Emma had changed—her surrender almost effortless, her passion quick to surface.

Lauren kept going, kept pushing Emma to face her unfaceable desires, just a little, just in theory. She could give Emma this.

"The slave disappears through an unmarked doorway, and I stroll back to the bar for my scotch. I'm looking right at you, waiting. I know you want to ask. You're burning inside to ask, to prepare yourself. But you surprise me—and please me—when you stare right back, saying nothing. That's when I decide I'm going to reward you. My good girl who doesn't ask questions that aren't hers to have answered."

Lauren kept her promise by popping the button on Emma's jeans and sliding her hand inside, cupping Emma's pussy. Emma's panties were already damp, and Lauren groaned softly in Emma's ear, trailing her fingers back and forth over the silk, right against her clit. "So fucking hot already, aren't you?"

"Oh, please."

"I love it when you beg." Lauren pressed firmly against Emma's center, pushing the cotton of her panties inside just a little. "I love it when you lose control."

Emma moaned, her hips lifting off the couch and into Lauren's touch. "Please."

"I lead you by the hand through the unmarked door, down a scrawny little corridor, and into a room designed for your pleasure. In the center, hanging from a solidly built metal frame, is a spreader bar. You don't know what that is yet, but you're about to find out. The slave is waiting, head down and hands clasped in front of her. She's naked and you can't help but stare. You stare at the slave. You stare at the ropes and pulleys hanging from the ceiling. You stare at me, lust in your eyes and in the pounding of your heart. I wonder if you're going to try to run, if you'll want to tell me no, but I don't think so, not this time. You want it too much to pretend.

"I drag an armless chair over to face the slave and lead you to the spreader. You whimper softly when I tie your wrists above your head. It's not very high, your feet are still firmly on the ground. I'm not going to push you too far, not today. With your arms like that, your chest pushes out, and that's all the invitation I need to take what I want. I snap the useless little straps of your silly dress, and you gasp. The material drifts to the ground as soft as a petal falling from a flower. You're naked underneath. You almost said no when I asked you to go without underwear tonight. Having nothing to shield from the world makes you uncomfortable. Being exposed makes you hot, too. I help you step out of your shoes.

"There you are—completely naked for me, flushed and straining. Absolute perfection."

Lauren slipped beneath Emma's panties and stroked her clit. She was wet and soft, already so close. Emma made a long, low, desperate sound, her hips rising, her belly taut. Her head lolled against Lauren's shoulder. Oh yes. She was completely immersed in the fantasy now. Time to keep her on edge and make it good for both of them.

"I run my hands all over you. Not rough, not this time, but firm and methodical. Sizing you up, examining every inch of your perfect body on display just for me. I pinch your nipples, press my hand against your sopping pussy. Oh, the slave is going to have so much fun with you, you're so ready for a good fucking. You pump your hips into my hand, your eyes begging for more. That's the thing about being bound and stripped. You have no secrets from the one who has you captive. I know how much you want to come, but I also know how much you enjoy the ride. I'm going to make you wait. I step away and wipe my fingers on my pants. Your arousal leaves a mark. Your need, a stain against my thigh. How dirty. I've barely even started, and you're already halfway there."

Lauren breathed out slowly through her teeth. *Don't fucking come in your pants like a horny teenager.* She didn't usually have so much trouble controlling her response when she was in a scene. It was all about the submissive and *their* need. But Emma flipped switches inside her that she hadn't even known were there to be flipped. Her responsiveness an irresistible infinity loop that fueled Lauren's passion.

"I step out of my shoes and undo the buttons on my shirt, letting it hang open to expose my breasts. You lick your lips, your eyes following my every move. I remove my pants and I'm naked except for the shirt. You pull against your restraints. It's so very unfair of me, isn't it? I almost never strip for you, not like this, not when we're in a scene and I have all the control. You want to touch me, but you can't. You just hang where I put you as your need for me soaks your thighs. I turn my back and walk away from you."

Emma whimpered as if Lauren really had abandoned her. Lauren pressed her fingers to Emma's opening, and made a quiet shushing sound in her ear. *Trust me. I've got you.*

"I sit in the chair, facing you and the slave, who still hasn't looked at either of us. Whoever trained her, trained her well. I spread my legs and drop my hand to brush over my folds. You pull at your restraints again. You say my name, half plea, half promise. It makes you crazy when I touch myself and force you to watch. You can't touch anyone, not even yourself. That's what the slave is here for. But you'll have to beg me for it. You'll have to watch me as I stroke myself. Watch me watch you come with someone else inside you. You don't want it to make you hot, but it does. You can't help it. You want it, even when wanting it makes you feel dirty.

"I instruct you to spread your legs and order the slave to kneel between them. She glances at me quickly, her gaze dropping between my thighs for a nanosecond, like she just can't stop herself. She bites her lip, and I give her a nod. It's okay to look.

"She starts out slowly. Barely caressing your folds with her tongue. So soft and gentle, you think you might be imagining it— but it feels so damn good. I lean back in my chair and spread my legs a little wider. I'm going to enjoy this. 'Please,' you beg me, your thighs trembling a little as you force yourself not to thrust into her mouth. You want it to be my mouth, not hers. You want to be between my legs, not have her between yours. You want me, but you want her, too, and it feels so fucking good when she licks you that you can't help but moan. It's so wanton to be getting off with someone else, when I'm right there watching you. Aside from your wrists tied above your head, this scene could hardly be called kink. I've gone so easy on you.

"If you don't account for the mindfuck."

Lauren dipped her fingertips inside Emma. In and out nice and easy, until Emma groaned.

"When she grips your thighs to steady you and dips her tongue inside, you cry out. I mimic her move, swirling my fingers around my opening as she circles her tongue around yours. I know just how it feels, Emma, just how much it makes you crave to be fucked. I thrust my fingers inside myself once, hard and fast, and you gasp, jerking against the slave's mouth. Your excitement makes her moan. Our slave likes to suck pussy. She knows how to do it well, hot and messy with your need painting her chin. I slide a finger on either side of my clit as I watch her make you tremble. As she rips cries and moans from your throat. As your eyes glaze and your breath comes in ragged gasps. You have no choice but to accept her touch. I wanted her for you, and all you can do is acquiesce. My pleasure is your pleasure, and your need is my need as we climb together, closer and closer to the inevitable.

"I've got you trapped. Not with the ropes binding your wrists and not with the woman giving you pleasure. You're trapped because you can't look away. This time you don't want to close your eyes, not even when she sucks your clit and you're so close to coming your knees give way and she has to hold you up with an arm around your thighs. You'd never look away from my desire, from my fingers playing over my clit, from the way I circle and thrust, hot and wet for you. Your eyes bore into mine, and you barely blink. You strain to catch every moan and sigh. I'm so turned on watching you teeter on the brink of surrender. Your begging is a ceaseless refrain now as you squirm and thrust into the slave's mouth. You need to come so badly, but you need my permission more. I almost give it to you, you've made me so fucking hot. Pleasure spins inside me, a tornado of passion that's going to rip us both to shreds. But I'm spoiled and your mouth is so much better than my hand. Too bad for you that you're so good at sucking pussy. Guess you'll have to wait a little longer.

"I tell the slave to get up. My voice is sharp. What sounds like anger masking the impossible desire biting at my sanity. I give her a signal, and she selects a harness and cock from a chest in the corner of the room. You watch her, your breath coming in whimpering gasps until I walk over to you, put my hands over your wrists, and press my body along yours. You're so fucking hot you arch against me, try to wrap your legs around my waist, your pussy against my stomach. I laugh softly in your ear. Nice try. I step back and, with your hands tied, you lose balance and stumble back, too. Your face is a mask of frustrated desire. So much need churning inside you and absolutely nothing you can do about any of it.

"I tell you, 'You'll allow me to untie your hands without trying to climb me like a ladder, or we go home now. Topping from the bottom is unacceptable, I don't care how turned on you are.'"

Emma jolted from her sexual trance.

Topping from the bottom is unacceptable.

Something didn't feel quite right. Not wrong exactly, not bad exactly, but not quite okay. She squirmed in Lauren's lap, her ears buzzing while Lauren's fingers circled her clit, so close to sending her over. Uneasiness spiraled around the pleasure until arousal and confusion, lust and panic, coalesced inside her and lodged itself, hot and sticky, in her throat. "Lauren, stop."

Lauren didn't so much as pause. "You know what kind of steak you like, Emma. I doubt you've forgotten already."

Emma's skin began to tingle and tighten. God, she was going to come.

She didn't want to come like this.

You know what to say if you don't want it.

"Filet mignon."

CHAPTER SEVENTEEN

Lauren instantly stilled and pulled her hand out from Emma's panties. Emma didn't know whether to cry out in frustration or gratefulness. The last thing she wanted was to come accidentally when things needed to be discussed. Needed to be changed.

"Should I leave, or do you want to talk about it?" Lauren's tone was deceptively casual, not a hint of frustration at having her scene shattered.

Emma's safe word was for her protection, and Lauren didn't make her feel guilty for using it. She was relieved about that, but she needed more than her body to be safe. How did she explain she needed her heart and their future to be just as safe?

Emma took a big breath and let it out slowly, giving herself time to decide. The last time they'd come up against an obstacle, she'd asked Lauren to leave. This time skipping out wasn't an option. She loved her. That was the thing about love, the sticking when things got tough part. The not running and not hiding, but facing what stood in the way. All the hitches and the monkey wrenches, and those times when life took a chunk out of your ass. Love was having someone who stuck.

Emma wasn't topping from the bottom, not really, but she needed to call this one shot. Just one. For Lauren, it would be the most important one.

She flipped over in Lauren's arms until she could look into Lauren's eyes. "I don't want to be in the club with a stranger."

Lauren raised her eyebrows and brushed her wet fingers against Emma's cheek, making her blush. Lauren was using her arousal to disagree with her. That was more than a little annoying.

"Yes, okay, it turns me on," Emma snapped. "This make-believe story you're concocting is hot, Lauren. Well done."

Lauren's face shut down just as Emma knew it would. Just as she'd witnessed every time Lauren came up against something that hurt. Emma couldn't have asked for a more compassionate and insightful lover. She'd never expected anyone to truly see her, and then to want the person they saw. Lauren had, and she did. The last thing Emma wanted was to be a source of pain for her, but if Lauren retreated every time things got hard, sticking would break them.

Emma had to say what needed to be said, and see if Lauren would come back.

"Well done? That's a bit condescending," Lauren said.

"Then maybe you should stop hiding if you don't want me to call you out on it." Emma dug her knees into the couch when Lauren tried to sit up and push her off. Emma knew exactly how she felt. She knew not wanting to face something. To have someone you cared about, someone you *loved*, tell you it was time to get over your self-judgment. Time to show up because they needed you to.

"Either explain yourself or let me up, Emma."

Lauren's voice was so quiet, so precisely controlled, that goose bumps spread down Emma's arms. Frost had crystalized over Lauren's detachment now, shrouding her in ice. This was a risk. Lauren's tone was a tiptoe away from legit pissed off. But loving someone meant you saw them for who they really were. You knew them for the good and the bad and all the ways they held themselves back from what they really wanted. That's what Lauren had done for her, and now she saw what Lauren was hiding.

"I'm getting a little bored being a pawn in your fantasies. Having you whisper in my ear is real hot and everything, but if you don't start acting on all this talk soon, I'll be disappointed."

She was such a liar her pants should be on fire. She would happily lie back and listen to Lauren weave a sexy world around her all damn day if she thought that's what Lauren really wanted. If she didn't finally *see* that fantasy and sex clubs and a change of scenery were Lauren's defense against truly owning up to her passions.

Emma didn't want fantasy. She'd lived in a fantasy world with Lauren as the star since high school, and as lovely as it was, it wasn't real. She wanted *Lauren*.

"A pawn? Disappointed?" Lauren hauled herself up with Emma still on top of her so they were tangled around each other in a sitting position. "Is that so?"

"Yeah," Emma shot back with all the bravado she could muster, "that's so."

They stared at each other, the fierceness in Lauren's eyes belying the remoteness of her expression.

Emma broke first. Of course, she did. She didn't even have half of Lauren's control, but it didn't matter. She had the truth instead. She knew it in her bones. Just because Lauren had more experience, didn't mean she didn't have demons. Lauren's wealth of experience was precisely why she got away with hiding behind fantasy. Fantasies were safe.

Emma knew all too well the cost of such safety.

"I don't want this fantasy," Emma said with all the certainty she could muster. "Not right now. I want you to tie my wrists to the metal rungs of my headboard. Then I want *you* to fuck me. I want *you* to take me. I want *you*. The real you. The one that's right here looking really damn put out by all of this. I don't want another fantasy. I don't want you to spin a make-believe story to get us off. I want real. I want honest. I want raw. You get annoyed when I close my eyes? When I struggle to be present? Well, I get annoyed when you distance yourself from what's genuine by layering a fantasy on top of it. By not really *doing* what you're describing. I want you to mean it, and actually do it, and to fucking *revel* in it."

I want heartfelt and wholehearted and heart-to-heart with nothing between us.

Lauren's gaze never wavered. Her stare peeled Emma inside out until every part of her was on display—her desire, her need, her heart—all there for Lauren to see. What Lauren stirred in her in that moment, her stare somewhere between a glare and a claiming, was too complicated to be love. Too big to be bound by emotion. She was laid bare and the feeling swamped her, wrapping around her, seeping into her pores, and becoming part of who she was. It was a feeling meant only for Lauren. This one woman who owned her heart.

Emma breathed.

"Is it so bad to want you?" She used a thumb to catch the tears that ran down Lauren's cheeks. "Wasn't it you who told me wanting something from someone is the damn point?"

Lauren's silence grew, like a slap stinging Emma's skin. She untangled herself from Lauren, pulled her knees to her chest, and wrapped her arms around herself. Swallowing hard, she tried to force away the burning in her throat that always signaled tears. They would never work if Lauren didn't stand up for herself and what she wanted.

Seconds and minutes and years bled together as Emma looked into Lauren's gray eyes, soft as cashmere and wild as storm clouds. Those eyes that had seen inside her from the very first moment. Those eyes had never looked away, never considered her too much to handle, and had always been patient, kind, sexy-as-all-get-out eyes.

Emma spoke to the woman behind those eyes. "Sex isn't as good if it's easy and simple and uncomplicated. I want vulnerability. I love you."

Lauren grimaced like the words made her bleed. "Emma."

"I love you."

"That's a really terrible idea on your part. I'm hell to love. I never remember anniversaries, and I leave my wet towel on the bathroom floor."

"Don't joke. Be vulnerable. Be real. Be you. Just you and me and nothing and no one else. I love you."

Lauren pulled her shirt over her head and pressed Emma's palm to her heart, where, in deceptively simple script, were the words *What doesn't kill me makes me stronger.* Her fingers wrapped around Emma's and held there, their joined hands against the phrase they'd have to break through for access to her heart.

Emma relaxed. Pushing Lauren to face her issues, ripping at her deepest secrets, wasn't what she wanted to do. Lauren had to *want* to expose herself. Lauren had to let her in. Asking, demanding, putting conditions on their connection, wouldn't get her what she wanted. Wouldn't do a damn thing to get Lauren to open up. Emma waited, and, for the first time, the waiting was comfortable, like they could sit there with her jeans undone and Lauren's shirt off all their lives. As if nothing and no one outside this moment mattered, and time was suspended and irrelevant.

"Mom was never a prostitute," Lauren said flatly. She squeezed Emma's hand. "She checked coats at a gentlemen's club in Albany, and she helped out the dancers sometimes, giving them a safe place to stay if they needed it. But she never had sex for money."

"Okay," Emma said.

"But bringing a procession of erotic dancers to your house, and treating them as if they actually mattered, as if they were as worthy as her church-going neighbors, well, that wasn't living up to small town values, at least not in Sunrise Falls."

Emma nodded and tucked a strand of hair behind Lauren's ear.

"I was eight when the rumors started. I've never been quite sure where they originated, but it got around fast that Mom wasn't just a coat checker, that she was taking cash for blow jobs, and God only knows what else. The kids at school, eight-year-olds, started calling her a whore. You know that's not a word they'd have figured out for themselves. They must've heard it from their parents."

"That must've been so hard." Emma's heart broke for Lauren. To be eight and struggling with such adult discrimination must have been agonizing.

"She lost her job at the bank. Back then, there wasn't any protection against workplace discrimination. What was she supposed to do? Sue them with no money and no job?"

Emma made a harsh sound, a laugh that caught in her throat and transformed into a sob when it reached her lips. Not even remotely funny how close Lauren's mom's history mirrored her current predicament. This town hadn't changed even a little.

"She had to take more hours at the club to make enough to survive, and even then, we struggled. There were days she didn't eat at all. Days she watched me cry and call her names because she had to deny me the apple sitting on the kitchen counter. I couldn't have the apple today. If I did, there wouldn't be any lunch for the next day. That's how I grew up after no one in Sunrise Falls would hire the whore who spent her nights sucking cock at the gentlemen's club and came home with a procession of pretty girls who just needed a safe place to sleep. Women who, it's hard to believe, were even worse off than we were."

Emma swiped at the tears on her cheeks and swallowed painfully. God. It was so much worse than she'd imagined. "Your mom sounds amazing."

Lauren's chin lifted and the smallest of smiles appeared. "She's the best, but poverty is debilitating. Life isn't about meaning or enjoyment. Nothing is as simple as going to school and playing with your friends, or worrying about your homework. Poverty is life. Every decision is about poverty. Do you put gas in the car to get to work or pay the oil bill to keep the pipes from freezing? Mom faced those choices every day, a weight on her mind every minute. That's the burden of poverty, not to mention the stigma of sex work. She did her best. She kept a roof over my head, kept me fed, kept me in school, but poverty came first.

"There was no one to watch me while she was at work, so I spent every night alone fending for myself. She had to sleep during the day so missed every school function. She was so sad, so fucking weary of the battle to just stay alive, she didn't have a lot left over for me. She loved me. She had the bone-deep decency to put her own worries aside and give shelter to girls who needed it despite the damage to her reputation. She did everything she could for me, and for them. It just didn't always feel like enough. Poverty always got the lion's share."

"I won't say I understand." Emma wished she could wrap Lauren in her arms and somehow heal all her hurt. "I'm sure I don't understand even half of what you went though, but I'm so sorry. It kills me that you suffered. That you're still suffering."

Lauren's shoulders lifted in a gesture too slow and exhausted to really be called a shrug. "Everyone suffers somehow. This was just my how. I got out, moved to the West Coast, and started over. But the past never really goes away no matter how much you stamp it down. What's that saying? No matter where you go, there you are."

"Is it connected for you?" Emma asked. "Your childhood experiences and your sexual expression as an adult?"

Lauren didn't answer for a long moment. "Yes and no. I don't think I'm kinky because of what happened when I was a kid. That's just who I am and what I like, and would be the same no matter what upbringing I had. But when I'm in control, it's easier to separate who I want to be from who I used to be. I like going to Kink's because the atmosphere, the role-plays, give me space to distance myself through fantasy."

"Why?" Emma felt the weight of those three letters like they were a sledgehammer about to come down on her heart. "Why do you do it?"

"Because I'm trash." Lauren put a hand up to stop Emma from voicing the protest that was instantly on the tip of her tongue. "I know I'm not *really* trash any more than my mother is. I know that her taking the only job available to her, and helping women even less fortunate, doesn't make either of us trash. I know trying to help Caroline doesn't make me trash, either. I *know*.

"But when I was eight, no one would play with me at school because my mom was the town slut. When I was fifteen, boys invited me to parties to get me drunk, thinking I'd be an easy lay.

When I was a senior, the school counselor told me that I'd have to focus on my grades, so I wouldn't repeat my mother's mistakes. It never ends. Now I've come back amid a scandal of my own making, and proved every single one of the naysayers right. That's who I am, Emma. And even though logic and reason tell me all those things don't make me trash, it's hard to really believe it.

"It's hard to be *me* with someone like you. Someone so good. Someone who excelled in all the ways I didn't. It's hard not to pretend to be a better version of myself. At the end of the day, at the crux of everything, it's just hard to believe that anyone would want *me*. Sexy, dominant, role-playing, fantasy-weaving Lauren who can make a woman come? That's given me confidence. That's helped me to find value in who I am. I'm *good* at that. But under it, I'm eight and afraid that this girl I'm falling for will discover I'm not really worth it unless I keep some distance between her and the person I am on the inside."

Emma swallowed past the tightness in her throat, hardly daring to breathe. This moment, this revelation, felt like the most important of her life, and the desire not to fuck it up was almost overpowering. She leaned forward, pressed her mouth to Lauren's, and whispered against her lips, "That's the biggest load of bullshit I've ever heard."

Lauren's laugh was genuine, if not exactly carefree. "I'll have to keep in mind you have an excellent memory and a propensity to throw my words back in my face."

"Can I help it if it's effective?" Emma got up and offered Lauren her hand. "I don't have the words for everything I need to say…for all the ways your history is heartbreaking, and for all the reasons you're wrong about not being enough."

Words would never heal the hurt shrouding Lauren's heart. Maybe nothing would. But Emma knew Lauren now, *saw* her now, and there was one way they could communicate without need for words at all.

"Come to bed."

CHAPTER EIGHTEEN

Emma made a sound that was two-thirds oh-my-God-hurry-up, and one-third don't-you-dare-stop-kissing-me, as they fumbled their way to the bedroom. Her need had reached the level of craving, the desire welling inside almost painful, as sheer want enveloped her so completely she couldn't separate her need for Lauren from her love for Lauren.

Love and lust were inextricably linked.

She landed unceremoniously on her back with Lauren on top of her. When Lauren grabbed her wrists and pinned them over her head, she didn't hold back the frustrated sound on the tip of her tongue. How was she supposed to convince Lauren that she loved her? That Lauren was worthy of all the love she had to give, if she couldn't touch her? She needed contact, skin, closeness. Emotional, sexual, spiritual…all of it.

Whose dumb idea had it been to suggest bondage, anyway?

"Stop trying to get away. You wanted this, now you're going to take it how I want to give it. I'm not inclined to hurry." Lauren's gaze glinted, half teasing, half hunger, as she rested her weight fully upon Emma.

Lauren caught her gasp in a searing kiss, and heat curled from her lips, burned down her belly, and blazed between her thighs. Emma marveled at how intense kissing was. No matter how many times Lauren took her mouth, her fingers tangling in Emma's hair, her lips and tongue urgently coaxing needy sounds from deep inside, nothing felt familiar. Kissing Lauren, or rather, Lauren kissing her, had adrenaline coursing through her veins, revving her up, making her breath catch and her skin ignite. Narrowing her awareness to this one point of contact, impossible to control.

Guhhh. Why did her mind have to screech to a halt right now? She had things to do, points to prove, feelings to express. Touch was Lauren's language, and she wanted to communicate just how loved and appreciated and goddammed worthy Lauren really was. She wanted to sooth a lifetime of pain with tender caresses and gentle explorations.

The trouble was, kissing Lauren made her want to fuck.

Emma wrapped herself around Lauren, rubbing her pussy against the bare skin of Lauren's stomach. "Please."

Lauren tortured her, cupping the back of her neck to hold her right where she wanted her, and grinding against her center. Emma whimpered. More, damn it. She wanted to be naked. She wanted Lauren to tip her head back and kiss down her neck, stroke her breasts, explore all her curves, use her fingers and her mouth to make her come. She wanted so much more. "Please. Please. Please."

"Such pretty begging," Lauren murmured against her mouth, crushing her hips into Emma's.

Need burned through Emma's senses, igniting her with reckless abandon. *Warning!* Extreme fire alert: uncontained blaze ahead, backup impossible. "I need you inside me. Please."

Lauren propped herself up on an elbow and looked down at her, a smile in her eyes. "A woman with a strap-on request at the top of her sex list must have one lying around here somewhere."

Emma considered denying it—for half a second. Lauren slowly moving against her was sending her whole world into overdrive. Embarrassment about sex toys would have to wait until after her hormones had been subjected to an ice bath. "Maybe."

Lauren laughed. "That'd better be a yes if you want me to fuck you. My treasure chest of erotic pleasures is back in San Francisco."

"San Francisco with its sex clubs and crazy vengeful bosses' wives can stay right where it is. There's a box in the top of my closet."

"I like a woman who's prepared."

Lauren was going to fuck her. Really fucking fuck her. No fantasy standing between her and Lauren's passion to claim her. Nerves, the anxiety a long lost not-a-friend, almost comforting in its familiarity, creeped into the edges of her mind. Instead of ignoring it, pushing it down and away and out of sight where it would still control her, Emma said, "I'm nervous."

Lauren glanced over her shoulder as she pulled a box from the top shelf of Emma's closet, her expression full of wicked intent. "Oh, goodie."

Emma laughed, the unexpected sound bursting from her as the tension melted away. So what if she was nervous? Lauren's desire for her, Lauren's desire for the very nerves that clouded Emma's thoughts, made them bearable. She might never fully understand how Lauren could find her nervousness hot, but Lauren did, and that made her nemesis something close to an asset for the first time in her life. Coming to terms with her condition wouldn't make it go away, but letting go of the shame that had always been a sticky aftertaste was a gift. *She* didn't have to hide, either.

"Thank you for saying that," Emma said.

Lauren raised her eyebrows as she sauntered back to the bed, harness and toy in hand. "Thank you, huh? That's a switch."

Emma's heartbeat climbed into her throat as she took in the mind-exploding image of Lauren's fingers wrapped around her favorite toy.

"Emma?"

"Huh?"

"I said that thank you is quite the one-eighty."

Emma nodded.

Change: check.

Love: check.

Excruciatingly turned on: check, check, check.

Lauren could fuck her now. Anytime. Right away would be ideal.

Lauren let the toy dangle from her fingers. "Want to help me out?"

Was there a place drier and hotter than the Sahara? Wherever, Emma was there. All the moisture in her mouth dried up in an instant. Her blood began to heat, radiating out through her skin. A nine-alarm fire was imminent.

"I'll warn you, I don't know what I'm doing. Someone else has always taken care of that part."

"Well, *this* someone wants you on your knees and ready for a lesson. You'll be responsible for this task in the future," Lauren said.

In the future. Their future. Lauren standing there, harness in hand and a devilish grin, conjured fantasies of spending every night getting fucked. Up against the door with her legs wrapped around Lauren's waist when they were too impatient to make it to the bed. Bent over the kitchen table with her thighs spread and her nipples rubbing against the wood with every thrust when she had a lesson that needed learning. On her hands and knees with Lauren fucking her hard, letting her have it all crazy and dirty and who the hell cared about decorum anyway. She wanted all kinds of futures with Lauren, but right now, the one that involved a lifetime of exactly this, was front and center.

Emma barely managed not to fly off the bed and knelt at Lauren's feet. She pressed her palms to Lauren's thighs. Kneeling in front of Lauren provided a stimulating view. Tough looking combat boots and jeans that poured down her legs like syrup. Lauren had a body made for jeans, tall and lanky, endless, endless legs encased in soft worn denim. She was unfairly good-looking. From this vantage point Emma had a prime view of the best-looking place of all. Her fingers twitched with the need to press her palm against Lauren's pussy. She wanted to make Lauren moan, wanted her to forget every terrible thought that had lodged itself in her head. "I'm ready."

"You are ready, aren't you?" Lauren cupped Emma's cheek, her thumb tracing the angle of her jaw.

Emma nodded. She *was* ready. For her lesson. For who Lauren really was. For everything they both needed.

She was ready for a lifetime. But she waited for Lauren's command.

"Take off my boots."

How did Lauren make such an ordinary sentence sound so blatantly sexy? She untied the laces, her fingers trembling, and Lauren toed them and her socks off.

"Put them aside, neatly," Lauren said.

Emma complied quickly.

"Now my jeans."

She popped the button on Lauren's jeans. The sound of the zipper descending slashed the air. Emma eyed the sexy expanse of Lauren's pelvis. She wanted to run her tongue along all that taut skin. "God."

Lauren cradled her chin and angled her face up. "Wait until after I fuck you to promote me to deity."

Emma just shook her head. "You make jeans look like lingerie. Only sexy, androgynous lingerie, not the frilly girly stuff."

"Thank heavens for that." Lauren tilted her hips so the button on her jeans almost brushed Emma's lips. "Hurry up. I've got things to do and patience isn't a trait I possess when a beautiful woman is kneeling at my feet."

She wanted Lauren's control, but there was something unspeakably erotic about testing her, and teasing her, and seeing if she'd lose it. Emma glided her palms slowly along Lauren's hips until they rested at the small of her back, slid inside Lauren's jeans, and squeezed her ass.

Lauren sent her a dark look, but her breath hitched. "Are you trying to get into trouble?"

Emma licked her lips. "My apologies. I got distracted."

She tugged Lauren's jeans down, coasting her palms slowly down the back of Lauren's thighs as she went.

Lauren kicked the jeans off in a movement just a bit too jerky to be casual.

"Now the rest," Lauren said, her voice like tires over gravel. "And, Emma? If you get *distracted* again, there'll be hell to pay."

Emma bit her bottom lip and dutifully pulled Lauren's underwear down and off while Lauren took care of her bra. A not insignificant part of her wanted to know what exactly Lauren meant by *hell* and what the payment would be. That would have to be a question for another night. Lauren West, stark naked and looming over her, was enough to melt her brain and make every thought run like a waterfall down to her clit. The woman was a damn work of art.

"Keep looking at me like that and I'll be tempted to forgo the lesson and fuck you blind right there on the floor. Your eyes are begging for it," Lauren said.

"Please. I'll beg as much as you want."

Lauren closed her eyes, as if Emma's words formed a picture she couldn't quite handle. When she opened them again, some of the edginess dissipated. "You're irresistible, if I was in the mood to be tempted. But I'm not. Pay attention and we'll both get what we want."

She'd never wanted to pay attention so much in her life. She had ambitions of graduating with honors from the University of Pleasuring Lauren. But she was having trouble focusing on anything except how gorgeously sexy Lauren looked naked, and the wetness seeping between her own thighs.

She was still fully dressed. She'd read in books that tops sometimes didn't ever undress as a sign of their power. Nakedness was part of what made the submissive vulnerable. It had made sense at the time. But undressing Lauren, stripping off her clothes while she didn't have permission to do the same? That was ten times hotter than anything she'd ever read about. Lauren wasn't following some well-worn script. This wasn't a fantasy she'd lifted from the pages of a *Fifty Shades* knockoff. This was real.

Lauren removed the O-ring from the harness and fit the base of the toy into it. "Always put the toy in and attach it first. It's not as easy to do once I'm wearing the harness."

Emma nodded, not trusting herself to speak. If she so much as opened her mouth, a string of incoherent pleas would come tumbling out. Heat flooded her cheeks and spread down her chest. *Stop being embarrassed that you want her. It's sexy.*

Allowing Lauren to see her need, to hear her begging, showing Lauren how much she wanted her, made her heart pound in a totally new way.

"Once it's snug in there, you attach it to the harness like this."

Emma tried to concentrate while Lauren showed her how to snap everything in place. She really really tried. There was no sexier lesson on the planet, and she wanted to do this for Lauren the next time. But it took everything she had not to moan out loud. Every time Lauren handled the toy, every word she spoke in that sexy professor voice, was making her crazier. She squirmed and her panties slid against her clit. Fuck, fuck, fuck. Kind of awkward if she came just from watching Lauren strap on. Was it even possible to come without being touched? That would be new, but if there was ever a moment for a spontaneous orgasm, this was it.

"Now it's ready to be worn." Lauren stepped into the harness and held the straps at her hips. "Adjust these straps first." Lauren tightened the leather. "Then the thigh straps."

"Can I?" Emma asked quickly, half afraid Lauren would say no.

"Eager, are you?" Lauren grinned.

"I think I used to be shy in another life, but not anymore. Please."

Lauren widened her stance and gave her a nod. "Every time you say please, my clit pulses."

Emma reached around Lauren's thigh to tighten the strap. "Please, I need you to fuck me." She did the same on the other side. "Please, I'm so wet right now." Emma sat back and rested her hands on her thighs again.

How the hell was she going to survive? A woman wearing a cock was vitally arousing. The genderbending. The blatant fuck you to the patriarchy and taking back that power. Using the symbol of masculinity to give female pleasure. Oh yeah. Strap-ons were at the very top of her sex list.

"So wet, huh?" Lauren said. "Let's see about that. Take your clothes off. On the bed, hands and knees. Close to the headboard."

Emma got shakily to her feet, pausing a second as her head swam from nerves and adrenaline. From all the blood that should've been in her head but was pounding between her legs instead. She stripped off her clothes with absolutely no desire to prolong the moment, tearing at the fabric like it burned. Lauren watched her, idly stroking her cock. No longer Emma's favorite toy. Lauren's cock, now—like it had always been part of her.

Emma positioned herself on the bed, her hands braced on her pillow. Her face flamed. She could feel the heat rise from her neck as if her body were a sauna. The way she was exposed and displayed in this position not only did it for her but rendered her completely self-conscious at the same time. She was beginning to understand that a shot of nerves only served to make her even more aware of her body, more in tune with exactly what she was feeling, and heightened her anticipation.

Lauren ran a hand down her spine in one seamless motion, as if she were smoothing a line. She stopped with her palm flat against Emma's tailbone. "Rest on your forearms."

Emma stifled the automatic protest before it left her mouth. On her forearms would lower the top half of her body. It would, as Lauren had so casually put it, leave her ass in the air. Her embarrassment and awareness multiplied to infinity.

Lauren crouched down beside the bed where Emma could see her. "You want me? The real me?"

She nodded. Nothing she said could match the emotion in Lauren's eyes.

"Then do as I say so I can tie your hands to the headboard, as you so passionately requested. You'll get it all." Lauren held up the soft bathrobe tie she must've grabbed when she'd gotten the toy and harness. "But this is the last thing I do simply because you asked me. If you want more, you'll have to earn it. Forearms. Now."

Emma bit the inside of her cheek and lowered into position, bringing her wrists together in an offering. Lauren looped the tie around the headboard and wrapped it around Emma's wrists, taking her time fashioning a truly beautiful knot. It was so fancy Lauren had to have practiced. She'd tied this knot before, maybe dozens of times. But no other woman had received what Lauren gifted her. No one had the real, true, vulnerable Lauren. Vulnerability made sex meaningful, not friction, and definitely not experience. Lauren had taught her that.

"Are you comfortable?" Lauren asked matter-of-factly.

If embarrassed arousal and head-spinning responsiveness equaled comfortable, then Emma was kicked-back-in-a-La-Z-Boy, oh-so-comfy. "Yes."

Lauren ran her hand down Emma's spine again, her palm coasting over Emma's ass and between her legs. Shivers rained in her wake and tendrils of hot sensation fanned across Emma's skin.

"Please."

Lauren made a tsking sound. "You told me you were wet. I have to find out for myself before I fuck you."

Lauren brushed fingers across Emma's pussy in a caress so light she moaned before she was even sure she'd felt the touch.

"Please."

Lauren casually traced the crease of her ass with wet fingers, and quivers exploded through her. She willed herself not to squirm. Her head swam, consumed with the desire for Lauren to fuck her. She ached and throbbed. So, so hollow.

"Please."

"So pretty." Lauren teased her opening, swirling a single finger across her pussy. Stroking her with an insanely slow caress. "So wet for me."

She was going to burn alive, or shatter into a million shards, or simply melt into hot sticky arousal. "Please."

"Ask me to make you come," Lauren said.

"Please, make me come."

"Tell me how much you want me to fuck you. Tell me how filthy you really are, Emma."

Emma let out a breath and plowed ahead before she could think too hard. "I've been imagining you fucking me like this for days. I want you so bad I can't breathe."

The tip of Lauren's cock pressed against her. Lauren grasped her hips, ready to pump into her. Emma dropped her head onto her arms, and a string of nonsense begging escaped. Soon. Soon now. Lauren would slide into her, fill her, fuck her...all but pound into her until her orgasm flattened her like a bulldozer.

"Yes. Please. Please fuck me. I need you."

"I need you too." Lauren pushed inside her in one long and steady stroke. Smooth enough for Emma's body to adjust, but not a moment of hesitation. Emma clenched around her, and a strangled sound erupted from her lips. *Yes, yes, yes.* All other words eclipsed. Shamelessly, she thrust back. Her nerves, like soldiers under fire, bolted into action and took over. *Yes,* and *more,* and *please,* all twisting and twining in her mind.

"Fuck, Emma." The ragged sound of Lauren's breathing was more erotic than all manner of dirty talk. She traced a finger down the crease of Emma's ass again. "One day soon I want to take you here, fill you everywhere, show you just how good it can feel."

Just the *thought* of that had Emma clenching hard around Lauren's cock. "Oh God. I want to come. Please. I can't wait."

Lauren thrusted steadily and reached between Emma's thighs. The dual sensation of having her clit stroked while being fucked had Emma's orgasm boiling inside her, each stroke bringing her higher, each plunge almost toppling her into oblivion. God, she was so close, almost but not quite there.

Lauren palmed Emma's pussy, applying pressure without stroking her clit, and slowed her thrusts. "You're very quiet. What do you need? How do I give you pleasure so you come for me?"

Emma felt the tears on her cheeks before she realized she'd started to cry. God. Was there a worse possible time to begin bawling than when the woman you loved fucked you, and stroked you, and was so goddamn in tune with your experience, she knew the moment you couldn't quite let go?

Lauren wanted the responsibility for her pleasure, but dominant didn't mean she was afraid to ask Emma exactly what she needed. *No one* had *ever* asked her before. The sadness at what she'd always deserved but never had, the joy of finally being seen, having her pleasure *matter*, coalesced inside her until her heart almost burst. Crying was so annoying right now, but the churning emotion had to come out somehow. Apparently, crying and sex were her new double act.

Lauren stopped moving. "Emma, what is it?"

"I need to see you." Emma gasped the words around her tears, the request choked and throaty. "I thought I wanted this. I thought it would make it easier if I couldn't see you. But I need you to see me. Well, more of me than my ass, anyway. I need, just…more. Closer."

Lauren pulled out and had her hands untied almost before Emma finished speaking.

"I'm sorry," Emma mumbled, wiping at the tears that still ran down her cheeks. "I don't know where all this is coming from. Usually, I love it like that."

Lauren's smile was one Emma had never seen before, as if it started on the inside and the tilt of her lips was only the tip of an iceberg a billion feet deep. "You want me to watch you come."

Emma's laugh came out a bit watery. "That sounds narcissistic."

Lauren kissed the tip of her nose. "Nope. It's being real."

Real. Present. Vulnerable. That was the *more* Emma needed. The more that, before Lauren, had always felt like too much.

"I don't want to close my eyes and turn away anymore," Emma said shyly. "I don't want to hide. I want you to see me."

There was a shine in Lauren's eyes that just might've been tears as she leaned down to kiss her. "You're beautiful and brave and I'm going to make you come so hard."

"Yes, please." Emma parted her thighs for Lauren to slide between them, so wet and ready she ached to be filled.

When Lauren slid inside her again, she arched up to meet her. Lauren cradled her hips and fit their bodies together, fucking her in long, endless thrusts. Emma's brain handed over control to her body. Passion swept like a forest fire across her skin. *Finally.* The war inside her ceased, the give and take of her mind, her body, her heart, all in perfect alignment and absolute agreement that she was going to come with Lauren above her, inside her, declaring her passion. Just exactly right.

"Please. You feel so good."

"You're so beautiful like this." Lauren's voice held awe and arousal as she reached between them and circled Emma's clit. "You're so sexy. So sweet. So needy and hot and crazy for me, aren't you? Do you even know how powerful you make me feel? When I am with you, inside you, stroking you, I'm a superhero."

Emma heard Lauren's words through the cloud of insane excitement that clung to her. God, she was going to come. She had to come. She'd fucking die if she had to endure Lauren's slow, deep thrusts and her fingers circling and pressing on her clit forever. Lauren's control wasn't just about calling the shots, but the unendingly slow and patient way she buried herself inside Emma, and the way her caress so completely forced Emma to the brink and then eased her away from the edge—leaving her hanging suspended in desire, slowly losing her mind—over and over again.

"If I dub you Mistress Orgasm will you let me come?" Emma asked.

Lauren groaned above her. "I'd better, with a superhero name like that."

Lauren thrust just a little harder, her fingers circling Emma's clit and finding all the places that made her clench. Teasing her, torturing her, as her orgasm built to unprecedented heights.

Emma stared unflinchingly into Lauren's eyes, fierce with power. Face-to-face, heartbeat-to-heartbeat, Lauren's cock driving both of them mad.

"I want to come inside you." Lauren ground out the words through clenched teeth.

Emma moaned. "Can you? God. Fuck, yes. Come inside me."

"Don't come yet," Lauren warned her, angling her hips. The cock hitting a spot inside her that made her eyes roll back in her head.

"Too late. I can't stop. Please."

"You can." Lauren ground out the words like she was using every ounce of willpower to prevent her own orgasm. "Look at me. Hold on for me. Remember this, Emma. This moment right now, this is me. Over you, on top of you, controlling your pleasure, making you wait just because I can. It's all me. It's us."

Emma's body was a taut live wire sparking electricity. She held Lauren's gaze and saw all the way inside. Past all her defenses, past the facade she'd created to keep herself safe, past everything, to her heart. Strong and steady and impossible to contain. "Please. Let me come."

That last desperate *please* must have done it. Lauren made a strangled sound.

"*Now.* Come."

"I love you," Emma gasped, right before everything inside her lit up and split apart. If there was a graph for measuring orgasms, the one that plowed through her would've been off the charts. She was spinning and flying, stiffening and convulsing, coming and coming and coming. She could hear Lauren above her, crying out her own release, throaty and passionate, raw, and best of all, absolutely, unequivocally *real.* Pleasure swept them away.

Emma would never have considered describing sex as making love. The idea was laughable. Candlelight, rose petals, and soft dreamy touches were so totally not her idea of a good time. The kind of sex she had with Lauren was definitely fucking, and unequivocally her thing. But it was also how they made love. Not the fantasy ideal some wanted, but perfectly, and romantically, them.

She had to beg Lauren to stop thrusting, her pussy clenching and her heart a jackhammer in her chest.

Stop and don't stop.
Pull out and never leave.
So close and not close enough.
More. Just, more.

Lauren eased out, pressing her palm against Emma's pussy when Emma moaned in protest.

"Shh. I've got you. I'm here. Let me take this off."

Emma closed her eyes and sank into muscle deep lethargy that was holding all her limbs captive. God. She wasn't going to be able to move for a month. "We might've killed each other."

Lauren settled next to her, pulled the sheet over them, and gathered Emma into her arms. "If this is heaven, God gave me a really good deal. You're so incredible. I don't even have words for all the incredible. Thank you for letting me see you."

It took a mammoth effort, but Emma managed to lever herself up on an elbow to look at Lauren. "Thank you for seeing me. No one has ever looked at me the way you do."

She hadn't really expected Lauren to say it. Part of her already knew Lauren wasn't going to, but her heart still took a punch to the solar plexus when Lauren pulled her in for a kiss in lieu of the, "I love you too," Lauren had to know she wanted.

Vulnerability had to go both ways, inside and outside the bedroom. Emma needed Lauren, and just as fiercely, she needed Lauren to need her.

She was going to need her own damn superpowers to save love.

Chapter Nineteen

Lauren pulled the SUV up outside Fishes and Loaves. She and Roxie jumped out and began hauling what seemed like two hundred dozen duck eggs from the trunk.

"Your mom is nuts." Roxie wiped her hands on her jeans and ran her fingers through her hair like she'd just run a marathon instead of standing back and letting Lauren do most of the work.

"She likes ducks." Lauren shrugged. The way people kept farm animals as pets was just one item on the laundry list of things she didn't get about Sunrise Falls. Thank God the town had an ordinance against roosters, or she'd be waking up to cock-a-doodle-doos at the crack of every annoying dawn. She wouldn't put it past her mom to try to sneak one by the Cupcake all the same.

Roxie grunted as she lifted a box like it weighed a million pounds. "It's weird to like ducks. Kittens? Totally get it. Puppies? The more the merrier. But ducks? What redeeming value do ducks have beyond the admittedly adorable duckling stage? If she wants pets, there are cute options."

"Eggs." Lauren slammed the hatchback closed and stacked the last box on the sidewalk.

"Eggs she doesn't even eat," Roxie said grumpily. "She must feed half the town with these. We're all going to die of cholesterol overdose."

"If I'm going to die from high cholesterol, it'd better be from ice cream and not eggs." Lauren piled two boxes into her arms and picked her way across the icy sidewalk to Fishes and Loaves' front doors. The ducks made no more sense to her than they did to Roxie, but her mom had dug a pond in the backyard just so they'd have a place to swim, and her face lit up whenever she caught one of their feathered butts waddling past the kitchen window, quacking up a storm.

Weird was accurate, but sometimes it took a bit of weird to make you happy.

On the second trip, she spotted Emma coming down the street. She almost called out, almost ran up to her like an overexcited chipmunk, she was so damn happy to see her. Pretty ridiculous. It'd only been a couple of hours since she'd dragged herself away to help her mom run errands, but hours felt like years when Emma was the bit of weird that made her happy.

Only Emma was with people. Jasper Wallings, cornerstone of the council; the Cupcake aka Brenda Baker, resident gossip and ass-pain; and another man Lauren didn't recognize and guessed must be relatively new to the council. Better rein in her chipmunk impulse. The last thing any of them would want was her bouncing over all smiles and enthusiasm. She ducked around the SUV so she wouldn't put Emma in an awkward situation, and the group walked into the council building two doors down from Fishes and Loaves.

When she came back around the car, Roxie was standing on the sidewalk, her hands planted on her hips and a what-the-fuck-was-that expression on her face. "Did you just *hide*?"

Lauren considered her options. Outright denying it probably wouldn't get her anywhere. Telling the truth would either earn her a lecture in how she should've had the guts to face the council or incite an interrogation into exactly what was happening between her and Emma. She went with the only choice she had. "Leave it, Rox."

Roxie didn't so much as slow down. "Seriously? You just hid behind your car like a douchebag rather than talk to Emma. I know things have been rocky, but hiding is a new low."

Lauren rolled her eyes. "I wasn't hiding from her. Things with Emma are good."

Better than good. Amazing. Superlative. Incredible.

"I was hiding from the council. We have to be careful. You know that plenty of people in this town won't like that Emma and I are together. I didn't want to make things awkward for her, that's all."

Roxie narrowed her eyes. "Wait. You're together? Like, *together*, together? Why am I the last person to hear about this?"

"Actually, you're the first, aside from Emma and Mom. It's just new and complicated. She lives here, on the hellmouth, in the center of my private run-away-as-fast-as-you-can horror movie set."

"And she can't leave because of the deal she made with the council," Roxie mused.

Really? Everyone but her had known about this deal? That was the way Sunrise Falls worked. If you wanted privacy, you didn't stay. And if you left, you were cut off like the illegitimate heir.

"So, you're staying here to date Emma?" Roxie looked pleadingly at the last box like she was hoping it would grow legs and walk itself inside.

"That's the plan." Lauren was grateful Roxie wasn't going to push her on how she and Emma ended up *together*, together. *I showed her what it meant to surrender by engaging in a consensual non-consent fantasy, and then she said I made her miserable while she went down on me.* There wasn't enough context in the world for all of that to make sense to anyone but them.

Lauren figured Roxie wasn't actually going to pick up that last box, so she hefted it and Roxie trailed behind her, chattering away.

"I'm *beyond* thrilled that you're staying, but maybe hiding from Emma isn't super smart if you're dating? What are you going to do? Develop agoraphobia and never leave the house so you don't run into someone who might disapprove?"

"If the house has a bed, and Emma's definitely does, that's not a bad plan." She deposited the last box with Doris Cranton, a woman with a face that resembled a stern headmistress, and a uncompromising demeanor that had always freaked her out. She skedaddled before she was forced to make actual conversation.

Her mom could've sold the eggs, not given them to the food pantry. She'd have made a mint at the farmers markets in Saratoga. But she donated them as a way of giving back. Fishes and Loaves had kept them alive once upon a time, and Stern-Faced-Cranton never missed an opportunity to remind her with those steely eyes.

They slid back into the car, but Roxie put a hand on her arm before she could turn the key in the ignition. "*Some* people are gossipy old hens who judge others to deflect attention from their own lives and problems. But not everyone hates you. If you're going to stay, you're going to have to grow some balls."

Lauren closed her eyes and rested her head against the seat. "I don't want balls."

"Lady balls," Roxie said, mock seriously. "It's where you keep your pride and all the sticky stuff that makes family."

Roxie had a way with metaphors that was funny bordering on so-completely-wrong, but she understood what Roxie was saying. If she was going to stay, she'd need to find the courage, *the balls*, to live her life, to perhaps build her family, without resorting to hiding behind her car. Hearing Roxie say it was surprisingly unsurprising. Lauren had known the second she'd agreed to stay, she just hadn't wanted to think about it.

"I need to talk to Emma first. This affects her. I can't just go advertising our relationship when she's the one who'll catch flak for it. Mom told me this morning there are already whispers about us."

"So?" Roxie launched the word like an arrow pointed directly at Lauren. "Who cares if people who you don't like gossip? You've got nothing to lose and everything to gain."

Lauren barely resisted the urge to yank her hair out of her head. "It's not about me. It's about what Emma will lose. She'll be gossiped about. People will be mean to her. Emma has history with this town and good memories. I don't want to be the reason that gets fucked up."

Roxie nailed her with a stare to rival Cranton's and launched another arrow. "Gee, Emma's a bit of a damp doormat then, isn't she? If she's going to run and hide, if she's going to let the town decide who she can date, you'd be better off without her. She's not worth your time if she doesn't want to be seen with you in public. You'd better ditch her immediately."

"Hey! That's completely unfair. Emma isn't like that at all." Roxie had gone too far. Best friend rules meant she could get away with a lot more than Lauren would take from anyone else. Roxie routinely toed that line, but too far was too far. "If it wasn't so cold, I'd make you walk home. Apologize."

Roxie held her stare. "I'm sorry for all the things I just said about you, even though they're true."

Lauren shook her head. "You said them about Emma. Talking about Emma like that is unacceptable."

"I agree," Roxie said softly, "so maybe you should stop blaming her for your own issues."

"I wasn't—"

"Yeah, you were."

Lauren rubbed a hand across her face. "I don't want to be the reason things change for her. I know you think it's only some people who judge, but it's everyone. You just don't see it like I do. I can't even donate to the food bank without a judgment day glare."

Roxie laughed. "Dorrie Cranton isn't judging you. She loves your mom. They have tea once a week, and she always asks after you."

Lauren blinked. "She does?"

"I'm not up on the social lives of the mom-contingent, but yeah, that's what I've heard. Whatever you think you saw, you're wrong."

"But she was glaring."

"Well," Roxie said, in an overly patient tone, "you didn't even say hello. Dorrie is old school. You have to make the first move, or she thinks she's being snubbed."

Huh. Not *everyone* in Sunrise Falls hated her. What a novel concept. Maybe not everyone was judging her, but she had sure judged them. She'd written off the entire town because of people like the Cupcake and Jessica Norman. Because judging everyone who might conceivably judge her back was safer than sorting the good from the bad and possibly getting it wrong. *Hello, trusty defense mechanism, so good to see you again.*

"I've been a dick, haven't I?" Lauren asked wearily.

"Uh-huh." Roxie grinned. "Now, if you had some balls to go with your dick, you could really create a stir."

Lauren snorted. "Stop, please. Emma would be really pissed that I just hid behind the car to avoid her."

"Yup." Roxie made it sound like Lauren had just discovered two plus two equals four.

"I thought I was doing the right thing by not creating a scene, but she doesn't need me to hide. She can handle herself. Actually, she's doing a lot better job of handling herself than I am."

"She needs what we all need," Roxie said, "someone who will stand with us through a storm. If you want to be together, you'll have to face this together."

"Why are you right? It's so annoying when you're right, and I'm not."

"I have to tell you something." Roxie placed a hand on her arm again when Lauren moved to start the car.

"Uh-oh. No good news in the history of forever has ever followed that phrase."

"I know why Emma is with Archie and Brenda and Jasper. I think you need to know, too."

"Isn't she working? The council controls the funding for the library, right?" Lauren asked.

"Yes, but…" Roxie hesitated. "Don't go away on me, okay?"

"*Okaay.*" A sick feeling took up residence in the hollow of Lauren's throat.

"The council is denying funding for a program Emma wants for the library. I don't know the details. I heard it secondhand off Doug. Something about e-books and circulation."

"That's a bummer, but surely they vote on this kind of thing all the time."

"They're saying no because of you." Roxie waved a hand in the air. "I mean, not *you*, but they think Emma is engaging in some risqué S and M stuff with you, and they're unhappy about that, and sending a message. That's what Doug thinks."

A strange buzzing started in her ears and spread through her head. At first, Lauren thought there must be something wrong with the car, but then her palms began to tingle, and her heart started thumping in her ears. She was…angry. It took a second to find the word, she was so used to blocking off emotion, but angry was definitely it. "They're making work difficult for her because of what they think we do in bed?"

Roxie nodded. "Not that I'm defending them or anything, but it's not exactly an unsubstantiated claim. Emma said it herself."

"What?" None of this made any sense.

"At the Christmas parade when she told Jess Norman you'd whipped her and that she should try it. That's what started it, and, well, the story just grew from there. Sami from next door told me the moms at the Tuesday morning K through Three Ravenous Readers group are planning to boycott the library."

Lauren was stunned. No. Stunned wasn't close enough. She was *rigor mortis* stiff. Dead from shock. "Roxie, you were *there*. Emma made an offhand comment, a joke. She was defending me. Was it a good idea? No, and I told her so. But also, so the fuck what if she's pro-kink? She should have her programs denied? Moms should refuse to allow their kids to use the library?"

"These things get twisted and blown up way out of proportion, and Jessica was pissed. So that's the way it looks, yeah. Jessica has a lot of power."

Lauren wanted to scream. She settled for squeezing the wheel hard until her knuckles turned white and her fingers began to ache. "It isn't fair. It's none of their business and the whipping comment wasn't true. Not that it should make a difference if it was, but it wasn't."

"It's not about truth, it's about perception. Who knows that better than you?" Roxie's smile was entirely humorless.

"She was standing up for me," Lauren said quietly, "and it might cost her her job. Right now, it's one program, it's one group, but if we start dating…"

The wince was all over Roxie's face. "There's at least a chance that things could go south for her if you're open about kink."

Lauren stared straight ahead down Main Street. The festively decorated shop windows and recently shoveled sidewalks were picturesque. Newly fallen snow, crisp, bright, and yet to turn gray and slushy. Tinsel still strung along power lines. The overt cheerfulness made the scene camera-ready for a Hallmark movie. So cutesy her teeth hurt. There was nothing cute about discrimination. Judgment wasn't cute. Using power and authority and money to force Emma to conform wasn't fucking cute. Lauren felt every ounce of rage she somehow couldn't seem to stop. Being with Emma, opening up to her, showing her who she was, had ruined her filter for good. Now every emotion was amplified and coming at her full force.

How could this be happening all over again? Everything that mattered to her being systematically dismantled by this town.

No. Hold up. Not the *town*, not everyone, just a few people who seemed to hold all the power.

Unfortunately, the most painful emotion, the one on the top of the pile, was hurt. Emma's future was in jeopardy, and Lauren knew she shouldn't be making it all about her, but it just plain *hurt* that Emma hadn't told her. Hadn't so much as mentioned any trouble. Why? Weren't they supposed to trust each other? Wasn't that what being in a relationship was all about? She could've been there to support her. They could've worked it out together.

Did Emma really mean it when she'd said, "I love you"?

"I can't believe Emma didn't tell me."

"I know it probably feels like she kept it from you on purpose, but you don't exactly make it easy," Roxie said.

"What does that mean?" Lauren snapped. She wished she could switch off again. Wished for every barrier imaginable to stand between her and her feelings right now, but there wasn't anything left to defend herself with. Emma's sweetness and bravery and mind-blowing strength had reduced her walls to rubble at her feet just when she most needed them to protect herself. Sometimes being all emotionally evolved completely sucked.

"You don't stand up for yourself," Roxie said in her usual, no-mincing-words way. "Why would Emma trust you to stand up for her? I expect she thought you'd push her away in some truly idiotic attempt to protect her. That sounds like you."

Lauren's laugh was bitter. "You don't think very highly of me, do you?"

Roxie pulled her in for an awkward hug across the car console. "I love you more than you love yourself. I know what you went through, and I know that kind of thing sticks. But I also know you can't blame your past forever. At some point, you have to take responsibility. You don't like yourself, and that's a real shame, because you're awesome and Emma needs all the awesome she can get right now."

Lauren wanted to be mad. She wanted to blame Emma for keeping her in the dark, and she wanted to rail about how unfair that was. But Roxie's words wouldn't stop repeating themselves in her head. *I expect she thought you'd push her away in some truly idiotic attempt to protect her. That sounds like you.*

Well, yeah. That's exactly what she would've done.

Having her actions called out before she'd even had a chance to make them wasn't exactly comfortable. She'd been more than a dick. Her past and her prejudices made it hard for Emma to trust her not to run if there was trouble. And she *might've* walked away, even if it'd ripped her heart out of her chest.

Is it so bad to want you?

I want the real you.

Am I the only one who has to be vulnerable?

Lauren ground her palm into her forehead like she could squish Emma's voice. But denying the truth was impossible when the truth was everything she'd always hoped for. "God. I've been an idiot. She loves me. She was trying to protect us from *me* and my idiot-ness."

Roxie punched her in the shoulder like they were bros in the locker room. "Obviously."

Lauren handed her keys to Roxie. "I have to go. Can you drive yourself home?"

"Sure. Where are you going?"

Lauren jumped out of the car. "To crash that meeting. To do what I should've done days ago. Emma is the best damn thing that's ever happened to Sunrise Falls. If they don't know that, they don't deserve her."

Emma was the best damn thing to ever happen to *her,* too.

Time for some lady balls.

Chapter Twenty

We simply cannot afford the expenditure. Thirty-five percent of circulation is picture books and young reader chapter books. Surely, kiddos won't be in on these newfangled e-book whatsits." Archie Franklin laughed at his own joke, the sound booming off the walls in the otherwise silent room.

Emma smiled politely. She got points for not immediately pointing out that e-books had been around longer than those kiddos. "Not currently, but young people are tech savvy and trends show that they're going to the internet for media. YouTube is increasingly popular with consumers over seven. I'd like to be able to offer an alternative to cat videos and music clips. The intra-library app would allow borrowers to select and download books right to their device. Some books contain interactive components and enhanced learning opportunities. We'll be able to work *with* the internet rather than against it, and compete for attention in the digital economy."

The Cupcake waved a hand in the air as if Emma's words were flies buzzing around her head. "I hardly think literature is in the same category as YouTube. Besides, old-fashioned ways and values aren't so out of style. Print books are gaining back market share."

What would the Cupcake say if she started weighing in on all the decisions the council made? She could figure out which roads needed repaving, and which buildings ought to be historic by eeny, meeny, miny, moeing the whole thing, if doing someone else's job was that easy. "Print is gaining, but it's a small amount compared to the seventy percent it's lost to e-books over the last ten years. We need this or the library will become obsolete."

Archie raised bushy eyebrows. "Library membership is primarily comprised of seniors and young mothers, all of whom prefer print books according to your last survey. Surely you're not suggesting that library patrons are wrong about what they want?"

She took a breath. It wasn't a bad point, and part of her job was to explain so the council understood. She wasn't usually so snappy, but the subtext around why they were denying her proposal, the elephant in the room that everyone was far too diplomatic to address, grated. She wanted to bring it up and force them to admit it, but she had no proof, and listening to them deny, deny, deny would just embarrass everyone. "Children under seven and seniors do prefer print books, but kids grow up. They're the readers of tomorrow. I'd like to encourage lifetime use of the library. E-books would increase adult membership and circulation."

"No." Jasper Wallings spoke up from his spot on the antique loveseat by the fireplace. "We didn't ask you here to debate with you. We're telling you, it's a no. You ought to focus your attention on the patrons the library currently has. I know Misty Granger would like a meeting regarding the Ravenous Readers group sooner rather than later."

"What—" Emma halted when the door to Archie's office swung open.

Lauren stood framed in the doorway looking about as innocent as the Cheshire Cat. "Oops. Sorry. I was trying to find the county clerk's office. Gotta pay those taxes."

She held nothing that resembled a payment, and the coincidence was just a bit too coincidental to be guileless. Emma's heart dropped out of her body and all the way to the basement of the building. What was Lauren doing here? The timing could not be worse.

Archie stood and peered at Lauren over his glasses. "The county clerk's office hasn't been in this building for more than a decade."

Lauren smiled charmingly. "I haven't been in this building for more than a decade, so I didn't know that." Rather than leaving, she walked right up to Archie's desk and stuck out her hand. "I don't think we've met. I'm Lauren West. I grew up here, but left town after high school."

Archie took her hand. "I'm aware. Principal Scarty and I play poker on Thursday evenings. He remembers you well. I'm Archie Franklin, chairman of the town council."

Lauren laughed. "Tell me good ol' Scarty is still teaching."

"He retired three years ago, having had quite enough of troublemakers."

Emma could only watch. Whatever Lauren was doing, she must have a plan. Mustn't she? Lauren seemed unperturbed that Archie, good-naturedly or not, had called her trouble. That was new—all the smiling and laughing and walking in on town council meetings and staying to make small talk. How could she be so at ease, the tension that usually bunched her shoulders noticeably absent, when Emma was so nervous she was half afraid she'd jump out of her own skin? What on earth was Lauren doing?

The Cupcake was having none of it. "You're interrupting a meeting, Miss West. Some of us have jobs to be getting on with." *Others of us don't have jobs at all.*

Lauren didn't even glance at the Cupcake. She gave Archie a help-a-girl-out look. "Would you mind if I took up two minutes of your time? I have something to say to Emma that isn't relevant to your meeting, but I've screwed up and it can't wait."

Archie seemed amused by the unexpected interruption and swept his arm to encompass the room as if it were a stage and Lauren was about to perform. "By all means."

The Cupcake harrumphed and folded her arms.

Lauren faced her, and the devil-may-care smile faded away. But there was a devilish glint in her eyes that had Emma's heart pounding.

Emma said, "Maybe we should talk later? We *are* in the middle of a meeting."

One Lauren had barged into on purpose for reasons unknown. What was she *doing* here?

"I got lost on purpose so the council could hear what I have to say."

Obviously. But why?

Lauren held her gaze in a connection that, as usual, turned her insides upside down. The truth hit her. Lauren knew exactly what this meeting was about. Bile rose in her throat. Was Lauren here to defend her? To defend herself? Emma couldn't blame her if she was, but there was no way the council would ever admit their reasons, and confronting them might make things worse. Plus, there was the tiny fact that she hadn't told Lauren what was going on.

Sorry. Really, really, sorry. But could you go away?

She tried to communicate with her eyes that Lauren should shut up and leave, but was pretty sure it looked as if she had a facial twitch. In any case, Lauren didn't catch on to her novice attempts at ESP.

Lauren knelt by her chair.

The air froze as if it too were waiting in anticipation for Lauren to speak. It wasn't a will-you-marry-me kneel, but when Lauren dropped to her knees and took her hand, squeezing hard, she felt herself flush.

Now is a really bad time to be thinking about kneeling in front of Lauren last night, begging her to touch you, you total pervert.

Heat flashed in Lauren's eyes, her smile hot enough to rival the sun that shone outside the window. She knew exactly what Emma was thinking. Lauren had reversed their positions on purpose. But why? More importantly, why *now*?

"I only have two minutes, so I'll get to the point. I love you, Emma. I'm sorry I didn't say it before."

Air that had frozen gained mass in an instant and crashed down on her, making it hard to think. "What?"

Lauren's eyes never left hers, her expression as exposed as she'd ever seen it. Vulnerable. Edgy. Entirely, undeniably, strikingly bare. Emma's breath caught. She was so used to Lauren withdrawing and shutting down when it came to anything of the heart. But she'd cast aside her walls and facades. There were no barriers. Not with her, or with the council.

Lauren's eyes shone, but worry creased around them. "I love you so much. Please say it back or I'll succumb to a broken heart, weeping from my gothic castle like Rochester or, you know, whatever. I want a life with you. I want you to be my forever."

"Lauren."

"I'm sorry I was a complete jackass and you felt you couldn't tell me about this meeting."

I want you to be my forever.

Emma pictured it. Sunshine filled days of love and laughter. Intense nights under Lauren's commanding touch.

She should probably be more concerned that it'd taken Lauren until now to say the words. She should harbor some doubts about how they'd handle their respective pasts and what it all meant for the future. But right this second, she couldn't muster any worry. Happiness filled her, spreading from their linked fingers and washing through her until she was sure it would overflow and drown them.

"I love you, too, but it's time you read *Jane Eyre* so you never massacre it quite that badly ever again."

Lauren grinned so wide her face looked as if it would crack down the middle. "Is there a version with two queers in love?"

Emma swallowed hard around the lump that was doing its best to cut off her air supply.

"We'll have to write our own kinky version."

She hadn't predicted kink to be an *us* thing. Kink was Lauren's thing, and she'd never expected, or wanted, her to stay in the closet. Only, kink wasn't just Lauren's thing anymore. Kink was her thing. Their thing. An Emma thing, too. She still didn't think it was anyone else's business, but if she was going to lose her job, she'd lose it because some folks in town weren't comfortable with *her.*

Lauren had said I love you and Emma had outed them as kinky to the council in no uncertain terms. No more running, or hiding, or silence. They *were* kinky queers in love, damnit, and whatever happened next, they'd have each other.

"God. I love you so crazy much. Why did I have to say it here where I can't kiss you?" Lauren glanced mournfully around the room, making Emma laugh again.

"Are you sure? We don't have to stay if you're unhappy. We can move." The council may as well know that she'd rather go to the ends of the earth to pay back her loan than force Lauren to stay where she wasn't wanted. Where *they* weren't wanted.

Lauren tilted her head to the side and smiled. "You're my happiness. I've had an empty place in my heart for too many years, and nothing to fill it with but bitterness. But loving you leaves no room for resentment, and certainly no room for the opinions of other people."

"God. I love you." She launched herself at Lauren, wrapping her arms around her and holding on as emotion swept her away. *I love you, I love you, I love you.*

She felt as if she'd waited a million years for Lauren to say it back, confessed in just that tone, filled with a certainty that settled into her bones. In the back of her mind, in a dark and dusty alcove she'd refused to fully acknowledge, she'd already known Lauren loved her. The way Lauren touched her, the passion of her caress, said what Lauren couldn't admit with words. Lauren had used sex and touch and desire to show her how she felt.

Lauren's world was touch, but Emma's world was made of words, and she'd needed them. Needed this moment. Lauren declaring her love, Lauren stripping off her mask, Lauren standing for her and what they both wanted by getting on her knees.

Emma needed all of Lauren, exactly as she was, wrapped in those three little words that magicked open her heart.

Lauren grabbed her around the waist and spun her in a circle, careless of the furniture they were about to bump into or the three pairs of eyes watching. She had come to claim her. She loved her. She'd crashed a freaking council meeting to tell her. Emma kissed her, proving to herself that this was really happening and not some school-girl dream.

Lauren loved her.

Lauren *loved* her.

Lauren—

Jasper cleared his throat. "That's quite enough of that. Now that you've made your spectacle, please go. We have work to do."

Lauren set her down but didn't let go of her hand. She turned to Archie. "I want to apologize if the rumors about Emma and me have caused confusion. What happens between two consenting adults in their bedroom isn't a public matter, and going forward we'll be more discreet. We understand the library services children, and such topics are inappropriate for kids."

The Cupcake looked as if she might explode, but Archie shushed her before she could erupt. He leaned back in his chair and considered Lauren. "The Christmas parade was a poor choice for such a conversation."

"I'm sor—" Emma began, but Lauren squeezed her hand.

"With all due respect, we were speaking in a group of adults, and Jessica Norman brought up kink. To my knowledge, no one heard that conversation but us." She smiled sardonically. "Well, and all the people Jessica relayed the conversation to. We will absolutely be more selective in who we share our personal information with, Mr. Franklin, but the only reason anyone knows is because Jessica told them."

"Everyone knows you're a walking scandal just like your mother," the Cupcake hissed like a snake releasing venom.

For the first time, Lauren glanced at her. She shrugged. "Fake news, and old news at that. Try not to let it bother you."

She turned back to Archie. "Does that clear up any lingering confusion?"

It took everything Emma had not to laugh. *Confusion* was such a useful word for prejudice. The council wasn't judgmental or stuck in its ways. It was a misunderstanding, and all Jessica's fault, really.

Silence hung in the air, broken only by the Cupcake's increasingly agitated sighs.

Finally, Archie stood up and walked around his desk. "Emma, you'll agree to make the library a welcoming environment for everyone, including children," he paused, a twinkle lighting his eyes, "and us non-kinky, non-queers?"

She didn't know whether to groan or giggle. "I promise. Lauren's right, we made a bad choice in whom we confided in. As far as I'm concerned, our personal life has nothing to do with my job, and the library won't be impacted."

"Well, then—"

"Wait one damn minute!" The Cupcake jumped to her feet. "You can't possibly be considering allowing this...this...*situation* to continue, Archie. The reputation of Sunrise Falls—"

"Is one that welcomes people from all walks of life." Archie leveled her with a stare.

Lauren said, "I hope it does. That'd make a nice change."

She looked about to say more, but Emma squeezed her hand this time. "Let me."

She squared her shoulders and looked Archie directly in the eyes. *Here goes nothing.* "I want to be clear that while we will agree to keep any conversation regarding sex of any kind age-appropriate, and I will maintain professionalism in my role as librarian, neither of us will hide, deny, or otherwise be silent about the fact that we're gay and kinky."

"Sexual matters ought to remain private." There was so much stiffness in Jasper's words, they could've up and walked themselves over to her.

She bit her lip. Jasper was an institution in Sunrise Falls, a war veteran, and tough as nails. He'd been on the council longer than she'd been alive, but he'd always been fair. She counted on that now. She crossed the room and put a hand on his shoulder. "You have my word we'll be discreet and appropriate. But I won't agree to keep it a secret. For some, kink is an identity as much as gay or trans or Christian. Yes, it's about sex. But it's also an expression of who we are as individuals. It's likely we aren't the only ones, and I'd like to be honest about it so Sunrise Falls can *really* be a place that's welcoming to everyone. Even people who don't fit in anywhere else."

Jasper's flint blue eyes bored into her, his mouth thinning into a straight line. She was sure he was about to tell her to go to hell and take her job with her.

"Please." Emma gave it one last try. "Don't ask me to live in shame. Don't ask anyone who might be a non-something feel as if they're the only ones, and they can't have a home here."

Slowly, Jasper nodded. He glanced at Archie. "I like you, Emma. You have pizazz. You've served this town well for years, and you deserve a chance. This is it, young lady. Let's make Sunrise Falls a town we can all be proud of."

As she had done only minutes earlier, Archie smiled and stuck out a hand to Lauren. "Welcome home. I hope you both decide to stay."

Emma ran to hug Lauren, laughing and so very, very in love. She wasn't going to lose her job. They were welcome to stay. The council wouldn't expect them to live in shame or judgment. Their future was an adventure she couldn't wait to start exploring. They'd done it!

It wasn't until they'd all turned to leave, that she realized sometime in the last ten minutes the Cupcake had left the room, and no one had noticed.

CHAPTER TWENTY-ONE

S o, wait, you waltzed in there, told Emma you loved her, came out as kinky, and Archie said *welcome home*? No fucking way." Roxie's mouth gaped comically.

Lauren grinned and kicked back in her chair. New Year's Eve celebrations were in full swing, and Grumpy's was the place to be. Almost every table occupied, and the noise level on par with a rock concert. Most of the noise centered around the TV over the bar. A dozen guys had their eyes glued to the screen and their fingers wrapped around sweating bottles of Bud Light, as if the game replay were the Second Coming and Jesus was the quarterback.

She watched Emma maneuver her way through the crowd, balancing their next round of drinks. Emma caught her looking, and her smile lit up the world. Well, it sure lit up Lauren.

Everything about her from the top of her head with its glorious dark hair falling in messy waves around her shoulders, to the tips of her knee-high leather boots, was insanely sexy. Emma had a knack for dressing sexy, even in the most inclement weather. And what was underneath all those clothes was even hotter.

But the best part? Emma was all hers. Her forever. Her surrender.

She waited for Emma to put their drinks down, and then tucked two fingers into the belt loop on her jeans and toppled

Emma into her lap, just because she could. "Yes, fucking way. My girl has *pizazz*."

Emma laughed. "It's actually not much of an exaggeration." She cupped Lauren's cheek and planted a smacking kiss on her lips. "My hero."

Roxie threw a balled up napkin at them. "Get a room."

"Oh, we plan to. We have a whole house of them and all the time in the world."

My forever and ever and ever.

Lauren kissed Emma again, prompting Roxie to cover her eyes. She peaked through her fingers to see if they were done. "You guys are real sweet, all disgustingly in love, but give a poor single girl a break already, would you?"

Lauren did her best friend duty and let Emma slide into her own chair. "Sorry, Rox. We can't help ourselves. We'll try to keep it PG."

"Although, we don't *have* to keep it PG, if say, someone is curious about kink, or a teen needs to talk about coming out as queer. We're out, and proud, and as in love as Jane and Rochester." Emma picked up her drink and took a delicate sip, smiling at Roxie's over-the-top expression.

"If I didn't trust the both of you, I'd swear you were lying. I *cannot* believe old Jaspy said you could be open about the kink thing."

"Discreet and appropriate." Lauren grinned. "But open."

Roxie toasted her. "You haven't done too bad for a homewrecking slutface. You should listen to me more often, especially when I dare you to sleep with the woman of your dreams."

"That dare was a *terrible* idea," Emma said. "I almost didn't forgive her. No more dares."

"None? That would be a shame," Lauren said.

No more going to bars to pick up women. Unless Emma was there, too. Maybe. Hell, no maybe about it. She had methods of convincing her that were more effective than any interrogation technique the CIA could come up with. Emma would enjoy being persuaded. One day they'd make it to Kink's and then…

Before her mind could wander too far down that inappropriate-for-a-public-venue avenue of imagination, a menu airplane hit Emma on the cheek.

"Gross, gross, gross," Roxie said.

Lauren laughed. "We could play truth or dare right now." There were so many things she wanted to see if Emma would dare to do. So many daring possibilities to explore together. "I dare you to—"

"Whoa!"

Roxie's next airplane menu missed Lauren and hit someone behind her. She turned around to find Ashton Kutcher standing awkwardly by their table.

"God. *Sorry*," Roxie said like she'd just hurled a brick at him instead of a paper menu. "Are you okay?"

"I dare you to kiss him better," Lauren murmured, covering her comment by sipping her drink.

"I'm fine, but your aerodynamics are terrible." He scooped the airplane off the floor. "If you fold the wings like this, it will have more forward momentum. Though, obviously, cardboard is better. This paper is too soft to hold the shape for long."

Emma grinned, her lips twitching in a way that said she was trying not to laugh.

Ashton the aviation geek was pretty adorable.

Roxie was going to eat him alive.

He placed the now wilting airplane in the center of their table and smiled at Roxie, who blushed. Then executed a superlative hair toss.

He said, "Would you like to dance? I didn't catch your name last time. I'm Patrick."

"That memorable, am I?" Roxie quipped, getting to her feet so fast she almost knocked over their table.

"I hope I find out." Patrick took her hand and led her to the dance floor.

Emma tipped her head to watch them walk away. "Oh my God, he is so *cute*. She's not going to be single for long."

"But who is that guy? Is he good enough for her? What are his intentions?" Lauren slung an arm around the back of Emma's chair and caught a lock of her hair, twining it around her fingers.

"I hope his intentions are very, very dirty. It's the nerds you have to watch out for. They're always the ones with the filthy imaginations."

"I have personal experience to validate your claim. Nerds are definitely sexy, especially in stockings and knee-high boots."

"Stop that." Emma laughed when Lauren tried to tug her back into her lap.

Without Emma to distract her, Lauren frowned at who-the-hell-was-Patrick-anyway?

"Best friends have sex too, you know. Roxie deserves some fun, and Pat's a good guy."

Lauren sighed. "I suppose I'm going to have to start meeting and, God forbid, hanging out, with people in town."

Emma linked their fingers together and leaned in for a kiss. "You are. Starting with the New Year's Day 5K tomorrow. I signed us up last night."

"Running?" Lauren stared. She couldn't have heard right. "You signed me up for running? Around town? With people watching? In the middle of winter? I thought you loved me."

"I love you so much I signed us up for every town event I could think of. But I'll make it up to you in very nerdy filthy ways," Emma said.

Lauren's heart all but pitter-pattered at the promises woven into the words. She downed her drink and pulled Emma to her feet. If she had to go running in the morning, she wanted a double payment in advance.

Time to go home. Just a couple of kinky queers in love about to dare for a lifetime in small town Sunrise Falls.

About the Author

Sandy has a master's degree in publishing from the University of Sydney, Australia, and is the senior editor at Bold Strokes Books. She's the author of *Party of Three* and *If You Dare* and is hard at work on her next draft.

Books Available from Bold Strokes Books

16 Steps to Forever by Georgia Beers. Can Brooke Sullivan and Macy Carr find themselves by finding each other? (978-1-63555-762-6)

All I Want for Christmas by Georgia Beers, Maggie Cummings, Fiona Riley. The Christmas season sparks passion and love in these stories by award winning authors Georgia Beers, Maggie Cummings, and Fiona Riley. (978-1-63555-764-0)

From the Woods by Charlotte Greene. When Fiona goes backpacking in a protected wilderness, the last thing she expects is to be fighting for her life. (978-1-63555-793-0)

Heart of the Storm by Nicole Stiling. For Juliet Mitchell and Sienna Bennett a forbidden attraction definitely isn't worth upending the life they've worked so hard for. Is it? (978-1-63555-789-3)

If You Dare by Sandy Lowe. For Lauren West and Emma Prescott, following their passions is easy. Following their hearts, though? That's almost impossible. (978-1-63555-654-4)

Love Changes Everything by Jaime Maddox. For Samantha Brooks and Kirby Fielding, no matter how careful their plans, love will change everything. (978-1-63555-835-7)

Not This Time by MA Binfield. Flung back into each other's lives, can former bandmates Sophia and Madison have a second chance at romance? (978-1-63555-798-5)

The Dubious Gift of Dragon Blood by J. Marshall Freeman. One day Crispin is a lonely high school student—the next he is fighting a war in a land ruled by dragons, his otherworldly boyfriend at his side. (978-1-63555-725-1)

The Found Jar by Jaycie Morrison. Fear keeps Emily Harris trapped in her emotionally vacant life; can she find the courage to let Beck Reynolds guide her toward love? (978-1-63555-825-8)

Aurora by Emma L McGeown. After a traumatic accident, Elena Ricci is stricken with amnesia leaving her with no recollection of the last eight years, including her wife and son. (978-1-63555-824-1)

Avenging Avery by Sheri Lewis Wohl. Revenge against a vengeful vampire unites Isa Meyer and Jeni Denton, but it's love that heals them. (978-1-63555-622-3)

Bulletproof by Maggie Cummings. For Dylan Prescott and Briana Logan, the complicated NYC criminal justice system doesn't leave room for love, but where the heart is concerned, no one is bulletproof. (978-1-63555-771-8)

Her Lady to Love by Jane Walsh. A shy wallflower joins forces with the most popular woman in Regency London on a quest to catch a husband, only to discover a wild passion for each other that far eclipses their interest for the Marriage Mart. (978-1-63555-809-8)

No Regrets by Joy Argento. For Jodi and Beth, the possibility of losing their future will force them to decide what is really important. (978-1-63555-751-0)

The Holiday Treatment by Elle Spencer. Who doesn't want a gay Christmas movie? Holly Hudson asks herself that question and discovers that happy endings aren't only for the movies. (978-1-63555-660-5)

Too Good to be True by Leigh Hays. Can the promise of love survive the realities of life for Madison and Jen, or is it too good to be true? (978-1-63555-715-2)

Treacherous Seas by Radclyffe. When the choice comes down to the lives of her officers against the promise she made to her wife, Reese Conlon puts everything she cares about on the line. (978-1-63555-778-7)

Two to Tangle by Melissa Brayden. Ryan Jacks has been a player all her life, but the new chef at Tangle Valley Vineyard changes everything. If only she wasn't off the menu. (978-1-63555-747-3)

When Sparks Fly by Annie McDonald. Will the devastating incident that first brought Dr. Daniella Waveny and hockey coach Luca McCaffrey together on frozen ice now force them apart, or will their secrets and fears thaw enough for them to create sparks? (978-1-63555-782-4)

Best Practice by Carsen Taite. When attorney Grace Maldonado agrees to mentor her best friend's little sister, she's prepared to confront Perry's rebellious nature, but she isn't prepared to fall in love. Legal Affairs: one law firm, three best friends, three chances to fall in love. (978-1-63555-361-1)

Home by Kris Bryant. Natalie and Sarah discover that anything is possible when love takes the long way home. (978-1-63555-853-1)

Keeper by Sydney Quinne. With a new charge under her reluctant wing—feisty, highly intelligent math wizard Isabelle Templeton—Keeper Andy Bouchard has to prevent a murder or die trying. (978-1-63555-852-4)

One More Chance by Ali Vali. Harry Basantes planned a future with Desi Thompson until the day Desi disappeared without a word, only to walk back into her life sixteen years later. (978-1-63555-536-3)

Renegade's War by Gun Brooke. Freedom fighter Aurelia DeCallum regrets saving the woman called Blue. She fears it will jeopardize her mission, and secretly, Blue might end up breaking Aurelia's heart. (978-1-63555-484-7)

The Other Women by Erin Zak. What happens in Vegas should stay in Vegas, but what do you do when the love you find in Vegas changes your life forever? (978-1-63555-741-1)

The Sea Within by Missouri Vaun. Time is running out for Dr. Elle Graham to convince Captain Jackson Drake that the only thing that can save future Earth resides in the past, and rescue her broken heart in the process. (978-1-63555-568-4)

To Sleep With Reindeer by Justine Saracen. In Norway under Nazi occupation, Maarit, an Indigenous woman; and Kirsten, a Norwegian resister, join forces to stop the development of an atomic weapon. (978-1-63555-735-0)

Twice Shy by Aurora Rey. Having an ex with benefits isn't all it's cracked up to be. Will Amanda Russo learn that lesson in time to take a chance on love with Quinn Sullivan? (978-1-63555-737-4)

Z-Town by Eden Darry. Forced to work together to stay alive, Meg and Lane must find the centuries-old treasure before the zombies find them first. (978-1-63555-743-5)

Bet Against Me by Fiona Riley. In the high stakes luxury real estate market, everything has a price, and as rival Realtors Trina Lee and Kendall Yates find out, that means their hearts and souls, too. (978-1-63555-729-9)

Broken Reign by Sam Ledel. Together on an epic journey in search of a mysterious cure, a princess and a village outcast must overcome life-threatening challenges and their own prejudice if they want to survive. (978-1-63555-739-8)

Just One Taste by CJ Birch. For Lauren, it only took one taste to start trusting in love again. (978-1-63555-772-5)

Lady of Stone by Barbara Ann Wright. Sparks fly as a magical emergency forces a noble embarrassed by her ability to submit to a low-born teacher who resents everything about her. (978-1-63555-607-0)

Last Resort by Angie Williams. Katie and Rhys are about to find out what happens when you meet the girl of your dreams but you aren't looking for a happily ever after. (978-1-63555-774-9)

Longing for You by Jenny Frame. When Debrek housekeeper Katie Brekman is attacked amid a burgeoning vampire-witch war, Alexis Villiers must go against everything her clan believes in to save her. (978-1-63555-658-2)

Money Creek by Anne Laughlin. Clare Lehane is a troubled lawyer from Chicago who tries to make her way in a rural town full of secrets and deceptions. (978-1-63555-795-4)

Passion's Sweet Surrender by Ronica Black. Cam and Blake are unable to deny their passion for each other, but surrendering to love is a whole different matter. (978-1-63555-703-9)

The Holiday Detour by Jane Kolven. It will take everything going wrong to make Dana and Charlie see how right they are for each other. (978-1-63555-720-6)

Too Hot to Ride by Andrews & Austin. World famous cutting horse champion and industry legend Jane Barrow is knockdown sexy in the way she moves, talks, and rides, and Rae Starr is determined not to get involved with this womanizing gambler. (978-1-63555-776-3)

A Love that Leads to Home by Ronica Black. For Carla Sims and Janice Carpenter, home isn't about location, it's where your heart is. (978-1-63555-675-9)

Blades of Bluegrass by D. Jackson Leigh. A US Army occupational therapist must rehab a bitter veteran who is a ticking political time bomb the military is desperate to disarm. (978-1-63555-637-7)

Guarding Hearts by Jaycie Morrison. As treachery and temptation threaten the women of the Women's Army Corps, who will risk it all for love? (978-1-63555-806-7)

Hopeless Romantic by Georgia Beers. Can a jaded wedding planner and an optimistic divorce attorney possibly find a future together? (978-1-63555-650-6)

Hopes and Dreams by PJ Trebelhorn. Movie theater manager Riley Warren is forced to face her high school crush and tormentor, wealthy socialite Victoria Thayer, at their twentieth reunion. (978-1-63555-670-4)

In the Cards by Kimberly Cooper Griffin. Daria and Phaedra are about to discover that love finds a way, especially when powers outside their control are at play. (978-1-63555-717-6)

Moon Fever by Ileandra Young. SPEAR agent Danika Karson must clear her werewolf friend of multiple false charges while teaching her vampire girlfriend to resist the blood mania brought on by a full moon. (978-1-63555-603-2)

Quake City by St John Karp. Can Andre find his best friend Amy before the night devolves into a nightmare of broken hearts, malevolent drag queens, and spontaneous human combustion? Or has it always happened this way, every night, at Aunty Bob's Quake City Club? (978-1-63555-723-7)

Serenity by Jesse J. Thoma. For Kit Marsden, there are many things in life she cannot change. Serenity is in the acceptance. (978-1-63555-713-8)

Sylver and Gold by Michelle Larkin. Working feverishly to find a killer before he strikes again, Boston Homicide Detective Reid Sylver and rookie cop London Gold are blindsided by their chemistry and developing attraction. (978-1-63555-611-7)

Trade Secrets by Kathleen Knowles. In Silicon Valley, love and business are a volatile mix for clinical lab scientist Tony Leung and venture capitalist Sheila Graham. (978-1-63555-642-1)